King Of The Jungle

A novel

By Scott McKay

King Of The Jungle

ISBN: 9798320615523

Copyright 2024 RVIVR.com

All Rights Reserved

Cover images and inside text by Scott McKay

King of the Jungle is a work of fiction. Unless otherwise indicated, all the names, characters, businesses, places, events and incidents in this book are either the product of the author's imagination or used in a fictitious manner. Any resemblance to actual persons, living or dead, or actual events is purely coincidental.

King Of The Jungle

For the villagers;

may they keep the pillagers at bay.

Contents

Prologue 6
Chapter 1 12
Chapter 2 32
Chapter 3 55
Chapter 4 73
Chapter 5 87
Chapter 6 96
Chapter 7 113
Chapter 8 128
Chapter 9 150
Chapter 10 179
Chapter 11 197
Chapter 12 211
Chapter 13 221
Chapter 14 241
Chapter 15 255
Chapter 16 269
Chapter 17 291
Chapter 18 301
Chapter 19 320
Chapter 20 333
Chapter 21 358
Chapter 22 381
EPILOGUE 404

King Of The Jungle

Prologue

March 10, 2024, Las Claritas, Bolivar

"Are the men ready, Hector?" asked the commander with an impatient scowl.

"*Si, coronel,*" came a simpering response.

The commander scoffed inwardly at his adjutant's subservience. *Mayor* Hector Carvajal had achieved his rank through favor rather than merit, an all-too-frequent occurrence in the *Ejército Bolivariano,* the land force of the *Fuerza Armada Nacional Bolivariana*, or National Bolivarian Armed Forces of Venezuela. Carvajal was only 29, a slight little man from a good family in a good section of Caracas, the capital, and he'd attended the best schools and then the *Academia Militar del Ejército Bolivariano,* the army's military academy at Fort Tiuna in the capital.

Carvajal, Cabrillo knew from his file, had not graduated with honors from the academy. He had graduated. And in the year since Carvajal had joined Cabrillo's command staff of the 53rd Jungle Infantry Brigade, he wouldn't go much further than that in his assessment of his adjutant.

Carvajal was there. He was adequate, if barely. He did what was asked of him, if barely.

Cabrillo knew that Carvajal was not where he wanted to be. Especially not here. Not in Las Claritas, a muddy little shantytown on a roadside at the edge of a wilderness where the 53rd had set up camp for the present on its way to destiny.

He knew Carvajal was likely to enjoy his future much less. The little major at least had a bedroom in a requisitioned house, though it was a servant's bedroom. Cabrillo's was considerably nicer, though he didn't use it much. There was too much to do.

And there were few bedrooms where they were going.

Cabrillo also knew Carvajal was not enamored with his commander. There was nothing surprising about that. After all, Manuel Lopez Alejandro Cabrillo, *Coronel* in command of the 53rd Jungle Infantry Brigade, was neither soft like Carvajal, nor even Venezuelan.

Cabrillo, like much of the command structure in Venezuela's military and intelligence community, was Cuban. And he knew that made him quite unpopular with not just the inferior men like Carvajal, but the more substantial ones as well.

That was a minor concern to Cabrillo. There was a reason why he and his fellow Cubans were here. They were loyal to the government of Nicolae Madiera, the president of the Bolivarian Republic of Venezuela, which wasn't exactly the same thing as loyalty to the people of Venezuela.

Cabrillo knew that well. He'd proven his loyalty to the regime often since arriving 20 years before. It wasn't easy, at least at first. There had been blood, more of it in recent years, as the regime had been forced to take more and more aggressive steps to hold power while the country declined.

The consequences of those steps hadn't been very friendly to the 53rd, as desertions and retirements had decimated its numbers. Just six months earlier, when Cabrillo had been promoted to his current rank and given command, his total strength was down to just 2,600 men.

The mission for which they were preparing would require twice that number.

Cabrillo had spent the past half-year recruiting and training – the latter a far harder job than the former. With conditions in the country deteriorating, young men with no other employment available and desperate to earn sustenance for their families were happy to join, and there were plenty of them available.

Finding men they could turn into soldiers, men who wouldn't wash out of a jungle infantry unit when things got tough, was a different story.

Cabrillo estimated that maybe 60 percent of his troops would fight in the presence of an enemy. The rest? Maybe they would run. Maybe they would hide.

That 60 percent might, he thought, be enough for the mission they were preparing to execute.

But the 53rd wasn't done training. And the stage of the pre-invasion process they were entering would hopefully harden the ones who didn't have the devil in their eyes.

"Lead the way, Hector. Let's see how this rabble looks today."

He and Carvajal walked from the command trailer, a cheap prefabricated building propped up on blocks on the edge of a potholed parking lot. The training ground for the 53rd in their current deployment was the site of an abandoned shopping mall; the men had turned the mall into a barracks where they were packed into close quarters. Conditions were less than optimal.

Which was how Cabrillo wanted it.

The 4,569 men of the 53rd Jungle Infantry were formed into their three battalions, all wearing battle fatigues draped with bits of excess cloth in various shades of green, making them well-suited for action in the rain forests of southern and eastern Venezuela – and parts nearby. They straightened and saluted at the call for attention, and Cabrillo smiled.

He and Carvajal took their time reviewing the men, a motley collection of veterans, peasants, criminals, kids, aging men. Some were well fed, others much less so.

"They have the legs for ceremony," he noted to Carvajal. "We will find out if they have *cojones*."

The adjutant's face betrayed worry at that.

"Hector, you have doubts?" asked Cabrillo, as they passed a final formation of men, a company of green recruits attached to the 533rd Battalion commanded by a porky captain named Perez whom Cabrillo had known from a rather ugly action in the suburbs of the capital the previous year.

Carvajal's mouth said nothing. His face said everything.

"*Jefe*," he finally said, as the two finished reviewing the troops and dismissed them to begin their day's training regimen, "this mission…I fear the men will not…"

"You doubt my leadership."

"I didn't say that, *Jefe*," said Carvajal. "But to invade another country will bring consequences."

"Which are those, Hector?"

"The Americans won't stand for it."

Cabrillo snorted.

"*Los Yanquis?* What will they do?"

"They could send their Navy. Or their Marines. Or they could send bombs or missiles."

"They sent no one to Ukraine. They sent no one to Gaza. Who are they sending to Taiwan?"

"To Taiwan, *Jefe*?" Carvajal said as they entered the trailer.

There was a man inside. He was as tall as Cabrillo, about six-foot. But he was husky, unlike the *coronel*. And his features were oriental.

"Hector Carvajal," said Cabrillo, "meet Mr. Xing."

"*Ni hao*," said Xing.

"*Buenas dias, senor*," Carvajal responded.

"To answer your question," said Xing matter-of-factly, "they will send no one to Taiwan, and you will see that soon."

"Yes, but…"

"They will send no one," said Cabrillo, "and our mission will be a success."

Chapter 1

April 4, 2024, Atlanta, Georgia

"Hey Mike," the email said, "I'm going to be in Atlanta tomorrow. What say we get together at the St. Regis? Dinner in the suite, bottle of Rip Van Winkle for after, and we'll shoot the shit and talk about old times."

"Sure, Pierce," I responded. "It'll be great to catch up."

Most people would view the chance to sit down for most of the night with Pierce Polk, founder and CEO of the giant conglomerate Sentinel Holdings, as a once-in-a-lifetime opportunity. I actually dreaded it.

Because I knew what was coming. It was going to be a classic Pierce move, and I really didn't want it. I also couldn't turn it down.

Pierce was my college roommate. We both graduated from Vanderbilt in 1995. By that point I'd more or less fallen in as the less-successful, less-fun wingman, the supporting actor to his lead role. And while Pierce was the hottest game in town, I was the recalcitrant and ungrateful friend who flew the coop rather than share in the glow of his stardom.

He'd already made his first million – hell, his first several million – by then. Pierce was an out-of-the-box thinker who could find big profits in utterly mundane things. He proved that by noting that the bars around the college, and even some of the bigger clubs on the strip, had a collection of weirdos, dunces and slobs as bouncers. So he found football players, fitness hunks, karate dojo rats and others who could handle themselves and he put them to work as private security professionals working those doors. You'd think that was a nothing business, but six months after he started it as a sophomore in college, he had half the watering holes in the city paying him top dollar for a guy to work the door, security cameras, pour regulation, inventory management and all kinds of other things.

Then he branched out into neighborhood private security. Then high-profile personal protection, with a bunch of Nashville country stars as clients. By that point he'd taken the bar security business interstate, with offices in all the big college towns in the Southeast and some in the Midwest.

Then Pierce sold the bar security business for a big chunk of change, and he kept the higher-end stuff.

All before he graduated college. Of course, it took him – and me – six years to do that. Pierce, because he was spending half his time building that business.

Me, because I was spending half my time getting wasted in the same bars Pierce was turning into his own personal ATM machines.

He put himself through college with what he was making in that business. He didn't need to. Pierce's father, who was a pretty strange bird, was a history professor at Catawba College in South Carolina who doubled as a clinical psychologist, and Connor Polk did an absolute number on his three sons.

Connor named Pierce's older brother Harrison Buchanan Polk. Pierce's full name was actually Fillmore Pierce Polk. The youngest of the three was Tyler Van Buren Polk.

Yes, Connor taught antebellum American history. So he named his kids for mediocre presidents from before the Civil War. And he told them he did it so they'd know they could never be mediocre.

Harrison joined the Marines right out of high school, then he went to Clemson for undergrad and Princeton for law school. He's a lawyer for a hedge fund in Connecticut now. And Tyler moved to Silicon Valley right out of high school and rose all the way up to Vice President at one of the big tech firms. You've heard of it.

These people were achievers, you understand. The kind of folks you started off being impressed by, and soon got completely worn out with, the more you were around them.

But Pierce was the most ambitious. Pierce had so much energy to him that he'd exhaust you.

By the time he graduated he didn't just have the personal security business. By then he'd rounded up some computer geeks and he was doing network security. And that took off so quickly that a couple of years after he graduated he ended up moving out to Palo Alto and took Sentinel Web Services into the stratosphere.

And by the time the 20th century ended and the 21st century began, Sentinel Security was doing port operations and logistics. Then Sentinel Construction popped up.

Then there was Sentinel Aerospace. Which led to Sentinel Communications, which was a satellite telecom firm which was launching birds into low orbit using the Indian and Russian space programs because they were dirt cheap. They've since moved on to using the domestic private operators, but they've got a ton of satellites in the air and profit very, very handsomely from those.

Everything Pierce touched exploded in a mushroom cloud of money. He hired great people and then he filled them up with all of his dad's behavioral psychology stuff, and it was basically a cult of capitalism he was running.

Every one of those companies got big enough to take public. But Pierce refused to do it. He said that the minute a company went public it went to shit. That the people who would take over would lack the soul and the balls of the founder.

So he had a giant empire worth billions of dollars by the time he was 32, and practically nobody on a corporate board, or stockholders that he had to answer to.

And by the time I was 32 I was, more or less, washed up.

While Pierce was turning himself into a captain of industry, or several industries as the case might be, I was – like I said – a lesser prodigy.

I'd gotten myself a job at the *Vanderbilt Hustler*, which is the school paper, my freshman year. By the time I was a sophomore I'd become something of a sensation. I managed to get a couple of tenured professors fired based on columns I'd written that exposed them for sundry matters of moral turpitude, and those two stories put me on the media map, at least a little.

They also made it so that I wasn't welcome at the *Vanderbilt Hustler* my junior year. But that was OK, because by then I'd caught on at the *Nashville Tennesseean*, not to mention freelance gigs for a panoply of publications left, right and center. I did a lot of public-policy stuff, and some cultural stuff, but what seemed to juice my career was when I'd do things on elections and campaigns.

I didn't really care at that point. I was agnostic about politics. What pissed me off was corruption, and at the time it was the Clintons who were the biggest crooks. And since I'd voted for Bill in 1992, mostly because he reminded me of my dad – and that's a whole other story – it really pissed me off that he was a scandal-a-minute as a president.

But then Clinton was gone, and next was George W. Bush. And his bullshit was little better than Clinton's, so before I knew it I was writing about what a clownshow the Bushes were.

And that, plus my telegenic face, I guess, was what got me the job at the American News Network, which led to me getting that prime-time show over there.

They called it *Mike Holman Tells The Truth*, which was a cool name, and I thought I mostly lived up to it. But it was criminal to give a 28-year-old kid a cable news show and all that came with that.

The show actually did pretty well. It lasted for four years, and it made me a household name. Lots of fans, lots of money, lots of ego. I was a mess. Ended up marrying Lisa, who was entirely the wrong girl. My mom said at the wedding, "I give it six months." I cut her off for that and didn't talk to her again…

…for seven months when that marriage ended in disaster.

And less than a year after that, *Mike Holman Tells The Truth* ended in disaster.

Not because of anything that happened on the air. Because of what happened at a New Year's Eve party the Rudolphs, who own ANN, threw.

Logan Rudolph didn't actually have a management role at ANN. He was Irving Rudolph's son, which essentially gave him free rein to make everybody at the network miserable. And Logan took a special dislike to me, for reasons I still don't understand.

That night he showed up at the party with Lisa. And got handsy with her in front of everybody. I was still pretty messed up about her — all these years later I still am, really, even though we're completely toxic together — and when I saw that, especially having had three cocktails too many, I got in that sniveling SOB's face and told him if he didn't leave her alone I'd break him in half.

And he knew I could do it.

But what he could do is break my career. And he did. Five days later I was out of a job, and that kick-ass apartment overlooking Central Park was my former address.

Luckily enough I had a couple of friends at WSB-TV in Atlanta, and I landed with a job as the investigative reporter there. But I didn't last long; local TV news was miserable, the money sucked, and I was done working for anybody else.

So I raised a little capital and started Holman Media, and for the last 18 years that's been me. It's a pretty good little website, a decently-successful YouTube and Rumble channel, and a little news operation I'm pretty proud of.

We don't earn shit for profit, and making payroll is commonly an adventure. But I'll say this – I've got a hell of a loyal staff. These guys are the best. Hell, I can't run them off – and for business reasons I need to, because they all make more than Holman Media can afford to pay them.

I'm house-poor, because I had to have a place in Buckhead to go with a smart-looking office in midtown, and I've been burning the candle at both ends trying to survive.

And I'm not a centrist, apolitical guy anymore. The eight years of Barry Omobba saw to that. If you've followed the podcast and the website over the last however many years, you know what that's about – the IRS scandal, Benghazi, the Clinton e-mail stuff and a few of the other things we managed to break some stories on. I even had Derrick Gripper, the Attorney General, call me a liar on national TV, which was the pinnacle of my career as far as I'm concerned.

The thing is, though, independent media has a massive target on its back. We get shadow-banned, fact-checked, censored and shit on by Big Tech and Big Media, which includes Big Advertising, and that makes it damn near impossible to bring in revenue. And so I've been at a real crossroads, because I really didn't think I could bump along like that much longer, even though keeping my team in their jobs had become a half-crusade, half-obsession and that had been more important than my own shitty finances.

Pierce knew I was broke. A few times he'd offered to buy Holman Media and make it a division of Sentinel Communications. I came up with unreasonable demands that he couldn't agree to as a means of turning him down and making it his fault.

He knew what I was doing, of course. And he knew it was a pride thing. He understood. But what made it worse was that he kept trying, kept sweetening the pot.

Three years ago he offered me $3 million cash for Holman Media, plus a five percent share in Sentinel Communications, full editorial control of the site and the podcast channels and a 10-year contract for the entire staff. It was utterly idiotic for me to turn it down and I still did.

Pierce stayed away for a while after that. I didn't hurt his feelings, it wasn't that. He just knew that my wall was too high. He told me, "Look, let's just leave that offer on the table, and when you're ready to accept it, give me a call."

That was the most infuriating part of all. Like an enduring reminder of my prideful dumbassery.

But if I took the offer, I'd be one of Pierce's guys. I'd be joining the cult. And my whole adult life had been an exercise in being my own man, as shitty a set of outcomes as that had generated. So I couldn't. I felt like an asshole, but I couldn't.

And the craziest thing about it is I called my whole staff in and told them "this is what Pierce offered, and I'm turning it down." And do you know that not a single one of the nine of them either gave me shit about it or quit? Three years later and every one of them is still with me despite the mad scramble it is to stay ahead of cash flow.

It's exhausting and inspiring at the same time. That's what running a small business is like, I guess. But after 18 years you're supposed to be at least a mid-sized business. Which is probably why I felt like I was coming to the end.

And yes, all of this was self-inflicted. All I had to do was take Pierce up on his offer and all those problems would go away. The Cult would take care of everything.

Ugh.

But now, there was this invitation at the St. Regis. I knew this was another round, and it would be harder than ever to resist him.

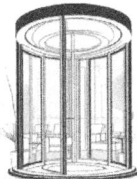

I made my way to the hotel – if you're going to stay in Atlanta and you have the means, by the way, you can do a whole lot worse than the St. Regis; the place is a palace – and Pierce had a new girl meet me in the lobby.

"Hi, I'm Courtney," she said, with that bubbly millennial aspirationally-inoffensive smartass thing that you get from the typical 33-year-olds. "You must be Mr. Mike."

"That makes me sound like a mail-order product," I said.

"I'm sorry?"

"Never mind, Courtney. You're here to take me up to Pierce's suite?"

"Totally! Do I need to get you validated?"

"I took an Uber."

"OK," she said, pulling out a business card and thrusting it in my direction as she shepherded me toward the elevators, "just email me the receipt and I'll make sure you're reimbursed for the ride."

"That's OK, Courtney. I think I can handle it."

"Are you sure?" she said, as she held a room key card over the scanner and punched the button for the top floor. "I mean, a free Uber ride…"

"Courney. Come on."

"OK," she said, "I guess I get it."

I looked her over as the elevator slowly took us up to Pierce's suite. She was a petite little thing, blonde, though not naturally so and I'm not sure it was a good fit on her. She was wearing a shiny silver pantsuit, with a boxy jacket that made it impossible to know if she was a skinny girl or fat.

I figured it was the former. She had skinny legs. That I could tell from the tight pants.

"I like your suit," I lied. "Is that the new style?"

"Oh my God!" Courtney said. "You don't know? All the influencers are talking about it. So at Saks they're…"

Just then, mercifully, we hit the top floor and the door opened to a hallway manned by a couple of Himalayas in charcoal gray suits. Their names were Bruce and Latrell, I found out later, and when we exited the elevator, they patted both of us down.

"Y'all are pretty strict up here, huh?" I asked Latrell, as he gave me a groping that I'd last received at a place in Amsterdam back in 2014. Latrell was a lot cheaper than the Dutch version.

"They got threats," he said. "Can't be careful enough."

I looked at Courtney. She nodded her head with as much seriousness as she could muster.

Courtney shepherded me to the end of the hall, then used her room key card to open the door to the suite. It was bigger than my house, and inside was the guy I'd been – unfairly, I guess – dreading.

"Holman! Damn, it's good to see you, dude!"

"Hey, Pierce," I said. "Thanks for having me up."

"Shit, man. I can't get you to come to me, so this is the best I can do. How are you?"

He asked that question, but I knew that he was extremely well informed about everything that was going on in my life and with Holman media.

"You already know that, Pierce. What about you?"

What followed was a good 15 minute monologue about business, geopolitics, women, cars and a few other things that came to Pierce's mind. It was a bit of an effort to follow – to listen to Pierce was to listen to two, or maybe three, or even four, conversations at the same time. He'd skip around between them. He'd be talking about the Maserati he'd just bought, and maybe he'd have it flown in so I could drive it, and speaking of that, did you hear about the stupid shit that was going on at Boeing? And then he'd note that sex scandal involving Olivia Rodrigo and that Delta stewardess on the flight to Salt Lake City, before telling me about the rocket launch Sentinel Aerospace, which was now a division of Sentinel Communications thanks to the brand-new reorganization, had planned in New Mexico the next week.

Then dinner arrived. Steaks, as always. Pierce ate steak twice a day, breakfast and dinner. Internally I was relieved that he wasn't insisting that the hotel serve his own private reserve Wagyu that he was getting regularly flown in from Hyōgo Prefecture. But I could tell that he had noticed the difference.

The conversation petered down to a somewhat manageable level, but then there was the apple trifle and the bottle of Rip Van Winkle that Pierce unearthed from somewhere.

And when he opened it and poured a healthy four fingers over a big, square block of ice in a glass for each of us, I knew I'd be getting both barrels. Not of the bourbon.

"Look, Mike," he said. "I know it's been a long time since we talked about this, but that offer is still on the table for sure."

"Jesus, Pierce," I said. "This again?"

"Hey, I'm your friend. I keep tabs on you. And I know you're in shit shape. The mortgage on your place in Buckhead is…"

"My business," I said. "It's my business. It isn't yours."

"Mike, you may not understand this, but you're actually an important guy. I'm not just saying that because we're close. The work you're doing is legitimate. You and your crew go where the corporate media assholes won't, and you've done more in the last two years to expose the White House and the people who run that show than anybody. The least I can do is watch your back."

"Yeah, well, thanks, I guess." I couldn't think of what else to say given that I knew what was coming next.

"Man, why don't you let me buy that company and give you the resources to turn it into a big deal? We'll buy a cable channel off the people at Discovery Networks and we'll turn it into Holman News, and it'll be your brand and your message, with a real opportunity to drag a shit-ton of ad revenue. Especially when we build a new app for it and bundle the website and…"

"How many times are we gonna talk about this?" I said. 'I'm not gonna work for you, Pierce."

"You wouldn't be working for me! I don't know anything about media. But I'm into telecom, so it's stupid not to have a media division. This would be *your* show."

"And you'd be on my ass about profit margin, which is something that journalism really shouldn't…"

"You're thinking about this all wrong, Holman. Remember – I don't have stockholders. I don't have a board I have to answer to."

"Yes you do."

"They're an advisory board, buddy. I can tell those guys to go screw themselves anytime I want. This is not like some soulless zombie corporation like the one you used to work for. It can be *our* thing."

I just looked at him.

"Fine," he sighed. "One day, maybe. But I have something else. If you won't let me buy your company, what if I hired you guys to handle Sentinel Holdings' PR?"

"You have a PR department already, Pierce."

"Yeah, but they don't really do all that good a job. I could use some help."

This was true – and it wasn't.

The problem Pierce had with public relations was that he never had a filter. The guy got so rich so fast that by the time anybody was paying attention to things he said he was no longer in a position to fear a public backlash.

Or care what anybody thought.

And then he had to essentially fight a war with the Omobba administration, first over its attempts to force him to take Great Recession bailout money that came with all kinds of strings, then over a bunch of lawsuits its agencies – EEOC, EPA, DOE, DHHS and a host of others – filed against him on a host of fronts over what I would call differing interpretations of federal regulations.

Pierce refused to hire lobbyists. He said it was morally wrong to do it. But he'd go and testify in front of Congress all the time. And one time the topic of lobbyists came up and he gave that really famous quote.

You've seen the YouTube of this, no doubt. It's when he essentially nailed the corruption of the system.

"I could hire an army of lobbyists," he said. "But I don't want to do that. Because I've seen how this works.

"Sure, I'll hire lobbyists. And they'll come up here and try to defend my interests in front of Congress. They'll go and see your chiefs of staff and your legislative directors, and they'll dig into the guts of whatever bills you're passing up here, and they'll attempt to protect Sentinel from all the awful things you could do to me.

"But when they've been successful doing that, and I don't have anything more to fear from you, the natural progression – and I don't count myself immune from it – is to ask, what's next? And I know what's next.

"Which is that since I'm paying these guys I'm going to get them to lobby you not just for our protection so we can succeed in a free market, but to warp that market so that we succeed by bending the rules to our favor. And that, folks, I can't live with.

"So I'll come up here and I'll tell our story myself, and I'll hire all the damn lawyers I have to in order to fight off whatever government aggressions you people and the bureaucrats up the street might dream up. But that's it. The things I really want from government, like a balanced budget, no stupid wars, common sense, I know I can't get. So you do your thing and I'll do mine, and we'll get along about as well as possible."

That was back in 2014, and it was a huge sensation with the folks. But that was when Pierce became "controversial."

He didn't care. He said whatever was on his mind. Then they pulled his Twitter account for saying that some prominent "transwoman" influencer was a man, and that nothing would change that fact, and that his bad imitation of a woman was disgusting. And they knocked him off Facebook when he posted that Joe Deadhorse, the Democrats' nominee in 2020 who beat the incumbent Republican Donny Trumbull under some weird circumstances, had stolen the vote in Arizona.

And he went from being a regular on CNBC to getting ghosted, not that he cared a lot. Fox Business still had him on all the time. And his head of corporate communications had been on his ass to shut up about politics, policy, economics and anything else not directly involving his business – which wasn't something Pierce was comfortable doing.

Larger-than-life guys like Pierce Polk generally don't hold anything in. Which was what made him so interesting and so exhausting all at the same time.

Just before he met me in Atlanta, Pierce had gotten himself in more hot water. He'd said Sentinel had a new company policy that they'd only hire Harvard grads in the janitorial departments because he didn't think a degree from there was evidence of any actual scholarship. Omobba himself rebuked Pierce for that, which led to Pierce responding to the former president during an appearance on Maria Bartiromo's show that his recent Netflix movie was "the worst damn thing I've ever seen."

Pierce was at the point where you either loved him or hated him; there was no in-between.

And naturally there were loads of people asking him to run for president, for the Senate, for anything. He said he didn't want any part of that, and besides, since he was a Republican – "not because I want to be, but because I have no freakin' choice" – there was already a guy running.

He was talking about Trumbull, naturally. And of course that got even more people mad at him. Trumbull was every bit the love-him-or-hate-him guy that Pierce was. You'd think they'd be peas in a pod, but … not so much. Uneasy allies, maybe, would be the way to describe them.

Pierce did actually need some help with PR, even if it was just somebody who could take his phone away.

"Seriously, Mike," he was telling me. "You're the only guy I would trust with the job."

"I dunno. Maybe," I said. "But I haven't done PR in a while, and it's not really my game. It's a sidelight at best. Let me think about it."

"OK, fine," he said. "But, now, *this* you can't turn down, and it's actually an urgent thing."

"An urgent thing?"

"Yeah. Walter Isaacson is begging me for a sitdown, because he says he wants to write a biography of me. He actually wants it to be an authorized biography. Man, I don't want Isaacson to be the guy who does that. I need you."

"Ahhh. OK."

"Look, *this* you *have* to do. All right? I'll pay you 250 grand."

I knew I couldn't turn him down. I knew everything about Pierce It would be the easiest quarter million dollars anybody had ever made, or so I thought. And I knew the book would sell. There were lots of people who thought Pierce was the distillation of the wildcat American capitalist, a breed that wasn't just dying, it was being hunted out of existence.

"Pierce, if I write that book I'm actually going to be objective. This isn't going to be some hagiography."

"What's a hagiography?"

"A blowjob, Pierce. And that's not happening. If I write your biography it's going to be a real story. I'm not just going to puff you up."

"Actually, I don't want you to. I think it would do me some good to read the truth about myself from somebody who really knows enough to have an opinion, and if that means there's some negative, so be it."

"Fine. Then under that understanding, I'll write your biography."

Pierce smiled, and he walked over to the writing desk, opened a computer bag and came back with a check for $250,000.

Some of you have held one of those in your hands. I did, once, when I was working at ANN. But it had been a long time, and when Pierce gave that check to me I felt a buzz.

And it wasn't the Rip Van Winkle we'd been drinking.

"All right, then," I said folding that check and thrusting it into my jacket pocket. "Where do we start?"

"Well, that's up to you," said Pierce, sitting back down to attack the rest of the bottle and beaming a billion-dollar smile

King Of The Jungle

at me. "But you really ought to see the new thing we're building down in Guyana."

"What? Guyana? What is this?"

"Oh, you'll see, Mike. In fact, you ought to clear your schedule the weekend and fly down with us."

"Well, hell, I guess I do," I said, the buzz of that $250,000 speaking to me telepathically from my breast pocket.

And I knew that after all this time, I was finally going to join the Cult of Pierce Polk.

Chapter 2

April 5, 2024, Atlanta, Georgia

I had a couple of hours to kill before the car was coming to take me to Fulton County Airport for the private flight to Pierce's jungle paradise, so I was playing around with an outline to his biography.

That check for $250,000 went into the bank as soon as it opened, which was not a moment too soon. It was a nice change to have payroll go through without having to tap into the line of credit, and the knowledge that I wouldn't have to worry about that for the next year had me sleeping like a baby the previous night.

I guess that was how being a member of the Cult of Pierce would go. Maybe it wasn't so bad.

I'd told my staff about the new plan, and reactions were mixed. Tom LeClair, our business manager, was excited. Megan Rivers, who handled our ad sales, said this was going to be her inroad into getting a bunch of sponsorship dollars from Sentinel and all the people they do business with. But Colby Igboizwe, who edits the website, said something that threw a bit of a damper on things.

"I thought we weren't going to sell out," he said. "Is that what this is?"

"It's me writing a book, Colby," I said. "How much do we cover Pierce Polk on the site, anyway?"

"Easily twice a week, boss," he retorted. "You know that."

"Yeah, well…" I struggled to find a comeback, "I don't know what this would change about that."

"If nothing else," Kaylee Russo, who's the producer of the three podcasts we do, chimed in, "every time we talk about something Polk says the folks will know that we work for him."

"OK – none of you guys work for him," I said. "I'm writing a book about him. That's it."

"That's not how it's going to be seen by the public, though," said Sammy Wu, our web/IT guy.

"Don't tell me you're opposed to this, Sammy," I said. "You're the biggest Pierce Polk fan-boy here."

"Oh, hell no," he said. "I don't care what the public thinks. Take the money, write the book, let him buy us. Seriously, But just know, they're going to think you're Pierce's guy from now on."

I didn't like that a whole lot. I looked around the room, though, and nobody was disagreeing with Sammy.

"What about you, Melissa?" I asked Melissa Swindell, my research assistant. Melissa was only 22, right out of Hollins. Her dad had a company which sold bedsheets, pillows, slippers and pajamas and they were our oldest sponsor. So when Pike Swindell called me at Thanksgiving and told me I needed a research assistant and sent me Melissa's resume, all I did was to tell Megan to go pitch The Right Side Of The Bed

– yeah, that's Swindell's company – a nice increase in their annual sponsorship package to pay for Melissa's salary.

We all thought Melissa didn't know how she got the job with Holman Media. She knew from Day One. She was a kid with a lot of goofy ideas, but she saw through things like she was a wise old woman.

It was irritating as hell, actually. Your research assistant is supposed to be a scared kid who does exactly what you tell her and doesn't offer opinions. Instead, I got a conscience with coke-bottle glasses and judgmental looks.

"Do the book," Melissa said. "The country needs Pierce Polk, and you might be the only one who can save him."

At that, there were nods all around.

"Well, then," I said, "he wants us to do something else for him. He wants to hire us to do PR consulting for him."

"Oh, thank God," said Megan. Before entering the exciting world of independent digital media advertising sales she'd done PR work for the New Jersey State Lottery, and over the last few years when we'd picked up the occasional PR client it was usually Megan who handled it.

"What's he paying?" asked Tom.

"Heavy," I said, and when I blurted out the number the whole staff broke into smiles.

"In for a penny, in for a million," Colby said with a shrug. "If we're going to be lackeys, let's be well-paid lackeys."

"Is this gonna be a problem for you, Colby?"

"Nah. I'll get over it. At least my paycheck'll be steady. And maybe fatter, right boss?"

"I think maybe the smart move is Christmas bonuses, at least this year," I said, and the gang all offered grudging acceptance to that.

And that was it. That was the rebirth of Holman Media in a nutshell. Especially when I emailed Pierce and told him we wanted to accept the PR contract.

"Awesome," came the response. "Hey, the car will pick you up at your office at 2:30. You're gonna love the place in Guyana! I just know it!!!!"

Four exclamation marks. That was Pierce. You thought only chicks punctuated messages like that, and generally you were right. Chicks and billionaire cult figures who think the world is their oyster.

I didn't know how I felt about this sudden change in my life. And as much as I valued the input from the staff, I couldn't really draw much from their reactions. End of the day, all of those guys were still driven by the pursuit of a salary, and so none of them were objective about the idea they would suddenly be working for a profitable company.

Of course, neither was I.

I called my mom to tell her the news. Amazingly, she answered the phone. Normally I'd get a return call.

"Michael, darling, so good to hear from you!" she said. There was what sounded like wind in the background.

"Hey mom. Where are you?"

"I'm on a boat! George is taking us fishing off Fernandina Beach!"

That was a pretty fair-sized hike from The Villages where she lived.

"Wow," I said. "Sounds like fun."

"I think he's going to pop the question. How about that?"

Mom was 75. She'd been a divorcee, then a widow after she and dad remarried. It's a long story. This guy George was 80; he'd been a broker on Wall Street and now he hustled golf games in the Villages, which was how Mom met him. When she moved down there from Cincinnati, where I grew up, after Dad died, she decided to take up golf, and she and George turned into an item.

It was idiotic that they'd get married, I thought, but nobody cared what I thought. If George made her happy, good for her.

Even though he was an asshole. George was worth millions, but he'd been a max donor to Sandy Bernard, the socialist senator from Vermont who kept running for president.

"We should have a wealth tax on billionaires," George told me the last time I was down there visiting Mom. "It's obscene what these people have."

"George, you're worth what? Twenty million?" I asked him. "If you think the rich don't pay their fair share, then you can fix that by writing the government a check. Nobody's stopping you."

"Well, I can't do that," he said. "I'm on a fixed income."

"Yeah, right. Like $2 million a year."

"I pay taxes on that!"

"How much do you give to charity?"

That was when Mom jumped in to shut us both up. But I knew the answer to the question. That blowhard SOB had never given a dime to charity in his life, and now he was the great philanthropist with other people's money.

I just smiled at him. He knew his argument was trash, which is why he glared at me.

"Mom," I said, "I have some news. Can you hear me?"

"You're going to want to talk louder!" she said. "It's windy out here, and George is running the engine flat out!"

"Okay!" I said. "Listen, I'm writing Pierce's biography!"

"His what?"

"BIOGRAPHY!" I said.

"Oh, that's nice, dear. Is he paying you?"

"Yes! And I'm flying down to Guyana this afternoon!"

"Did you say Guyana, honey?"

"Yes, Mom!"

"Why Guyana?"

"Pierce has a place down there! He wants me to see it!"

Just then Megan poked her head into my office with a scowl on her face.

"Why are you screaming?" she mouthed at me.

"My Mom," I said. "She's on a boat. What's up?"

Megan shook her head. "Nothing," she mouthed, "but you're too loud."

"OK," I mouthed back and gave her a thumbs-up. Away she went.

"…and that's where that psycho Jim Jones killed all his people," my mother was saying. "I don't think you should go."

"This is not like that," I said. "And come on! Pierce is nothing like Jim Jones!"

"Isn't he, dear?"

"Of course not!"

Then again, I'd been referring to Pierce as a cult leader since college, and now I was going to Guyana with him, and I felt like I'd check-mated myself a little.

"It'll be fine, Mom!" I said. "I'm just checking in. Be back in a couple of days and I'll call you!"

"All right, honey," she said, the connection breaking up a bit. "Be careful!"

That was it. Then I called Ashley, who I was not-all-that-seriously dating.

Or better put, Ashley was not-all-that-seriously dating me.

"Hey, Ash," I said when she answered. "I've got a little bit of news. I'm flying out this afternoon on a work thing and I'll be gone a few days. But I'll check in with you when I get there."

"Oh," she said, somewhat disapprovingly. "Where are you going?"

"South America. It's a work thing."

"Like Rio? Or Buenos Aires?"

"Nah, a little north of there."

"Mike, there's nothing north of there," she said.

"I think that's probably true, but anyway…"

"Well, I thought we were going to dinner on Saturday."

"Did we make plans? I'm sorry. I didn't know that I…"

"No. It's fine. You're right, we hadn't put anything on the calendar."

"Ashley, I apologize if this jams you up. It's kind of a big deal. I'm writing a new book, and I've got to head down to Guyana to do some interviews…"

"You're writing a book about Jim Jones? I thought all the people you'd interview about him are already dead."

"No, Ash. This is a book about Pierce Polk."

"What's Guyana got to do with Pierce Polk?"

"He's building…something down there. He wants me to see it."

"Hmm."

"What?"

"And you didn't invite me to go with you."

"It's apparently in the middle of the jungle, sweetie. Probably a good idea that I scout it out before I'd make you come down there."

"Oh, right. Like I'm some delicate flower who can't handle herself."

"Well, they say that the black caiman that lives in the Essequibo River can grow as big as 20 feet. Not to mention the Bushmaster snakes that grow up to 10 feet long…"

"Fine. I get it. You don't want me there."

"I have no idea what Pierce has going on down there. He just said I'll find it interesting. Maybe I'll take you down there on the next trip."

"Sure. Whatever. It's…whatever."

"Hey, I'm sorry. I'll make it up to you when I get back."

"OK. You do that. I'm hanging up now."

And she did. That wasn't Ashley being rude, it was Ashley being Ashley. I was sort of hoping that I could tell her what was going on and how it might change things with me and the business, but at the end of the day I was beginning to realize that it wouldn't.

To Ashley, I was the sort-of-famous guy she was dating. That was basically it. I wasn't rich, I looked good in a suit but not so much in a swimsuit, at least not anymore, I couldn't claim that I was overly successful, really, and she'd told me that I was "emotionally unavailable," which I thought was more like projection on her part.

Honestly, I don't really know why I cared what Ashley thought. She was the sort-of-hot-and-interesting woman I was dating. She was 40, she was a single mom with a daughter who was an absolute wreck of a teenager – the whole blue-hair-and-piercings-and-never-ending-angst game was super-strong with Jordan – and she was an associate at a law firm in downtown Atlanta which was never going to make her a partner. Ashley had amazing blue eyes and a fitness-model body and she could carry a conversation when she felt like it. But she loved to talk about how terrible her life was and how her daughter was such a disappointment. She'd even complained that Jordan had demanded to move in with her father.

"Well, isn't he married with two little kids?" I had asked her during that conversation. This was about a week before Pierce and I did our deal.

"What difference does that make?"

"Maybe she wants to connect with her brother and sister."

"Half-brother. Half-sister."

"Right, but that's still probably a big deal for her."

"She's just trying to get back at me. That hair, her appearance, they're just an effort at pissing me off."

"But you complain about her a lot, Ash. Maybe you ought to let her move in with her dad if that's what she wants."

"Oh my God! Are you kidding me? Never!"

"I'm just saying," I said, and caught the laser beams she was shooting at me from her eyes, "but I'll stop. It's not my place to say anything."

Especially when I would have had to admit what I was really hoping for was to get rid of Jordan. She was a bitchy little kid who hadn't said a civil word to me in the three months since I'd met her.

It struck me that the thing to do was to tell Ashley it was time for both of us to move on, because this wasn't really going anywhere. I could do better, especially with the new lease on life that selling my soul to Pierce had offered me.

Right? The whole point of taking the deal was that my life would get easier and my professional batteries would get recharged. Why hang on to things that don't work?

I figured I'd think about that on the plane. Hell, maybe Ashley would do us both a favor and break up with me when I got back.

So as I was jotting down notes for the chapter outline of Pierce's biography, I pulled up a link on YouTube that I'd saved.

It was Pierce. He was testifying in front of the Senate Energy and Natural Resources Committee back in November of 2023.

The subject of his testimony had been about how America was dangerously vulnerable to EMP and cyberattacks. Like, our power grid would collapse if it was hit with an EMP, and we needed to harden our ports, industrial facilities, communications and other stuff. Pierce had actually spent a few billion dollars on hardening Sentinel's assets against EMP strikes, and Sentinel had launched a TV ad campaign bragging about that and asking why other big companies hadn't.

He mentioned that – obnoxiously, I thought, but on the other hand he had a right to, because it was criminal how little most of Corporate America, like the electric utilities and cell phone providers and others, had done on that subject – during the opening statement he gave.

But no sooner had he finished his statement but Pierce got waylaid.

The chairman of the committee was George's hero Bernard. And this wild-haired dipshit was pontificating about Pierce's greed.

"In a fair society," Bernard was bleating in that crappy Brooklyn accent of his, which you'd think would grate on Vermonters but apparently it didn't, "there would be a significant wealth tax on men like you for hoarding your resources away from the public."

This came literally right after Pierce had bragged about the money he had spent to safeguard his company's operations against an EMP attack, that the country was otherwise vulnerable to thanks to the inaction of the federal government. Bernard hadn't listened to a word Pierce said.

"Excuse me, Senator," said Pierce, "but how is it fair for the government to confiscate the assets of private citizens without recompense?"

"I'm sorry?" asked a confused Bernard.

"The Takings Clause of the Fifth Amendment," said Pierce. "'Nor shall private property be taken for public use, without just compensation.'"

"What does that have to do with what I said?" asked Bernard.

"You're talking about stealing my money," said Pierce. "You're not really talking about taxing anything. You're talking about making me poorer with no other purpose than that. Where's my just compensation?"

"We'd use those assets to fund the government," said Bernard. "That's your compensation."

"With all due respect, Senator, "nothing the government would do with my money or my businesses would be remotely as good as what I could do on my own. Take dealing with the EMP threat, for example…"

"For you, Mr. Polk," said Bernard. "For you. Not for the masses of the people who suffer (he pronounced it "suffa" in that Brooklyn brogue of his) as you go along your way making a profit at the expense of the planet…"

"The planet? Somehow the planet is mad at me now?"

There were chuckles audible in the crowd, and Bernard was not amused.

"As I was saying, the profit you make is used for your benefit and not for the world."

"My companies protect high-value people who might otherwise suffer physical harm. We make sure ports operate efficiently, so that needed items get where they need to go faster and more cheaply. We have a construction company which builds residential, commercial and industrial facilities, not to mention roads and other transportation infrastructure. We provide network security for major companies so their assets aren't stolen by our enemies. We're in telecommunications, which enhances the ability of people to exchange information and ideas. Are you telling me that those things only benefit me?"

"How many houses do you have, Mr. Polk? How many does one man need?"

"I have eight houses, Senator. And I'm considering building another one."

"No man needs eight houses."

"I see. Don't you have four? So if I sold half of my places I suppose I'd then become virtuous enough for you?"

The chuckles turned into laughs. Bernard was becoming flustered.

"In fact," said Pierce, "I can't think of a single thing you've contributed, Senator, which benefits the world rather than you. How'd you make the money to afford those four houses?"

"You're not asking the questions, Mr. Polk."

"That's OK, Senator. I already know the answer. Your scam is that you sell books. But your presidential campaigns are the buyers of those books, not the public. Essentially what you're doing is you're running a money laundry, and then you want to come to me and tell me I don't provide enough value to deserve to keep what I earn. It's a joke, and you ought to be ashamed of yourself. Now – can we discuss cybersecurity and the EMP threat like I had hoped to do today?"

I remembered watching that exchange and thinking Pierce would be lucky to get out of DC alive after he had it. Bernard, after all, was the dickhead who had run around the country in 2016 running for president and demanding a "political revolution" in America, and then one of his supporters had shot up the Republican congressional baseball team's practice and nearly killed the Majority Whip. Bernard got away with a mealy-mouthed denial that he was ever for violence, and that was it.

Pierce had emailed me after that shooting and said it was a turning point for him. "I can't take it anymore," he said. "These politicians are killing the country and we're just letting them do it."

He hadn't been political prior to that. That was when he started.

And now he was a bull in a china shop.

Not long after he was done with Bernard at that hearing, Polk caught a line of questioning from Suzi Hirohito of Hawaii, who had a reputation as one of the dumbest people in the Senate. Hirohito was about to burnish that reputation nicely.

"Mr. Polk," she began, "how many stockholders do you have?"

"Oh, I don't know," he said. "Between the six companies, maybe…a dozen or so. Including my two ex-wives, who definitely don't have a voting share."

There were giggles from the audience.

"How is that possible? They're big companies."

"Yes, they are, ma'am."

"But they have such a small number of shareholders!"

"That's because they're privately-held. We've never taken any of the Sentinel companies public."

"Why not?"

"Because we've never needed to. And I don't like public companies."

"I don't understand."

"Senator, if I were to take one of my companies public, it wouldn't be mine anymore. And that would make it a worse company. I don't like making things worse."

"Why would your company be worse with public shareholders?"

"Too many cooks spoil the soup. I would then have a board to answer to and the SEC to deal with. It isn't worth it."

"But can't you raise more capital by going public?"

"We've never had trouble raising capital. Our credit is excellent. We borrow at advantageous rates."

Hirohito was getting exasperated.

"Let me help you, Senator, because I know where these questions are coming from," said Pierce. "I'm well aware that a very large percentage of your campaign contributions come from RedGuard Capital, so much so that one could say they own you. And while we're telling the truth here, let's recognize that institutional capital funds like RedGuard tend to gobble up all the public companies worth owning stock in, and when that happens they're able to dictate all kinds of stupid things to the management of those companies."

"Stupid things?" scoffed Hirohito.

"Yes, Senator. Stupid things. Like ESG and DEI, and all kinds of other uneconomic, fantasyland ideas that serve neither the bottom line nor the public. Why would I play that game when I don't have to? Thanks, but no thanks.

"And yes, I can see what's coming because I've heard lots of rumors that at some point next year your side is going to launch a legislative – and probably regulatory – attack on privately-held companies like mine. This little conversation between us is a prelude to that. You didn't hide it very well. Do you have any questions about cybersecurity or EMP? Have you considered that an EMP over Oahu would result in making Honolulu unlivable for six months? Are you even interested in that question?"

Bernard was banging the gavel furiously and scolding Pierce about how he wasn't allowed to ask questions at the hearing, while all of the Republicans on the committee were standing and applauding him, and Pierce was just sitting there with a shit-eating grin and looking at Bernard. He'd torn apart a couple of planned-out attacks, stupid though they were, that the majority on the committee had laid in for him, and it was clear they weren't in his league.

I was thinking that the majority of the potential buyers for the book would want it to focus on Pierce's newly-minted political relevance, and all the red meat he'd splattered all over the walls would need to be featured in order to reach them. But what was a lot more interesting to me was the rest of it.

Sure, he didn't want to take his companies public, and what he told Hirohito was the truth. But maybe not all of it. What I knew was that Pierce didn't want shareholders because Pierce couldn't stand the idea of somebody else having the power to tell him what to do. I knew that was part of the psychology of the man.

But do you write that? If you do, how do you write it? Is that a strength, or a weakness?

It's both, obviously.

I knew I'd have to kick that around a bit. And I'd want to talk to Pierce about it. I needed to gauge just how uncomfortable I could make him without him shutting down or shutting me out.

And how much of this was I even going to discuss with Pierce before the book was finished? Was this biography going to be Pierce's story, or mine?

His, obviously. But I was the guy in control of it. I needed to figure out what that meant.

I'd told Megan to come up with a PR strategy document I could bring down to South America to discuss with Pierce, and I noticed that she'd knocked it out in less than a morning. I knew that because it popped up on my email, and 20 seconds later she popped into my office.

"Got your paper done," she said. "You packed?"

"Not really," I said. I don't even have a clue what I'm supposed to wear down there. I have a bunch of t-shirts and shorts and shit like that. I assume it's hot."

"Mike," she said, shaking her head, "the last thing you want to wear in the jungle is shorts."

"Why not?"

"Mosquitoes? Hello?"

"Shit. Well, I did pack a pair of jeans…"

"Is that your bag?" she asked, pointing to an ugly plastic box with a half-protruding handle and a couple of worn rollers that was leaning against the couch.

"You know it is."

Megan grabbed it and dropped it onto the couch, unzipping it and cracking it open.

"No, no," she muttered. "No, no and definitely no."

"My choices don't meet with your approval?"

"You're going to look like an idiot American tourist," she said. "How much time do you have before they pick you up?"

"I have…" I said, looking at the clock on my laptop, "…one hour and 45 minutes."

"Great. I'll be back before then. Give me your Visa card."

"Oh, I don't think our relationship has progressed quite that far, honey," I joked.

"I don't have time for this, goofball," she snapped at me. "I'm going to hit Orvis and Dick's Sporting Goods and get you something appropriate for this trip."

"Huh," I said, proffering the instrument of my financial diminution. "Seems like you're more excited about this than I am."

"Maybe so," she said. "But I'm definitely not going to have our CEO looking like he doesn't belong."

"OK, fine. But I'm not wearing a pith helmet or jodhpurs."

"Oh, shut up," she said, shaking her head and leaving.

Colby came next, asking if I was going to file any stories or recording any podcasts when I was on the trip. I said yes, I'd probably do something.

Then he asked me if we were going to have any extra money in the budget, because he wanted to hire a kid out of Texas who'd built an X following of half a million people with hilarious memes mostly making fun of Joe Deadhorse, the president. Specifically, there was the recent claim Deadhorse had made that he was a Lakota Sioux Indian, something that was perfect fodder because (1) Deadhorse had never claimed to have Native American blood before, and (2) Deadhorse made lots of idiotic claims like that lately, lending an air of hilarity to current events that just screamed for satire.

And this kid, whose X handle was MemeCracker110 but whose actual name (we found out his name because MediaMatters had doxxed him and then some asshole had swatted him four nights in a row) was Billy Ray Olivera, was a genius. I especially liked the stuff he was doing that called Deadhorse "Chief Spreading Bull."

"If we capture that and start up a Meme O' The Day page on the site," Colby was telling me, "it could increase site traffic by 20 percent. Maybe more."

"How much does this kid want?"

"Fifty grand a year, plus traffic bonuses. Pretty cheap."

"To make memes? Are you kidding me?"

"He'll pay for himself. Megan can tell you. Where is she, anyway?"

"Off buying me jungle gear with my credit card."

"She's the most valuable one here."

"Probably true."

"Anyway, I'm talking to Billy Ray now. Give me the go-ahead and I'll lock it down."

"Does he do anything else but make memes? Can he write? Can he do a podcast?"

"Billy Ray?" Colby was snickering. "I don't think that's a good idea."

"What is he, like an idiot savant?"

"Ummm…"

"He's an idiot savant."

"Let's just say he has a lot of time for Photoshop on his computer."

"Fine, whatever. Yeah, hire him. If he doesn't juice site traffic I'm gonna leave you in Mechanicsville after dark."

Colby gasped. "That's it. I'm going to the EEOC. My boss is a racist and this is a hostile work environment."

I gave him a smirk. Colby was always joking about playing the race card. The guy had a signed picture of Clarence Thomas on the wall of his office.

"Shaddap, Iggy," I laughed.

"Don't come back a jungle bunny," he said as he left. I shot him the bird.

Chapter 3

April 5, 2024, Atlanta, Georgia

Megan came back just before the car showed up with a brand-new suitcase full of brand-new clothes and other brand-new gear.

"Throw that disgusting thing away," she said, looking at my suitcase. "You don't need it, or really anything you packed in it."

"How much stuff did you get me, Dear Megan?" I asked.

"Enough," she said. "Plus, you should put this on."

She handed me a couple of plastic hangers containing a "river guide shirt" and a pair of "Jackson quick-dry pants" from Orvis. And a bag containing hiking boots, socks and a rain jacket from Dick's Sporting Goods.

"What's wrong with what I'm wearing?"

"A Hawaiian shirt and jeans? No, you may not."

Just then Melissa came in.

"I agree," she said. "By the way, the car is here."

"Sheesh. I thought I was the boss of this clownshow."

"Hurry up," said Megan. "Melissa, will you pack up his computer gear for him?"

"Yup," she said, shooing me out of my chair.

A few minutes later, dressed like an Eddie Bauer model or something, and having waved goodbye to the staff, I was sitting in the back of a giant Suburban listening to Aaron Lewis belting out "Am I The Only One" – not my choice; that was what Raul, the driver, had on – as we fought our way south on I-285 on the way to Fulton County Airport.

"It's probably longer as the crow flies," he said, "and I know it's bumper-to-bumper, but at least there's no traffic lights. I hate the traffic lights."

"I'm with you," I nodded. "Besides, it's Atlanta. There's no escaping this traffic."

"Am I the only one not brainwashed?" Aaron was asking, on the stereo. "Makin' my way through the land of the lost, Who still gives a shit, and worries 'bout his kids, As they try to undo all the things he did?"

"Hmmph," I said.

"Music all right, Mr. Holman?" asked Raul. "I can put on something else."

"Nah, Aaron's fine," I said. "Just thinking about those lyrics."

"They're true," said Raul. "I think it's lost. Just a matter of time."

"You may be right. That's a common feeling, I notice."

"We're run by freaks and psychos. You know it, Mr. Holman. I listen to your podcast. You had Riley Gaines on talking about *los transgéneros*. Taking over girls' sports. I got a daughter; what am I supposed to tell her about that?"

"I don't know what to tell you, Raul. It's stupid. Not like when we were growing up."

"My parents grew up in Nicaragua under the Sandinistas," he said. "My Papa won't stop talking about how this country is just like that now. It freaks me out."

"Yeah, not good."

"You tell Mr. Polk that if he needs a driver down there I'll go. I just want to bring my family."

"Raul, I don't think they have a lot of roads where he's building his place."

He laughed. "Good point. But there's a lot of us who'd go with him."

"You need to fight for *this* place, Raul. The country is only lost if you let it be."

"I hope you're right. You would know better than me. But it's hard to keep faith. Did you hear what Deadhorse said this morning?"

"What, about how Catholics of all people ought to be for abortion?"

"Yeah. What the hell was that?"

"Raul, I have no earthly idea. I'm not even gonna try to analyze that one. But I'm almost positive that the *Washington Post* will explain it for us in tomorrow's edition."

"Freakin' gibberish, is what it is," Raul said. "That's all we hear. And I used to be a Democrat. Now I'm not anything. I can't stand any of them."

"You don't like Trumbull?"

"Yeah, he's OK. I'll probably vote for him. But his party won't even back him. Look at the ones here."

"Also a good point," I said, since the Georgia governor had a long-running feud with Trumbull for which both sides shared ample fault.

Finally, after 45 more minutes of Raul's desperate harangues and a playlist of country songs featuring a lot of Oliver Anthony, Kid Rock, and Jason Aldean, we pulled up to Fulton County Airport, which was the private-jet venue of Pierce's choice. Raul hustled the Suburban through the checkpoint and drove us right up to a big hangar. We got out, he grabbed my bags and I walked in…

…to find Pierce with a half-dozen other guys drinking beer.

"Hey, here he is!" said Pierce. "Mike, glad you could make it. Here, I want you to meet these guys. Fellas, this is Mike Holman, my old college roommate. I'm assuming you know who he is. Mike, meet some of the folks who are making Liberty Point a reality."

"Hey Pierce, hey everybody," I said. "What's Liberty Point, again?"

"Liberty Point is what we're calling the little colony in the jungle," said an older guy with a cowboy hat and an iron handshake grip. "I'm Ted Kournis, project manager for Sentinel Construction. Liberty Point is my thing."

I nodded, enduring that handshake until Kournis let go.

"And this is Bill Abbott," said Pierce. "He's the architect. Absolutely brilliant."

"Nice to meet you, Bill," I said.

"Likewise," said Abbott, who came off as bookish until I noticed the tree-trunk forearms he had.

"That there is Roman Jefferson," said Pierce, pointing to a bald-headed black guy with a badass look to him. "He's a guest and a potential inhabitant."

"Good to meet you, Mike," said Jefferson. "I'm a fan."

"Yes, sir," I said. "What line of work are you in?"

"Private security, mostly. Some other things."

"All right."

"These two guys are Todd Allen and Chad Burkhardt," Pierce said, pointing to a couple of bankers. "They're bankers."

"Guess that's obvious," said Allen, who had a pinstripe suit on. His handshake was like a pillow compared to Kournis'.

"And I think you already know Mark Smith," said Pierce. "He's building our IT setup down there."

"What's up, Mark?" I said. He'd gone to Vanderbilt, a couple of years behind us. Mark graduated at the same time we did. And he'd been with Pierce from the get-go.

"Long time," he said. "Good to see you, Mike."

"OK, guys, let's get on this sucker and get moving. I've got lots of liquor and I think we have all kinds of snacks and there's a chocolate cake and some other stuff…"

He droned on a while as we boarded.

Oh, and did I mention the plane was a Gulfstream G700? The most gorgeous thing I'd ever seen. I made the mistake of complimenting Pierce on it and before I knew it, I was getting all the specifications. It would seat 18 and sleep 12. It'd do Mach 0.925, which was more than 700 miles an hour, its wingspan was 99 feet, 9 inches, and they'd had to build their own airstrip for it because the one at Mahdia, which was the closest town to Liberty Point, was only about half as long as they needed.

"This guy can make the trip down there and back and down again," Pierce said. "Awesome range, right? We could go halfway around the world until we'd need a refuel."

"It's amazing, Pierce," I said, half-exhausted from his dissertation. "Really. Some kind of beautiful plane."

"Definitely nicer than that Bombardier Challenger 300 you used to have," said Smith. "What a lemon that was."

Pierce cocked his head and nodded. "At least I got a decent resale out of it."

I looked at Roman, figuring that he and I were the two broke-dicks on this flight. Then I noticed his watch. It was a

King Of The Jungle

Cartier something-or-other, which had to be worth seven or eight grand.

Roman smiled. "You fly private much, Mike?" he asked.

"Not that often," I said. "Business class is usually the top of my game."

He chuckled. "I feel you."

"Makes this a fun trip," I said. "At least until we get there."

A pair of stewardesses came aboard and saw a cocktail party going on, and after some scolding and cajoling and a dose or two of the kind of sexual innuendo that would make for a considerable legal problem but for the fact, as Pierce told me, that Stacey and Allie had heard it all before and had signed an NDA before coming aboard, we were all in our seats and the jet taxied out onto the runway.

And when the pilot punched it, in the blink of an eye we were airborne.

"Smooth," I said to Pierce, who was seated next to me.

"Right?" he said. "Guys, Mike is comin' out of an oath of poverty he took a bunch of years ago. We gotta get him acclimated to the big-time!"

"Hear, hear," said Burkhardt, lifting a glass. He wasn't drinking beer.

And before I knew it Pierce was handing me a glass of…

"It's Perrier-Jouët Belle Epoque 2002," he said. "Only about six thousand Euro a bottle."

"Oh, come on," I said.

"No big deal. It's just sparkling wine. But these guys like it."

I shook my head, but I joined in his toast, which was "to a new world in the new world." And then as the other passengers commenced to their own conversations, Pierce started peppering me with details.

"So it's a four and a half hour flight," he said, "and then we'll land at CPX. This will blow your mind."

"What's CPX?"

"That's the airport code for Connor Polk Airfield."

"You named it for your dad, huh?"

"He's always been into aviation. I thought he'd get a kick out of it. Mom sure did."

I nodded.

"Wait until you see Liberty Point," he said. "It's a bad-ass little place. It's obviously not done, but we've got the main lodge finished, and we put together the hydro plant, the airport, the water treatment and the sewer system, and…"

"Pierce, how many people are you expecting this place to hold?"

"Well, we can house 2,300 now. Comfortably. In a month when the second phase is finished it'll be more like 4,000, maybe more if the weather cooperates. And in two months when the big condo buildings come on line that'll be another six thousand people."

"Where are you going to get all these folks from?"

"Lots of Sentinel employees, mostly. But also, I've got some friends of mine who've bought in. It's kind of a just-in-case thing for them, but they're all making their way down to visit. You'll see some pretty famous folks at dinner tonight."

"Interesting."

"OK, I'm overloading you. I get it. Hey, there's a master bedroom back there. You want to rack out? You want me to send Stacey with you to tuck you in?"

"Tempting, Pierce. Really. But I'm good. I think I'm gonna work some more on my outline for the book. Got some ideas rolling around in my head that I want to put down."

"Hey, great idea! So you'll know, the wifi on this is like eight times faster than anywhere on the ground. Part of that is Gulfstream, and part of it is Mark's wizardry."

"Cool. Thanks!"

Then he left me alone for a while, and I got to work.

But before I knew it, Pierce was harassing me again.

"Hey," he said, "you're going to want to check something out. We're coming up to the coast of South America, and we're going to come in low and slow over Guyana because there's something you'll want to see."

"All right," I said. "What is it?"

"Only the tallest waterfall in the world. Come on!"

We were descending pretty rapidly, and I could tell the engines were powering down. The coast of Guyana was visible below in the fading daylight. I couldn't see any evidence of civilization.

"Why's the beach unpopulated?" I asked Pierce.

"The whole country's unpopulated," he said. "There's like 800,000 people in all of Guyana. It's pretty much one of the most unspoiled places in the world."

"Until you came along to spoil it, right?"

"Yeah. Something like that. We'll be landing right at sunset, so you won't get to see the night-time view, but it's one of the most amazing things – you can fly at 35,000 feet above the jungle and you won't see any lights at all from the ground at night. Like nothing. Just a black void."

"I hope that's not supposed to make me more comfortable."

Pierce laughed. "Hey, don't worry about it. If we crash, it's pretty much a done deal we're all dead. Better if the impact kills us."

"Hilarious, Pierce."

"You and I aren't meant to die in the jungle, buddy. Trust me."

A little while later I could feel the jet making a sharp turn.

"Oh, here it is!" said Pierce with all the enthusiasm of a ten-year-old. "You're not gonna believe this. OK, everybody, look out the right-side window!"

King Of The Jungle

Just about everybody but me had their phones out, mashing them against the window as the plane tilted right.

Then I saw why. It was glorious.

"That's Kaietur Falls," said Pierce. "It's a 750-foot drop, which is the biggest in the world. We're not in the rainy season yet so you're not getting the full force of the water, but look at that!"

"I never heard of this thing," I said. "It's the tallest?"

"Yeah," said Mark Smith. "It's not the biggest waterfall in South America overall, that's Iguazu Falls down in the three corners. But this'll do."

"That it will," I said, as we banked around for another look.

"There's a little airfield down there," said Pierce. "I told them I'd pay to put down a runway big enough to land a jet like this, but for some reason there was resistance to that."

"Probably because you'd put all the little plane operators who run tours in there out of business," I said.

"Yeah, maybe so. But still – big hotel on the river at the top of the falls, cantilever deck so you could see the whole thing, somebody would make out like a bandit!"

"They don't want it, Pierce."

"They don't know what they want. I guarantee you in five years somebody will build it. Guyana is exploding. Exoil found something like 12 billion barrels off the coast here and they're pouring in the resources. Guyana's GDP went up

SIXTY percent last year, and it's going to do probably better than that this year."

"Jesus."

"The place has gone from one of the poorer places on earth to, I think, fourth-richest country per capita in the Western Hemisphere in the space of a decade. All that wealth coming in means development. You know it, and I know it."

"Guess that means Georgetown…it's Georgetown, right? The capital?"

"Yeah."

"Georgetown must be a happening kind of town right now."

"Sort of. It's a shithole of a place but it's got lots of potential. We bought a port facility on the Demerara River close to its mouth, right by downtown. Servicing a lot of the offshore stuff. Running helicopters to the platforms and back. It's pretty rich little business."

"So you're, what? The oligarch of this country?"

"A little. Mostly I just want to help. They have super-nice people here. Most of 'em have no idea how to live in a rich country, but that's actually part of the charm. They're simple, but they're buying BMW's and day-trading on the NASDAQ. There's tons of inflation, because it's all so remote and they can't buy enough stuff to satisfy all the money they're making. So mostly everybody trades in dollars. We're building a first-class mall next to the university in the capital."

After we made a second pass over the falls, the jet turned southeast and then northeast, and in just a couple of minutes we were dropping down over a thick carpet of statuesque trees into a narrow fenced-off clearing and setting down onto a well-constructed runway. I could feel the brakes kicking in, and I must have shown some panic on my face, because Pierce laughed at me.

"No sweat, pal," he said. "This runway is 8,000 feet. Plenty long enough."

"I wouldn't expect otherwise," I said. "What are the fences for?"

"Keeping out the critters."

"What critters?"

"Caiman. Capybaras. Anteaters. Jaguars."

"Jaguars?"

"Oh, yeah. We have a couple of them who visit us from time to time. It's why we have a couple of game wardens at Liberty Point."

We taxied to a large hangar painted with the Sentinel logo and the plane slowed to a stop inside.

And when the door opened I expected a blast of steam to rush in. Instead, it was actually just a little on the warm side.

When we walked down the little stairway, I asked Pierce if this was normal.

"This time of year it'll get up to 90 degrees or so," he said. "The low is 72."

"Shit, that's only a little hotter than back home. How are the summers?"

"This is about as hot as it gets, actually. What's not good about the summers is the rain. You've never seen rain like this place gets."

"Is that right?"

"Oh, yeah. Last June I think we got 14 inches in a month."

"Good Lord."

"Wasn't easy on the construction, I'll tell you that."

A couple of Jeep Grand Cherokees pulled up, and we all piled in. We motored out of the hangar and onto a road which took us around the runway, up to an electronic gate which opened as we approached it, and into a dense forest down a hill.

"Damn," I said, looking out of the side window. "It's freaking dark out here."

"Yeah," Pierce said, as Kournis and Smith chuckled. "We haven't installed the streetlights yet."

"Very funny, Pierce."

"No, we'll put them in. When's that scheduled, Ted?"

"Six weeks," he said. "Need the power transmission lines first. Maybe sooner."

"Well, wait – where does the power at the airstrip come from?"

"We've got a couple of diesel generators for that," said Pierce. "But that'll change when we hook the place up to the hydro plant on the Potaro."

"The Potaro?"

"That's the little river. It's the one that big waterfall is on. Upstream from here."

"What's the big river?"

"That'd be the Essequibo. You'll see that one in a minute when…"

Just then the road straightened and headed northeast, and we stopped at another gate. A wall of solid wood stood in our way.

"Looks like something out of Jurassic Park," I said. "What's on the other side?"

"Civilization," said Kournis.

The gate opened and the road became a boulevard, and I broke out in a laugh.

"You've got to be joking," I said.

A lot of it was under construction, and I could see there were people working, even now under project lights since the sun was down, but what it looked like was that I'd found my way to Florence. Or maybe Marseille.

"We decided on a Mediterranean feel," said Abbott. "It sort of fit the territory, plus the local sources of building materials are a good match."

"Great stone in the quarry on the other side of the Potaro," said Pierce. "And we have great clay for mortar."

"I'd have thought you'd use wood," I said, "since there's so much of it."

"Nope," said Abbott. "Wood attracts termites. And *these* termites are real sons of bitches."

I chuckled and shook my head.

We made our way about a half-mile down the boulevard and then the Cherokee made a right turn under an archway into a courtyard.

"Welcome to the lodge," said Pierce. Everybody got out of the vehicle.

I could see what looked like an expensive restaurant on the ground floor to my right. The building surrounding us had three stories and it was done in a renaissance Italian style with white sandstone walls.

I followed Pierce to a lobby-slash-concierge station in the corner of the building where he was greeted by a pretty Latin girl as we passed through the door.

"Hey, Consuela," he said. "How's it going?"

"Very well, sir," said Consuela. "They're waiting for you upstairs."

"OK, great. Thanks."

He led us to an elevator, and as we got to the third floor and the door opened I got to see the Essequibo as I looked out of the window.

"Damn," I said. That's a big freaking river."

"It's half as wide as the Mississippi," said Kournis. "Flows at 200,000 cubic feet per second. Which is about a third of the Mississippi's volume."

"How navigable is it?" I asked.

"To here, pretty navigable," said Abbott. "Boat comes with supplies a couple times a week."

"Where does the boat come from?"

"Bartica, downriver," said Pierce. "Hey, come this way."

He opened a door and inside was a penthouse suite-looking place that would put the Ritz to shame.

"Jesus, Pierce," I said.

"This is really a temporary thing," he said. "Tomorrow I'll show you where I'm going to build my place. It's a little upriver from here, which means south of here. Decent-sized hill overlooking the town. Perfect for a villa!"

"And you'll get to see the town," said Kournis. "It's growing fast."

"How much is all of this going to cost?"

"Eight billion," said Pierce. "Pretty cheap."

"We'll come in under budget," Kournis said. "Not a lot of red tape down here."

Pierce led us into the dining room. The other guests were already there. Among them: a couple of very recognizable singers, a retired Super Bowl-winning quarterback, the president of Lincoln Mining Company's South American operations, the CEO of Magpul and the former head of the Brexit Party in the UK.

And we all sat down to dinner. Steak, obviously. That's what you ate when you were at Pierce's table.

Chapter 4

April 8, 2024, Atlanta, Georgia

I spent a weekend down at Liberty Point, and I don't mind saying it – the place blew my mind.

It was basically a little village in the middle of a vast jungle, but the way they were building it was like some sort of medieval/renaissance European city. They'd walled it off, though the walls were built to be temporary and modular – they'd move them when it was time to expand the place.

Wide streets, little courtyards in the middle of all the city blocks, all the buildings were three stories high. Everything was stone and concrete, with those Italian-looking terra cotta tile roofs. They were making the tiles on site with river clay from a quarry on the Potaro Pierce had acquired. He had bought 20 square miles of property, and that included five or six quarries and mines, along the Potaro and Essequibo and heading inland.

He showed me the plans for Liberty Point on a map. It was essentially a square bordered by the Potaro to the north and the Essequibo to the east, stretching into the jungle part of the way toward Mahdia, the little mining town west of Liberty Point and into, well, nothing but wilderness to the south. It was pretty clear this was going to be the center of commerce and wealth for the area around it, if for no other reason than that there wasn't much in the way of commerce and wealth other than Liberty Point.

But Pierce said that was a crime, because it was his opinion that a proper effort at exploiting the natural resources in that area would make every single human around there rich as Mansa Musa. He started rattling off the stuff that was under the ground, beginning with gold and diamonds and moving on to all kinds of other things, and he said all it would take was a little bit of real infrastructure and this could be one of the richest places on the planet.

"It's all small-time shit here so far," he said, "but it doesn't have to be that way. I really want to help these people get what they deserve."

Pierce was especially proud of the hydroelectric power plant they'd built. The Potaro was pretty rapid in its downflow into the Essequibo, so what they'd done was to wall off part of the river and repurpose an old set of land dredges that somebody had put in to harvest gravel decades ago into a firmament to install a series of vortex turbines that ran along the south bank of the Potaro. Each one of them supposedly spat out 15 kilowatt/hours of power, and there were 100 of them along the river. I met a guy named Fred Tranh, who was the engineer in charge of this thing, and he was giddy about the project.

"There's a weir on the Potaro just upriver from the Liberty Point property," he said, "and we're negotiating the rights to it. When that's done we're going to install six big-ass turbines along that weir and it'll set us up with enough hydroelectric power to juice up this whole region. Won't need any more generators for 40 miles."

"You don't need a dam for that?" I asked him.

"Not with this new tech we're using. It absolutely kicks ass. And it'll run almost completely without outside support. Total fire-and-forget project."

Tranh said there was a company out of Belgium which supplied the turbines. They'd had to fly them into Georgetown, then put them on ferry-boats up the Essequibo to get them to the landing site, and then truck them along the little road they'd carved to the sites. He showed me all the video of the hydro plant construction, and I've got to admit it – even though I don't have a drop of construction enthusiast blood in me, this was fascinating stuff.

I could hear Tim Allen oinking while I was watching Tranh's video. And I wondered when Allen, or maybe Mike Rowe, was going to make it down here.

Everything about the place was fascinating. They'd gone in with three of these single-grip forest harvesters which can turn 100 trees a day each into stacks of logs, and they'd cleared out first a path from Mahdia, which was about 17 miles away from the confluence of the Potaro and the Essequibo, to Liberty Point, and then they started clearing the site itself.

Kournis told me that the first thing they'd built was the Landing, which turned out to be a pretty cool deal. It was this big restaurant/bar facility with an outdoor amphitheater that faced out onto the confluence of the two rivers, together with a bunch of piers and moorings for boats just west of it where there had been a strip mine and a deep pit somebody had dug. What they'd built just west of the Landing was not really a marina, but sort of like one.

Kournis said that after they opened the man-camp where the first two hundred or so construction workers had come in, they'd cleared the trees from the confluence point and built the Landing, and that was where they'd feed and entertain the folks.

And eventually, they'd built enough buildings that the man-camp was dismantled and the workers started crashing in the apartments they'd built. Kournis said it was amazing how much faster the work went once that had happened.

I noticed there was a bug-zapper under every single streetlight, and there were lots of lights, all of them a good 25 feet off the ground. I asked what the deal was.

"Do you notice all the mosquitoes?" was Kournis' response.

"Not really," I said.

"Exactly."

He said the bug-zappers had been an on-site idea because in the initial stages of the construction process the mosquitoes were so bad that the men were essentially having to work in hazmat suits. Clearing the forest set loose every manner of hostile natural response possible, and insects turned out to be the most irritating.

So the answer was lights, high up, and bug zappers. And over the course of four months or so when the first phase of the

King Of The Jungle

project was finding its footing, the zappers greatly diminished that mosquito population.

"I'm surprised the eco crowd hasn't thrown a fit," I said.

"Well, you're pretty well-informed. How much did you know about this project?"

"Until Pierce mentioned it Thursday night, nothing."

"Right. Nobody knows about Liberty Point. We'll keep it that way as long as we can. Then it's a fait accompli and if they don't like it, screw 'em."

Later, I asked Pierce about the bug zappers. He laughed and said I hadn't heard the best part.

"We're emptying the catch bins and boxing up the products," he said, "and at some point I'm going to ship those little boxes to Klaus Schwab and John Kerry and Bill Gates and whoever else with a note that says, 'Eat Ze Bugz.'"

"Want to see the video of one of those guys opening that up," I said.

"Hell yeah."

The people at Liberty Point were mostly Sentinel Construction guys, and they were getting triple wages down there. It was a level of hustle you just never see in American construction; there were barges bringing in steel for the structures of those buildings, and it was immediately dumped into a materials yard along the shore of the Essequibo, then trucked to the next building site where cranes would set the girders into pre-set foundations, rivet them together into a skeleton, and then came the concrete-and-stone blocks. All the buildings were designed the way the old Spanish and Italian cities – and some of the ones in southern France, too – had been set up. They were essentially hollow squares that took up a city block and had courtyards in the middle. Everything was three stories, and the first story would have a parking garage – though there weren't really any cars; mostly everybody went around in golf carts – and space for stores, coffee shops, restaurants and whatever, though there weren't much of those businesses in place yet.

Then the second and third floors were where people lived.

There was a decent-sized little park in the middle of the town and there was a movie theater – that was where lots of folks congregated at night. Pierce said the theater could also be repurposed for live music, and that they were going to start flying bands down to do weekly concerts there.

"Sounds cool," I said, "but wouldn't your amphitheater be better for that?"

"In the dry season, yes. In the wet season, nope. It's gotta be inside once the rains start coming."

The buildings all had cisterns equipped with water filters collecting rainwater from the roofs and, when full, those were supposed to enable each building in Liberty Point to be self-sufficient in generating its own potable water supply. But they also had a water treatment plant along the Potaro and a full sewer and water system that would accommodate up to 10,000 people.

"You went all out on this thing, Pierce," I said. "Is this just some erector set for you? I don't really get the motivation to go through all this trouble to put this together in the middle of nowhere."

"It's *because* it's the middle of nowhere," he said. "When we've got Liberty Point fully built, and we're racing to get that done before the rainy season fully kicks in, we'll be a little paradise that almost nobody can get to."

"What, like a hermit kingdom?"

"More like a refuge for when the world goes absolutely to shit."

"So you've bet eight billion dollars that the world will go to shit."

"Yeah, and I'd say it's the safest bet going. You pay attention to current events. Watching what's happening to Taiwan? The Chinese are going to get that place without firing a shot."

The Taiwanese president, who had been overwhelmingly elected on a platform of opposing unification with mainland China despite the ChiComs backing his opponent to the hilt, had resigned the previous week with no explanation given. The Parliament had gone into emergency session and appointed an interim president who gave a speech stressing "conciliation" with China. A flood of Taiwanese had taken to the air and sea to get off the island, with lots of them turning up in Hawaii and the Philippines. The Deadhorse administration had congratulated the Taiwanese on their "peaceful governmental transition."

"I'm just not gonna give up on America," I said.

"Me neither, Mike, but I have the means to hedge my bets, and so I'm doing it in a place that I can control. Liberty Point is that place."

"You're likely to have a flood of immigrants when the folks find out about it."

"And the interesting thing is, between the fresh water and the natural gas and the minerals and the other assets we have in the area, we could very easily build a first-class city of a million people here."

"You know there's one flaw in your plan, though," I said.

"What's that?"

"What happens when the Venezuelans drop in out of helicopters and declare that all of this is theirs now?"

"Oh, that? Screw that. They wouldn't dare."

"Let's say you're wrong. What then?"

"It'll be the biggest mistake they ever made, I'll tell you that."

Back home in Atlanta Sunday night, I was visited by a pair of feds.

"We're agents Smythe and Muhammad, FBI," said the black guy.

"I take it you're Smythe and she," I said, pointing at the white lady, "is Muhammad?"

"Very funny," he said. "Can we come in?"

"What's this about?"

"We understand you were out of the country this weekend."

"So what if I was?"

"We'd like to ask you some questions about your trip."

"I see no reason why anything that went on this weekend would be of interest to you guys," I said. "What's more, I'm not an idiot, and therefore I don't talk to the FBI without a video camera recording and an attorney present. Sorry, y'all."

That earned me a stink-eye from Smythe. Or maybe she really was Muhammad. Either way, that visit freaked me out enough that I texted my old buddy Morris Moskovitz, who I'd known going all the way back from my time living in New York.

Morris was, he called himself, The Perfect Jew. Except he wasn't perfect. He was an old fart, about 70, and the hair atop his head had decided at some point to grow out of his ears instead. Morris ate too much and he drank too much and he didn't care about the consequences, which were advancing on him.

Most of all, Morris was the funniest human being I knew. I had told him that he was born too late.

"You should have been in your grandparents' generation," I said. "You could have gone into comedy and shared the stage with Youngman and Rickles and Dangerfield."

"Oy vey," he said. "And scratch out a living in the Catskills? Whaddya, special?"

Instead, Morris was a lawyer. A pretty good one.

I had met him because every day he'd eat lunch at a delicatessen that was on the ground floor of ANN's building in Manhattan. I'd be in there all the time and there he was with his newspaper, his legal pad and his Reuben sandwich. The little conversations we struck up became big ones, and when Logan Rudolph got me shitcanned at ANN Morris handled the severance negotiations and did very right by me. He'd been my lawyer ever since.

Especially when he decided in the middle of the COVID lockdowns that he'd had it with New York.

"I guess I'm not The Perfect Jew after all," he told me. "A Perfect Jew would move to Miami. I'm only going so far as Atlanta. What does that make me?"

"Like a two-thirds Perfect Jew," I said, figuring that was about the difference in distance between the two destinations and Manhattan.

"Heh," he said. "Anyway, you have me to complain about now. I'm moving to your town."

And he found a nice Jewish deli in Buckhead where he plopped down daily, and the two of us would eat lunch once or twice a week.

But I texted him an invitation to a diner open late, and included the words "dying to see you" at the end.

"Twenty minutes," he said.

And twenty minutes later, Morris was sitting down and asking me "what the hell are you doing interrupting my spring football game?"

He was the only human being I know who gave a damn about the new UFL the TV networks were pushing, but Morris was a die-hard Birmingham Stallions fan for some strange reason.

"I had a visit from the FBI," I said, and told him the story.

"Ahhh, you don't need me," he said. "I do contracts! I look like a criminal lawyer to you?"

"I'm not gonna get into what you look like, Morris," I said, which earned me a smile. "All I know is you're my lawyer. So if I need counsel on this thing, can you help me find somebody?"

"This is what I would do if I was you," he said, slurping on a black coffee the waitress had brought him. "I'll find you a criminal defense lawyer, you hire the guy not just for you but for everybody on your staff. I doubt they've hit any of them up but it's probably coming. If everybody is covered, you then have an unbroken line of defense."

"Fine."

"What you don't need is somebody on your staff ratting you out to the feds."

"Morris, I haven't done anything. All I did was agree to write the biography and take on the PR job."

"Yeah, and you didn't bring me the contracts! Whaddya doing, you zhlub!"

"What the hell is a zhlub?"

"A schmendrick! A meshuggeneh! A fool!"

"Morris, we don't even have a contract yet."

"And he paid you already?"

"Yeah."

"Pierce Polk does business on a handshake?"

"With me he does."

"Oh, look at you then! I'll get you contracts, have him sign them. And you should make him front you the cost for the lawyer. Understand?"

"Sure, that makes sense. But why would the FBI be up in my face, anyway? That's just strange."

"Intimidation, Michael. You went with Polk to Guyana, that means you're in his circle now. And they know that you are."

"But so what?"

"So he has a target on his back."

I scowled at Morris. The idea that my college roommate, who for all of his flaws was an especially upright and moral man and whose professional and personal ethics were generally head-and-shoulders above those of his competitors and acquaintances, would be treated as a villain, really offended me.

I hadn't fully processed the idea that I was now one of Pierce's guys. Pierce did a company-wide thing once a year, and when he did it he would literally rent out an NBA or NHL arena, like the Bridgestone Arena in Nashville that he'd paid for last year, for an all-day "Sentinel Reset Summit" that Tony Robbins would put on.

Robbins' stuff and the stuff Pierce's people bought in on were very similar. And honestly, I couldn't argue with it. These folks regularly kicked the ass of the competition, and they did it by winning with better productivity and better price. They were kicking the shit out of the Chinese, for crying out loud; most American companies were busy selling out to the Chinese, and Pierce's guys were whipping them.

And this guy was a crook?

Maybe I was settling into the cult. On the other hand, you didn't have to be part of the cult to be supremely pissed off about the feds and their heavy-handed bullshit where Pierce was concerned.

"It's not like he's a criminal," I protested to Morris. "He has armies of lawyers. He turns a profit the old-fashioned way. What do they have on him?"

"The fact that Omobba and Deadhorse hate him. That's what they have. And in case you haven't been paying attention, that's a lot."

"Terrible."

"Yes, Michael. It makes me glad I'm a septuagenarian. I'll be long gone when this all goes to hell. You, on the other hand, will be neck deep in this mishegoss. And now I'm going home to watch the second half. I'll text you the number of someone to call in the morning."

And then he left, prompting me to fulminate over a hamburger steak.

Just then I got a text. It was from Ashley. "Check your email," it said.

So I did, and at the top of my inbox was a message which had as a subject…

"Dear Michael."

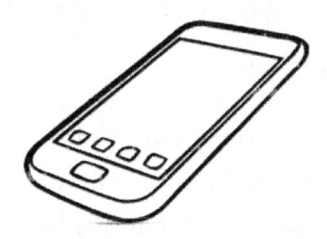

Chapter 5

April 16, 2024, Atlanta, Georgia

"Hello America, and welcome to Episode 334 of *Connected, With Mike Holman*. In this edition of the podcast, we've got one of the most interesting people in the world, talking about things of interest to the world. Pierce Polk, CEO of Sentinel Holdings, has just announced plans to launch a wireless internet consumer service early next year with coverage all over North America, and no sooner was that announcement made but the opposition spiked immediately. Calls for an investigation into Sentinel issued forth from several quarters, including the Department of Justice. A letter from Garrick Wreath, the attorney general, claims that Sentinel is engaging in "hegemonic" business practices and decries the "dangerous trend" of "hyper-vertical integration" that Sentinel's plan represents.

"But that's not all which is happening in the world of Sentinel Holdings. The FBI announced an investigation into Sentinel Port Management, alleging in leaked documents that its operations in Victoria, Texas and Hueneme, California are fronts for the global drug trade. Mr. Polk has denied this, and he has offered $100,000 to anyone who can provide definitive proof that drug trafficking is ongoing with participation or assent of Sentinel employees at any of the company's 31 U.S. facilities.

"Legacy corporate media outlets are now calling Pierce Polk an 'embattled' CEO. But if he's embattled, he's battling. He's got a lot to say and a clear desire to say it, so it's a pleasure to welcome to the show Mr. Pierce Polk. Pierce, thanks for stopping in. Which one of these kerfuffles do you want to start with?"

Pierce gave me a perturbed look, not that I cared. I'd told him that the podcast wasn't the best idea and that I wasn't going to use my show as a vehicle to give him a hummer. I made it clear, or at least I thought I did, that if he was coming on the show, I wouldn't be hostile – but I also wasn't going to bury him in cream puffs, either.

The thing was, we didn't do much show-prep. He just told me that he thought it would be a good idea if we did a podcast to talk about the things Sentinel had going on that were in the news. I went into the podcast largely blind as to what he had to say, which pissed me off. I'm big on preparation, and I'm in control of my show. That's how I work. All of a sudden, I was part of Pierce's cult, like I'd been afraid of, and I was reduced to the status of a spectator, essentially, on my own program.

Obviously, the guy you interview is going to drive the conversation a little. This was going to be more than that.

So yeah – I waylaid him with the open. Tough shit if you don't like that, Pierce.

And when he saw that I didn't melt from the stink-eye he gave me, Pierce immediately snapped out of his irritation and went into Charming Cult-Leader mode.

"Mike, it's a great pleasure to be with you, and let me say that America desperately needs more Mike Holmans who actually do their jobs in media. The legacy press that you referenced is full of political operatives disguised as reporters, and most of them don't even know what journalism is. So, thank you for what you do."

"Appreciated, sir. Is there any truth to the allegations about the ports?"

"No. in fact, we're going to release, as soon as we can and as soon as some legal protections are established for the sources of our information, several documents which prove the origin of this so-called investigation. It didn't come from FBI field offices in Texas or California or anywhere else, and not even from the FBI at all. Instead, it came from the White House."

"Well, *that's* an allegation."

"You bet it is. And it's by no means all I've got. Mike, you've reported on your show and website for several years just how radical and corrupt this government is, and you've inspired me to do my own work. We at Sentinel have been in the network and private security business for a long time and as such we have investigative resources of our own. We've begun to marshal those and look into corruption at the highest levels on down, and today will be the first of many disclosures that will shock the American public."

"It seems like this might be one of our most-watched episodes."

"I would hope so, because the American people really need to know just how bad things are."

"Before we get to that, we should talk about the wireless internet project and the Deadhorse administration's threats to that business expansion. What about Attorney General Wreath's letter?"

"I was amazed to see that, Mike. After all, this attorney general and this administration, and the previous one of the same party that this administration is the rump end of, had absolutely no problem with one Big Tech company after another vertically integrating themselves. Or horizontally integrating, which is even worse. They allowed Silicon Valley to turn into a very tight oligarchy, especially in the consumer marketplace, and they've done nothing as the cable companies and cell providers have built, essentially, monopolies in all the markets in America for internet service.

"So along we come – and by the way, this would really be our first foray into the consumer market for anything, because most of what we do has always been business-to-business – and now he's concerned. Why? Because Garrick Wreath made millions of dollars doing work as a lawyer and lobbyist for the cell phone companies, owns a whole lot of stock in two of them…"

"Yes, but that stock is held in a blind trust," I interjected, trying to keep it fair. Wreath, like all of the political hacks in this administration and lots of others, hid behind that cover story as they profiteered from their positions. But on this one,

King Of The Jungle

I knew what was coming. I was like John Stockton feeding Karl Malone for a one-hand jam.

"Oh, right. A blind trust. And the administrator of that trust is Excelsior Capital Management, the CEO of which is Keith Bradbury, who is Wreath's brother-in-law."

"Whoops!" I said.

"Right, exactly. Whoops. Here's the problem with Garrick Wreath, and it's a lot worse than his crooked attacks on our proposed expansion. We've been looking into something that had gotten a lot of viral traffic on social media, at least for a little while before it was suppressed on Facebook and YouTube and a few other places. Namely, that there's a ring of child predators operating in New York and DC who engage in human trafficking and sex slavery."

"But those allegations were supposedly debunked."

"Were they? There were elements of them which were clearly untrue, but the 'debunking' was more like suppression and hope they would go away. Well, our team decided to do some real digging, and that's when we found a 14-year-old named, well, I'll call him Pedro."

"This is something new."

"Yes, it is, Mike. Pedro comes from a country in Central America, and he was trafficked across the border as an 11-year-old. First year of the current administration, when the border was thrown open. The coyotes took him to Piedras Negras in Mexico, across the river from Eagle Pass, Texas, and sent him to cross the Rio Grande into the hands of the border patrol. And from there, our own government transported him to 'relatives' who lived in Hyattsville, Maryland."

"I take it those relatives weren't really relatives," I said.

"No, Mike, they weren't. Instead, these were people working for the Mexican cartels who handled kids being trafficked. And in Pedro's case he was taken to a house in Bethesda, Maryland, where he was then abused in ways I won't describe by people who, he says, paid a lot of money for that sick privilege."

"That's awful."

"Yes, it is. And a couple of weeks ago Pedro managed to escape from that house and by a spot of luck he saw a flyer our team put up on a telephone pole giving a number that runaways and kids being trafficked could call for help. That's part of Operation Lifeline, a nonprofit we founded a few years ago which has delivered hundreds of kids who've been trafficked back to their families all over the world."

The website and phone number for Operation Lifeline appeared on the bottom of the screen.

"Anyway, Pedro called the number and said he'd been held by bad people and he was afraid to call the police because he believed the cops were compromised, and he asked if we could help him. So we did. And Pedro identified the house in Bethesda where he'd been subjected to the most disgusting abuse known to man."

"I haven't heard about a raid on that house or any arrests made in the legacy media."

"Neither have I, which is one reason I'm here. While we were waiting for the FBI or state or local police to do something about that house and what was happening there, we had a crew surveilling it from the street and overhead. And we watched as it was cleared out of all the people and stuff that was in there."

"That's disconcerting."

"What's more disconcerting is that we looked into the ownership of that house. We thought it was unusual that the house was owned by a small real estate investment trust, a company with a very uncommon investment profile. All it owns is large single-family houses in declining neighborhoods of cities around the country, places with six and seven bedrooms, lots of trees on the property, and garages. Always garages."

"Potential houses of ill repute, you're saying?"

"I'm not sure what I'm saying…just yet. We're investigating dozens of these places, but we're trying not to burn the evidence like we might have done in Bethesda."

"But I take it you do have something on that REIT."

"I do. It's a privately held entity, but among the listed investors in the initial paperwork filed with the state of Delaware 17 years ago is…one Garrick Wreath, now Attorney General of the United States of America."

That wasn't all Polk had to say. He then said he had written proof that the Vice President had taken a bribe from a Mexican cartel kingpin, and that the Federal Reserve was deliberately devaluing the currency.

Then at the end of the podcast he made a confession – that Sentinel's announced move into consumer wifi was a bluff to smoke out Wreath.

"We have the capability to offer that service," he said, "but we're not doing it yet. We need an entirely different regulatory environment so that a company like ours could compete in a free market rather than this rigged system we're currently in. But when we do enter that market, we'll cut people's monthly internet service costs by 50 percent.

"But I do thank the Attorney General for taking the bait. He can't say that I started this fight. That's on him, not me. He should know that he's not beating me, though, not when he's coming from so weak a position as he is."

No sooner was the show uploaded to YouTube but it immediately came down. It didn't matter. That podcast set a record for downloads on Rumble, and within two days it was over 100 million views on X, a number that had doubled a week later.

Congress called for hearings, the police raided that house in Bethesda and found nothing, of course, there was a smattering of calls for Wreath's resignation in the legacy media. Conservative media went ballistic, as it often does, but anyone who was looking for this to provide some collapse within the administration was going to be disappointed.

Four days later Joe Deadhorse's approval rating in a new national poll ticked down from 37 percent to 35.

And the day after that, the FBI, NYPD and the New York State Police raided the corporate headquarters of Sentinel Port Management in Manhattan's Upper West Side, pursuant to separate warrants issued by judges from the Southern District of New York and The Criminal Court of the City of New York.

They found the offices empty.

Chapter 6

April 19, 2024, Los Claritas, Bolivar

"Here they come," said Xing, from behind his binoculars.

"It's certainly about time," said Carvajal, who Cabrillo had noticed was less and less successful in his efforts to hide his contempt for the Chinese emissary.

This was a failing of the diminutive major, Cabrillo was aware, but on the other hand he couldn't quite fault Carvajal's dismay at their situation. Their effort at preparation for an invasion of the wilderness to the east was increasingly dependent on foreign assets.

The Chinese were suddenly everywhere in Venezuela.

This was something the Madiera regime had resisted for years, while other countries were embracing things like the Belt and Road Initiative and other "cooperative agreements" with the Chinese Communist Party.

Cabrillo had seen what China could do. Would do.

There would be investment. The Chinese would send in engineers and workers, and they would open a mine or a quarry or some other facility drawing raw materials from the earth. Here and there, the local citizenry might make a few dollars, pesos or dinars off the trade, but in the main, those materials – the lithium, the diamonds, the oil, the cobalt, etc. – would make their way onto ships bound for Shanghai or

Quanzhou where their products would be turned into all kinds of consumer goods.

Or weapons. Or whatever.

And the local economy? Other than a few jobs and some graft swung the way of the indigenous ruling class, the locals would barely feel the effects of their mineral wealth being packed off to the Orient.

Cabrillo didn't pretend to know much of commerce. He was a military man, as three generations of his family before him had been. His father had been a colonel in the Castro regime and had fought for *la revolucion* in Angola and Nicaragua, which had earned him a villa near the beach in Playa Larga. And his grandfather had been a general – but not for Castro, at least not initially. The old man had been with Bautista and had fought against the communists. He stayed until the end and was captured. After three years in the prisons, several times nearly personally executed by Che Guevara, Eladio Jorge Cabrillo had been brought to see Fidel Castro himself, who made him an offer he couldn't refuse.

"You will join us," Castro said, "and you will see your wife alive. If you do not, you will see her die. And your children, too."

Eladio had then agreed to rejoin the *Fuerzas Armadas Revolucionarias,* which is what the regime was then calling the Cuban army. He was never treated without suspicion, but the Castros found themselves with so few competent military commanders that they tolerated Eladio nonetheless. And eventually, the Cabrillos became communists.

Manuel was a communist, but as he would joke among his friends, he wasn't very good at it. Manuel actually liked the idea of private property, and when he wasn't here in Venezuela commanding a brigade of peasants and Amerindians, he was busily burnishing his "bug-out bag," as the Americans called it.

Or as best he could, given his less-than-perfect command of the free market system.

His wife Esmerelda, who he'd brought to Venezuela from Havana and stashed in an apartment in a well-secured area of Maracaibo, was a much more accomplished entrepreneur. She managed his properties. There were apartment buildings, sugar plantations, a small shipping company which did a brisk little business moving certain agricultural products from the Colombian hinterlands to Merida, on their way north, and a few other investments, most of which were managed out of a financial institution in the Cayman Islands.

It was cheap to conduct business in Venezuela, if you had the right stroke within the regime. Which Cabrillo did.

But Madiera was putting much of that at risk with his foreign ambitions.

It wasn't that the mission Cabrillo was training the men for was particularly problematic. The Guyanese had no military to speak of; their official force strength was just under five thousand men. Cabrillo had almost that many in his brigade alone, and there were two others just like it in the Venezuelan army's Jungle Infantry Division.

He didn't know if the others were any better prepared for offensive action than his was, and frankly, he wasn't all that confident in the 53rd.

But against a lightly populated nation of farmers, miners and fishermen, most of whom barely had pistols and other small arms much less any real military hardware? This was not a difficult mission.

They would conquer the area to the west of the Essequibo River, which the Venezuelans had claimed as their own for hundreds of years. The Madiera government had renewed an old complaint that in 1899, when the border between the two countries had been settled by a commission of British, American and Russian diplomats, with the Americans representing the Venezuelans owing to a lack of diplomatic relations between Venezuela and the UK at the time, what resulted was a corrupt bargain due to an American sellout.

Cabrillo figured that argument was probably correct. His experience and indoctrination had it that the U.S.A. was always engaged in some manner or other of depriving the people of Latin America of their due. But he also knew that most of the world wasn't all that interested in the claims of the Madiera regime of Venezuela.

And when the regime, the previous December, had staged a national referendum on annexing Essequibo pursuant to its age-old complaint, the planning of the Jungle Infantry's mission had begun, which led Cabrillo to Las Claritas.

Given no outside interference, that mission was clearly destined to succeed.

And while Cabrillo's assessment of the American administration, headed – at least nominally – by the deranged old man Joe Deadhorse, was that it was utterly paralyzed by a lack of leadership or even any conviction over its own national interests, he was nonetheless a bit worried that their adventure to the east would bring the Americans into a war. And if the Americans came into the theater, he'd need an elite force just to survive.

Which he most certainly did not have. He knew he was right to be worried about that.

Carvajal was more than worried. He wouldn't shut up about it. Cabrillo had told him to stop his whining several times, but the little major had confined his complaints to their private conversations and never expressed doubts about the mission to the men. Like always, he'd stopped short of conduct Cabrillo could justifiably discipline; he had to give his adjutant room to privately express his judgment, or else he would be closing off a potential source of information and good advice.

And while he didn't welcome Carvajal's doubt-casting, none of it was ill-founded. The Guyanese they would sweep aside easily; any other force in their path, whether it was American, British (a possibility), Jamaicans or Dominicans if the Caribbean defense organization CARICOM got involved, or whoever else, and things could grow problematic very quickly.

Cabrillo found himself praying – a relic of his family's pre-communist heritage – that their mission didn't bring them in conflict with the Americans or others.

And if as to represent a sideways answer to those prayers, the Chinese continued to arrive with gifts for the 53rd Jungle Infantry Brigade.

Today, those gifts were to include two dozen Harbin Z-9 helicopters capable of transporting 10 soldiers each.

Xing, the sweaty apparatchik who styled himself a military adviser though he appeared to be nothing of the sort and decked himself out in a trilby hat and a gray seersucker suit rather than fatigues, was cackling into his binoculars as the choppers noisily made their way into Las Claritas.

"They're nearly here. Aren't they beautiful?" he exclaimed.

"They're fine," said Carvajal, who was looking at the approaching choppers through his own binoculars.

"These will put your men in position to secure town after town when the signal is given," Xing beamed. "And then our cooperation may truly begin."

Cabrillo rolled his eyes.

Three days before, there had been a food riot in El Dorado, about 45 minutes up the road to the north, and he'd had to send some of his men there to suppress it.

Cabrillo knew that Venezuela was in no position to start a war with anyone. He also knew that the Chinese were perfectly well aware of that fact and happy to take advantage of it.

Those Harbin Z-9's were only part of the shower of military assistance the Chinese were dumping not just on the 53rd but all the elements of the National Bolivarian Armed Forces. Cabrillo also knew that Xing wasn't there so much to supervise that assistance but also to direct their progress when he saw fit to do so. Cabrillo had been informed of that very thing in a communique from headquarters.

What he hadn't been informed of was exactly who Xing was. Was he with the People's Liberation Army? The Ministry of State Security? He didn't think it was the latter. He'd thought to ask, but had stopped short. Cabrillo's experience and training told him that curiosity was not a virtue.

Xing was Xing. If the powers that be wanted him to know more, they'd tell him.

He didn't like any of it, but he couldn't do anything about it.

But something else troubled him. The 53rd was building up quite a store of ammunition and supplies while the locals found themselves more and more desperate. Cabrillo's quartermasters were under orders to stock up on all manner of foodstuffs and other supplies which might be useful to sustain a military occupation of the Guyanese hinterlands to the east, but he knew that was inherently problematic when the locals were suffering deprivation. He expected that ultimately his men would be living off the land – and that meant living off the locals in ways that big stacks of *Bolívar*

Soberanos, suspect value that those already carried, wouldn't suffice to facilitate. There had already been incidents; three days before, some of the men had shot a cow which was loose in the jungle and brought the carcass back to the base for butchering – only to endure a lengthy harangue from a local farmer with what amounted to an angry posse armed with machetes, pitchforks and a few pistols standing behind him.

It was a scenario which held the prospect of a major incident, not to mention a major setback in the training of his troops. Cabrillo, arriving quickly to the scene, had managed to placate the farmer with a stack of Bolivars and the promise of a new cow, which he was able to procure from a ranch in Brazil thanks to a regime contact in Caracas who had talents in such acquisitions. But it struck him that his men were the best-fed and certainly best-armed of all the occupants of this far southeast corner of Venezuela and the locals still showed up ready for blood if satisfaction wasn't at hand.

That wasn't a good sign. He knew that, while he wasn't in charge of the timeline, the best thing that could happen was to get orders sooner rather than later for moving his men out of Las Claritas and into Guyana.

And for taking whatever they could off the people of Essequibo.

Xing's choppers landed, and Cabrillo halfheartedly participated in the ceremony which ensued thanking the Chinese for supplying such a gracious bounty. When it was over, he and Carvajal reconvened in the small trailer that was brigade headquarters. They found Xing already there, boots off, stretched out on the little couch watching the large flat-screen TV along the far wall. Xing had sneaked away while Cabrillo was attempting to communicate with the Chinese chopper pilots, who left in a bus after officially turning the helicopters over to Venezuelans from the Army Aviation Command's helicopter battalion.

Cabrillo had noticed that. Even before Carvajal had griped about it. He thought to upbraid Carvajal for his complaints, but again checked himself; while listening to his adjutant protest about Xing was unpleasant, it was nonetheless a reasonably accurate summation of their situation.

"We're an extension of the Chinese Army," Carvajal groused quietly. "We're an instrument of our country becoming their colony."

"Oh, stop moaning like an old woman," Cabrillo said halfheartedly. "Without the Chinese we would be short of every necessity. Instead, we could support a force 30 percent greater than our present size."

"That might be true," said Carvajal, "but the question is whether Venezuela actually profits from this operation, or does that honor go to our oriental friends?"

"Excellent question," Cabrillo said cheerfully. "Does it really matter at the end of the day? Your orders are still your orders."

Carvajal was starting to respond, but then he stopped himself.

"What?" asked Cabrillo.

"I think if the men are asked to brutalize the Guyanese, they will refuse," he said. "Especially if they believe this is all for the benefit of Xing and his friends."

"Whose friends?" asked Xing, missing most of the conversation amid the TV show he was watching intently.

"Nothing," said Carvajal.

"I'm very interested in the Z-9," Cabrillo interjected, trying not to ruin Carvajal's career.

"What are you watching?" Carvajal blurted out as he noticed something disturbing on the screen Xing's eyes were glued to.

Cabrillo saw it as well and did a double take.

"It's SuperLolita," said Xing. "The latest from our American friends."

Cabrillo had heard of the show. It was a controversial offering from the giant U.S. media conglomerate XYZ/Sidney which had appeared on its streaming platform SidneyAlso.

SuperLolita was a comic book made into a TV series, though Cabrillo had no idea if it was ever actually a comic book. The gist of the show, as he understood it, was that the main character was an early teen Latino trans-woman street hooker with super powers who fought for social justice on behalf of the LGBTQIA+ community, the differently abled and the undocumented migrants of inner-city Houston. She, or at least it was Cabrillo's understanding that SuperLolita was to be referred to as a she, had two super powers: the ability to hear conversations even through brick walls from 1000 yards away, and the ability to shoot deadly laser beams from her nipples.

Glancing at the screen, Cabrillo saw that the latter power was real as SuperLolita pulled down her tube-top and let forth a pair of considerable beams of light which destroyed a police car. Xing bellowed a laugh, followed by several words of indecipherable Mandarin.

"Why would you be interested in this filth?" Carvajal asked the Chinese emissary.

"To watch the Americans destroy their own culture without help?" Xing responded. "How can you not be entertained?"

Carvajal looked at Cabrillo.

"He isn't wrong," Cabrillo said.

"You don't find it depressing?"

"I have nothing to do with it. If they want to destroy themselves, it isn't my problem. The mission is."

Xing was cackling loudly as SuperLolita was climbing on top of a burly white policeman as he crawled away from the burning cruiser.

"You gonna learn to respect the new trans matriarchy, sugar," she was telling the terrified cop.

"Yes, ma'am," the suddenly subservient cop said, as SuperLolita took his handcuffs from his belt and clasped them around his wrists.

"This is filth," Carvajal said.

"I don't understand the casting," Cabrillo noted.

"What's wrong with it?" asked Xing.

"First, the actress is not a Latina."

"Amy Nguyen is excellent," Xing said. "She's very popular in China. Half-African, half-Vietnamese. Very exotic."

"And a man," Carvajal said. "She has a beard."

"Enough of this," said Cabrillo. "It's time to go over the order of deployment so that we can calibrate the mission preparations."

Xing sighed and pressed the "pause" button on the remote control just as SuperLolita was crushing the policeman's hand under a spike heel. "Fine," he said. "Let's go over this again."

A map of southeastern Venezuela and central Essequibo, the area of the 53rd's planned operations, was laid out on a cheap card table. Cabrillo approached it with Carvajal and Xing in tow.

"Now," he said, "the first wave will go out as follows: nine helicopters straight to Kaietur Falls, and three each to capture the towns of Ekereku, Paruima Mission, Waramadan, Opadai, and Kamuda Village."

"Yes," said Xing, a mild exasperation in his voice, "we've been over this."

"And then we will be joined by a second wave of helicopters, so that we will then send 10 of them to the next target, which is Mahdia, plus two each to the secondary targets Ajimpepai,

Kwiokrebaru, Isseneru Village, Assura Village, Pipillapai, Opadai and Kokadai."

"These places are so small it's hardly worth it to spend the gas," Xing muttered.

Cabrillo gave him a sideways look, irritated that the interloper would carp about his plan. If executed correctly he would effectively occupy what points of communication and transportation existed in his area of operation within a couple of hours of the opening of hostilities. And what did Xing know about it?

"And then the major target," said Carvajal.

"That's correct," Cabrillo said, looking defiantly at their Chinese guest. "The American settlement at Liberty Point."

Chapter 7

April 27, 2024: New York, New York

I was in Manhattan for a meeting with ClearHeart Broadcasting, a big corporate radio company that I'd flirted with for years over the idea of doing a daily syndicated radio show, when one of their suits stormed into the conference room.

"You guys have to see this! Turn on ANN!"

So we did, and there was a breaking news report about a massive cyberattack that had taken down the servers for all of New York's state government and for New York City as well.

Both of them had made a large show of firing Sentinel Security as their firewall provider in what was essentially a political retaliation for Pierce evacuating the company headquarters. But they obviously hadn't done much preparation for the change, and the guy who'd been in charge of the New York state server had made a very public resignation.

It was gorgeous, actually. What he'd said was that DEI and wokeness doesn't build a bridge, fly a plane or run a firewall, and he'd put up with a lot over the last few years, but he'd never seen anything like the attempt to cancel Sentinel over politics.

His name was Aidan Park Hoo, and we had him on the *Connected* podcast the next day. He was a geek's geek, but a hell of an interview. When I asked him what he was going to do next, he said he was thinking about buying a cabin in the hills.

"There's a lot of that going around," I said.

"Well, yeah. Just pay attention! Lunatics are running everything. And they definitely don't listen to advice. All you can do is try to get away from them."

That same day, Deadhorse gave a speech at an assisted living facility in Arizona where he'd attempted to attack Pierce as an outlaw, but he ran off script and got him confused with Ross Perot. That after letting it slip that the Justice Department had been "secretly investigating" Sentinel for months.

It was awful and hilarious at the same time, but the upshot of it was that before the end of the news cycle the New York state legislature passed a bunch of changes to its criminal fraud statute that were clearly aimed at Pierce.

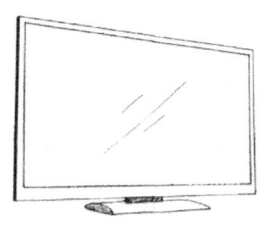

That night the cable news shows were full of lawyers arguing over what the state legislature in New York had done. The public hadn't heard terms like "bill of attainder" and "ex post facto law" in a long time, but that had changed.

Pierce sent me a text message letting me know that there would be a big party in Georgetown soon. I knew he meant the one in Guyana, not the one in DC.

And the meeting with ClearHeart was largely a waste of time.

The thing was, I didn't really want to deal with all the time a daily radio show would take up. Between the two hours in the evening ClearHeart was pitching, and the show prep time before that, it was going to be a monopolization of my schedule. But the big sticking point was that they were insisting on gobbling up the podcast for their own app, and that would have largely been the end of Holman Media.

I would have considered it had I not done the deal with Pierce. In fact, the ClearHeart meeting was already scheduled when I made the deal with Pierce. But now that I had that deal and I was becoming the hottest thing in media – or something like that – I said I'd only consider it if there was a verifiable shit-ton of money on offer, and that had to be up-front money.

It wasn't.

I had a cable network TV hit in a midtown studio that night, which was a debate with Juan Williams about the threat rogue billionaires presented. Williams blew a gasket at me when I noted that for all his complaints about Pierce, he'd never attempted to do anything damaging to the rest of us like pumping chemicals into the sky to deflect the sun's rays, he wasn't in the Epstein flight logs, he hadn't tried to fix an election or censor anybody.

"Well, you work for him," said Williams, "so of course you'd say that."

"I'd say it regardless," I shot back. "It's the truth. Why aren't you angry that a government full of political hacks is trying to destroy him simply for having a different opinion than you?"

"He's destroying the economy! He's putting his competitors out of business!"

"Really? Who? And how? And did you say this about Amazon and what they've done to Mom and Pop retail in America?"

Williams didn't like that. The debate got nasty, and the host cut to a commercial break early and the segment ended.

Then as I was leaving the studio, I got a text from Kathleen Lemoine, Pierce's personal assistant, letting me know a car was waiting to pick me up in the building's garage and take me to Teterboro Airport where a jet was going to take me to Guyana. She said she'd have somebody check me out of my hotel and bring my bags.

"OK," I texted back. This was probably better than having to get up at 4 AM to catch that Delta flight back to Hartsfield the next day.

I landed in Georgetown at 1 a.m. and a car was waiting for me at the airport. The guy driving it called himself Vinesh, and he spoke with an accent that sounded like he was from Calcutta.

"Are you one of the newly-arrived?" I asked him as he wheeled around onto a two-lane road leading out of the airport.

"No, sir," said Vinesh. "My people have been here for two centuries."

"You're kidding."

"Most of us in Guyana are descended from Indians brought here as indentured servants."

"I see."

"Most of the rest are of African descent. We were indentured to them."

"Wait, the Africans were the landholders and you guys worked in their fields?"

"That's correct."

"How about that?"

"Now we run the country."

I just nodded. I had a feeling this was going to turn into a lecture of some kind.

"Hey," I said, "I heard your economy here grew like 60 percent last year. This place is booming, huh?"

"It is. But you can't really tell. You can make more money now, but everything has become very, very expensive. When it isn't bought up immediately."

"I can imagine."

"Guyana was always one of the more reasonable places to live. But now there are Americans, British and the Latins, and they are buying up everything. Pricing us out."

"I would guess they'll be putting up subdivisions and apartment buildings and so on."

"Pierce Polk already is. You know him?"
"I do. He's building things here in Georgetown?"

Vinesh nodded.

"Sentinel Construction is building a big place in Land of Canaan, which is south of Georgetown, for a headquarters. And they're buying up land for, who knows?"

"That sounds like him. Always ahead of the game. I hear he's building a mall around here somewhere."

"I like him," Vinesh said, nodding. "But he should stay in America, not have his jungle Shangri-la in Guyana."

"Why so?"

"Because they will take it from him. It is too much, what he is trying to do."

"He'd be a little dismayed to hear you say that. But I expected you were going to give me a Guyana-for-the-Guyanese speech."

"No," he said. "But this is South America. It isn't like the United States where good things just naturally happen."

"I hate to tell you, Vinesh, but most people in the States don't think that's true of the States anymore either."

"I know. I have a nephew who lives in Baltimore."

"Yikes. Baltimore?"

"The suburbs."

"Right."

Vinesh pulled us in front of a little boutique hotel along a big east-west drag of a road. The marquee said it was the Grand Coastal Hotel; it wasn't all that grand, but it was tidy and had a little bit of a tropical-colonial vibe to it.

Once I was inside, a friendly rotund lady gave me an actual metal key to a room with a king-sized bed, and I didn't even undress before I crashed.

The next morning when I checked my messages I saw that all hell had broken loose back home.

At a press conference in Manhattan, the U.S. Attorney for the Southern District of New York announced he'd secured an indictment of Pierce Polk and "twenty of his confederates" on a RICO beef. I wasn't sure what the details were, but my attention was really piqued when he said that it was important that Polk be arrested seeing as though he was a flight risk.

Arrested? Guys like Pierce, you call his lawyer and negotiate a surrender. This clown was talking about sending feds out to get him like he was a drug dealer or a rapist.

I texted Pierce then, asking what the hell was happening. The response was a question: are you in Georgetown?

When I said yes, he told me to chill out and enjoy the pool, and he'd be down there later that day.

Of course, the hotel carried ANN, and of course, they were breathlessly following the Pierce Polk saga. There was a special graphic flashing on the screen about the "NATIONAL MANHUNT" for the "rogue billionaire," and a few minutes later there was a correspondent in Dallas reporting that the U.S. Marshals had him trapped at Sentinel's offices in Dallas. But the Texas Department of Public Safety was also on the scene and there was something of a standoff. Sentinel's people were heavily armed and refusing to allow the Marshals into the building. And Texas DPS was siding with Sentinel and not the Marshals.

There I was, texting Pierce asking what the hell was going on. "No big deal," came the response.

And ANN's cameras caught a helicopter taking off from the roof of the building. "He's escaping!" cried the reporter. "They're letting him get away!"

Melissa, my research assistant, called.

"I think you should come home," she said. "As much as I like him, do you really want to be associated with Pierce Polk now?"

"I pretty much have to see this though at this point," I said. "If nothing else it's one of the biggest stories in modern journalism, don't you think?"

"Yeah. If they let you tell it."

"Hmmm."

"What are you doing down there?"

"Right now? Answering emails in a hotel room. Maybe later I'll go and hug a sloth."

"Smart-ass," she said. "Be careful."

"Everything OK at the office?"

"Yeah. Colby is ecstatic. Site traffic is through the sky today. We're live-blogging the Pierce Polk manhunt like everybody else is."

"OK," I said. "I have some sort of lunch meeting down here that I got a calendar invite for. I don't know what it is."

"Again, be careful."

King Of The Jungle

A little later on, there was a report that the Sentinel Holdings Gulfstream G700 jet was forced to land at Belle Chasse Naval Air Station south of New Orleans. Some press flack from DOJ was on TV bragging about how they were arresting Pierce. That was pretty impressive, I thought, considering that he was texting me with laughing emojis.

"You OK?" I replied.

"Fuckers got my jet," came the response.

"Where are you?"

"I'll be there in a couple of hours. We're meeting with the PM."

So that was my lunch meeting.

Vinesh brought the car to the front of the hotel, and now in the light of day we were following the main drag, which was the Rupert Craig Highway, westward into the downtown.

"I think you might be stuck with our friend from now on," I said.

"Pierce Polk?" he asked.

"Yeah. Seems like they tried to arrest him in the States today and he decided he'd relocate to your fine country instead."

Vinesh sighed and nodded.

A little later on, he put us in front of another hotel. This was the Marriott, and it backed up to the beach.

"Damn," I said. "Wonder why they didn't put me here."

"Because there's no room," said Vinesh. "It's booked weeks out."

"Really?"

"It's like I told you. Everything is expensive when you can even get it. Too many people here now."

"Wow," I said as I got out.

"I will wait for you," said Vinesh.

Inside the hotel, a pretty black girl in a flowery pencil skirt met me and directed me to the presidential suite. She said her name was Mathilda and she was an assistant to the president – a guy by the name of Mahandas Ishgan.

"Your boss is already in with him," she said. "His flight got in early."

Chapter 8

April 30, 2024: Georgetown, Guyana

Mathilda took me up the elevator to the top floor of the Marriott, and there I found the presidential suite.

Which really was the presidential suite, of sorts, because apparently it was permanently rented out for the president.

And when we arrived, I met a pot-bellied little guy with a droopy face wearing a seersucker suit and — I'm not kidding — a sash draped across his body from one shoulder.

"Mike Holman," said Pierce, "this is President Mahandas Ishgan."

"It's a pleasure to meet you, Mr. Holman," Ishgan said. "I'm a fan."

"That's quite a compliment, sir," I said. "I had no idea my little podcast had an audience all the way down here."

"Oh, yes," he said. "Yes, indeed."

I knew he was lying. He was a politician, after all. But as lying politicians went, he was one of the most polite.

"Shall we adjourn to the dining area?" asked Ishgan. "We've much to discuss."

"Of course," said Pierce. "But wait. Don't we have one more coming?"

"We do," said Ishgan, rolling his eyes. "The Prime Minister will be here … when he gets here. We can begin without him."

"The Prime Minister and the President are political enemies," Polk explained. "It's fun watching them hate on each other."

"He was once President," said Ishgan. "He was removed in a corruption scandal. But he's in the middle of a comeback and he'll run against me in the next election."

"Then why is he invited to this meeting?" I said as we sat down at the dining table set out on a large balcony covered by an awning. A couple of servers brought glasses of beer and chilled shrimp with a red sauce.

Ishgan looked at Pierce.

"It's Banks Beer," Pierce said. "Stuff is terrific. It's becoming my favorite."

"So Pierce invited your PM," I chuckled. "Always ask for forgiveness rather than permission, right Pierce?"

"The things we're going to talk about, everybody in Guyana will need to be engaged in them," he said. "It's only fair."

Ishgan said nothing. But I could tell he was less than enthralled.

Just then an elegant, but quite old, bald-headed man with a caramel complexion and a thin gray moustache made his way to the table.

"I apologize for my tardiness," he said as we all stood. "You must be Mr. Holman. It is nice to meet you, Sir. I am Moses Jaganoo."

I shook his hand and then we all sat down. Ishgan was glaring at Jaganoo, who was ignoring the politician who was, at least nominally, his boss.

Gonna be one hell of an election, I thought to myself.

"Your meeting, Mr. Polk," said Ishgan.

"All right," Pierce said. "Listen, first of all, I should explain that Mike is here as an advisor. His company is consulting with Sentinel Holdings about our public relations. But he's also probably the smartest guy in the room and I want him to give us something of an outside opinion about what we're going to discuss. Are you guys OK with that?"

"Naturally," said Ishgan. Jaganoo waved his hand in acquiescence.

"Then fine. So as you've likely heard by now, I'm going to set up residence as a Guyanese pretty much permanently owing to the…"

"Outrageous," said Jaganoo.

"I must believe it will be sorted out in time," said Ishgan. "You surely have access to the finest legal counsel."

"You'd think so," said Pierce. "But something interesting is happening, which is that we're finding ourselves being turned down by a lot of the big New York law firms. It seems they've put the word out that I'm untouchable. And not in a good way."

"Well, that's news," I said.

"I'll find somebody," said Pierce. "But it seems like I'm not in very good odor with the people who run my country at the moment."

"Again, outrageous," said Jaganoo.

"I believe we can get our parliament to extend Guyanese citizenship to any of your men and their families who desire it," said Ishgan. "We would be delighted to have you."

"Given the contributions Sentinel has already made and will be making to our economy," said Jaganoo. Ishgan nodded enthusiastically.

Pierce shot me a sideways look, and it dawned on me at that point that he'd bribed the shit out of both of these guys.

"So the thought is this," said Pierce. "Mike, what do you think of us putting up a website that would process applications for Guyanese citizenship to any American who wants to come and then advertising it on independent media all over the country?"

"Depends," I said. "Who and how many are you looking for?"

"We've got room for 10,000 at Liberty Point right now," he said, "or at least we'll have it inside of six weeks or so. Construction's going really well. Better than we expected when you were last down here."

"I imagine you're going to want folks who are, sort of, hardier souls," I said.

"You've got to be outdoorsy to really enjoy Liberty Point," Pierce said. "These guys are gonna be hunters, gun owners and, we hope, military vets."

"Venezuela," I said. "Are you still thinking they're not coming?"

"The threat is not diminishing," said Ishgan.

"Which is why we're going to need to get Guyana caught up," said Pierce.

"Meaning weapons?"

"We have no air defense capability," said Jaganoo. "And our naval capacity is quite meager."

"OK, let me get my head around this," I said, "because I've not done my research on this situation. The Venezuelans want to annex Essequibo, which is, what? The western two-thirds of the country?"

"That's correct," said Jaganoo. "They would have everything west of the Essequibo River."

"So across the river from here would be Venezuela, or … no, that's wrong."

"That is the Demerara River," said Ishgan, pointing out of the window to the mouth of the river just west of the hotel. "The Essequibo is not far to the west of here, though."

"OK. And if they came, they'd be rolling tanks in?"

"Helicopters," Pierce said.

"It's all jungle in Essequibo," said Ishgan. "There are very few roads. In fact, there are no roads from Guyana to Venezuela other than the one which runs south through Brazil."

"So they'd be air-dropping troops in."

"And it's likely a naval invasion," said Jaganoo. "They would bring troops on boats along the Atlantic coast and into the Essequibo and land along the western shore."

I nodded.

"I'm not a military expert," I said, "but I've covered a few conflicts. It would seem like they'd turn this place into a very nasty battlefield."

"We are poorly poised for defense," Ishgan said.

"Wait a minute," I said. "There is no way Venezuela invades here without drawing the U.S. in. Right? Isn't that what's stopping them?"

"They don't fear American involvement," said Jaganoo.

"They don't think it's coming, Mike," said Pierce.

"That's insane," I said. "Doesn't Exoil have a pretty massive drilling complex off the coast?"

"We're going to meet Exoil's guy running their operations here later today," said Pierce.

"Yeah, but the Navy would shut down any move they'd make on Exoil's assets, right?"

"They didn't when the Venezuelans nationalized all of their assets in that country about 10 years ago."

"Yeah, but this is an actual invasion of another country," I said. "If Deadhorse and his gang would throw a hundred billion dollars into stopping the Russians in Ukraine, they'd have to help here."

"We've received no guarantees," said Ishgan. "In fact, your State Department is telling us it is not confident that the legalities of the 1899 treaty are fully sustainable."

"What does that mean?" I asked.

"The border between our two countries was established in negotiations between Great Britain, Russia and the United

States," said Jaganoo. "The British negotiated on behalf of Guyana while the Americans negotiated on behalf of Venezuela, with Russia as the intermediary. The Venezuelans have long since complained that your country sold them out."

"Did we?"

"It doesn't really matter," said Pierce, "or at least it shouldn't. The reality is that Guyana is a free country and Venezuela is a communist dictatorship. And this is right in our back yard."

"Hmmm. Wait, I remember reading not long ago that you guys were doing joint exercises with the Air Force, or the Marines, or somebody."

"We did," said Ishgan. "But in the last month, it seems that American cooperation has simply evaporated."

"That's concerning."

"So the plan is, we need to make this the hardest target we can," Pierce said. "That's why Sentinel Security is busy recruiting."

"Mercenaries?"

"And we've opened up procurement offices in Belgium and Colombia," he said, nodding. "MANPADs, small arms, mortars, artillery, choppers where we can. Plus the Argentines are kicking in with a bunch of their surplus gear."

"How soon is this invasion coming?" I asked.

"We do not have a military intelligence capability," said Ishgan. "We do not know for certain."

I looked at Pierce, who smiled.

"They're training troops just across the border," Pierce said. "We've got a satellite kicking down real-time imagery."

It struck me that Pierce had more or less assumed control of the country. Ishgan and Jaganoo might have been nice guys, but clearly neither one of them had the first idea how to handle any of this, and they were both looking at Pierce with every question.

Maybe as a means of keeping from looking at each other.

"When it comes, if it comes," Pierce said, "it's going to be helicopters dropping troops in villages all around west of the

Essequibo. We need to be able to shoot them down, so we're trying to get trained shooters placed in all those places. And…"

"Wait," I said. "Mr. President, do you have a general in command of your army? And is he going to join this meeting, or…"

Ishgan gave me a look I couldn't discern.

"There's concern Brigadier Darke is, er, compromised," Jaganoo said. "As such, our strategic discussions are being held at a level above his pay grade."

"Perhaps you should do more than that," I said. "Compromised how?"

"China," said Jaganoo. "And perhaps Venezuela as well."

"I don't understand."

"China is behind all of this," said Pierce. "They want Essequibo, and they've already bought Venezuela to get it."

"And Brigadier Darke is bought off?"

"I don't know," said Pierce.

I looked at Ishgan, who was stone-faced. I got the impression he didn't want to say anything in front of Jaganoo.

"It's going to take some time to figure out who the patriots are," said Pierce. "I'm sure we have some in this room."

I noticed a very uncomfortable look coming from Jaganoo. Ishgan noticed it as well, and I think he noticed me noticing it, because he gave me a glance that said more than if he'd talked to me for a month.

Lunch came, and for the first time in a while I noticed that Pierce wasn't eating steak. Instead, we were eating bowls of pepper pot, which I was told was the national Guyanese dish. It was a thick, dark stew with chunks of mutton and a variety of peppers. I thought I was going to have a heart attack over the spice.

"It's pretty potent," I said, downing the rest of my beer after the first bite.

"You'll get used to it," said Pierce. "This has some cinnamon and nutmeg in it? Fantastic!"

Ishgan agreed, slurping happily from his bowl.

The meal ended, and then the conversation turned to a host of economic projects that Pierce was initiating. He'd bought a small port facility in Georgetown just upriver from the Baker Hughes plant that was servicing the offshore rigs and that was going to be Sentinel Port Management's facility until he could build the bigger port across the river that he'd planned. He said Liberty Point was going to be the site of a sizable network security hub and server farm. There was the Sentinel Construction facility upriver from where we were. They talked about the mall he was building. And he was snapping up real estate all over the country. Ishgan and Jaganoo were like a couple of fan-boys letting him run the meeting; I noticed about an hour later that neither had objected to anything he said.

"Well, fellas," Pierce finally said, "I know I've monopolized your time this afternoon, and for that I'm sorry."

"That's quite all right," Jaganoo said.

"A pleasure," said Ishgan.

Then the president invited Pierce to address the parliament the next day. He thanked him for that, and then he essentially dismissed Ishgan and Jaganoo.

"Thanks, guys," he said. "Let's reconvene tomorrow. I'll give that speech before I head back to Liberty Point."

And at that they both shot up from the table and made their way out.

Then Pierce and I were alone.

"You're a lot further along here than I expected," I said.

"I'm an idiot, is what I am," said Pierce. "Here I figured that this would be a great investment — it's a free country, the locals are cooperative as hell…"

"For sale cheap, you mean."

"Well, yes, but it's more than that. They like investment and they aren't communists. You grease the wheels for 'em, sure, but they're actually interested in growing this place. And they know they have no idea what they're doing."

"What about this Ishgan versus Jaganoo thing?"

"Yeah, they hate each other and they're going to run against each other next year. It doesn't really matter who wins from our perspective."

"You've got them both on the payroll."

"I learned my lesson back in the States. If I'd been smart, I would have played both sides against the middle rather than going to war with Omobba, as disgusting as the thought of throwing in with communists is. I'm not making that mistake again down here."

"So how do you keep the Venezuelans out?"

"I have no idea at this point. It's like I said: it's all China. The Chinese are in all those villages paying off Indian tribes, buying up mines and other stuff. They're everywhere."

"You think Jaganoo is bought by the Chinese? I can tell Ishgan does."

"I wouldn't be surprised if Ishgan was on their take too."

"This is a hell of a fix you've gotten yourself into."

"Not to mention I'm stuck here."

"What? The indictment?"

"I have my suspicions about that. I think that's also China."

"Shit, Pierce."

"Network security? We're the only people who can consistently stop their hackers. Port management? We're one of the last remaining competitors to the big Chinese firms. They're trying to stop us from that interport rail project we're working on in southern Mexico that would kill their investment in the Panama Canal. Telecom, construction … if they could get me out of the way they'd have a hell of a nice run."

"You think they have the Southern District of New York?"

"I think they have Wall Street. And Wall Street wants me down for the count so I have no choice but to take Sentinel public and go away. So it's hardball now."

"I imagine so. They're going to seize your assets for sure at this point."

"They'll try. We've done a pretty good job of offshoring everything that's liquid, and most of our domestic assets are leased, rather than owned."

"You have cutouts?"

"Yes, I do."

A little later, Tom Burnham, who was Exoil's Vice President in charge of Guyana operations, paid a call at the presidential suite. He came by for a meeting with Pierce.

"So you're the new sheriff, I see," said Burnham to Pierce, when we were sitting at the balcony table. "Regretting your new acquisition?"

"Not yet," Pierce said, "but who knows? How goes your effort to keep Madiera's greasy hands off your rigs?"

"We're in a similar boat as you," said Burnham. "We're here and we're committed, and that means we're likely screwed."

"Seems like Madiera is aiming to un-commit you," said Pierce.

"We took on a Chinese partner. If nothing else, when the Venezuelans come we can sell out and recoup something."

"But the payoff," I said. "What are you turning, a million barrels a day out there?"

"Not quite yet. It's about half that right now. But it'll be a lot more than that when it's fully developed. Twelve billion barrels, is the size of the reserve we're looking at."

"Losing that would be a major hit," said Pierce. "I noticed that your stock is losing altitude."

"We've definitely got some exposure," said Burnham. "Houston is under pressure to negotiate an exit, but dumping these assets at a fire sale price would be tantamount to surrendering our status as the big dog on the porch in our own hemisphere."

"To the Chinese," I said.

Burnham looked at me and nodded.

"And Madiera's people are demanding that we license the whole block through their government if we want to continue producing. Which we won't do. But it does create a problem if and when they come. They're warning us we'll be considered as pirates and they'll confiscate our end of the block."

"I can't understand why Deadhorse isn't standing in the way of this," I said.

"It's oil. His people won't lift a finger to help an oil company," said Burnham. "And we've fought off the institutional money demanding that we join the ESG cult, which makes us only slightly less objectionable than Pierce here."

"And it's China," said Pierce.

"What, you think Deadhorse is bought on this?"

"All those business deals with the idiot son of his?" said Burnham. "They were energy deals."

"All right," Pierce said, pulling out a sheet of paper and handing it to Burnham, "Hal had me put this together for you. Try to get back to me with how much of this you guys can pull together."

"Who's Hal?" I asked.

"Colonel Hal Gibson, retired, United States Marine Corps, and head of security at Liberty Point," said Pierce.

I knew who Hal Gibson was. Everybody who'd been following the news since Deadhorse's collection of limpdicks at the Pentagon purged out half the officer corps knew exactly who Hal Gibson was.

"And he's effective commander of the defense of Guyana, I assume," I said. Pierce smiled and nodded.

"How many has he got, Pierce?" Burnham asked.

"All told, like about 6,500. And counting."

"That's half again what the Guyanese have."

Pierce nodded again.

"And a hundred times the capability."

"Pierce," said Burnham, as he perused the document, "what kind of Navy contacts does Hal have?"

"You mean the submarines," Pierce said.

King Of The Jungle

"You're getting a sub?" I asked.

"We're trying."

Chapter 9

May 3, 2024, Liberty Point, Guyana

It turned out that while I was in Georgetown the FBI had paid a visit to Holman Media. Tom had called Morris, who in his polite, old-school way, had shooed the agents out of the office. Then he'd recommended the attorney for the company to hire – a New York ball-buster by the name of Karen Lugowski who didn't agree with a damn thing on our websites or podcasts, but hated the feds a lot more than she disliked us.

I'd had to sign her retainer agreement via email while I was in Georgetown. I got Pierce to agree to foot her bill in person; he was in the room with me when the document arrived in my inbox. And when I came home, Karen had already flown in and was waiting in my office.

"Lookit," she said, "as your attorney I'm going to recommend that you stay far away from Pierce Polk. He's on the list, and you're going to be on it as well."

"The list? What list?"

"Enemies. People who need to have bad things happen to them. He took off down to the jungle for a reason, you know. They aren't going to let him back in, not while this gang is in office. And now you're part of Polk's crew so you're a suspect."

"For what?"

"It doesn't matter for what."

"You're a criminal defense lawyer. There has to be a charge."

She looked at me like I was a moron.

I'd read online on the flight back that the feds had raided Pierce's place in Telluride. It had been completely cleaned out but for a velvet painting of Elvis on the wall above the big fireplace in the den. And Pierce was not an Elvis fan, so that gives you an idea of just how much contempt he had going for these people.

I'd also read that Joe Deadhorse's approval rating had dived to 32 percent in one poll and 28 percent in another. A major airline, which had launched a TV ad campaign touting its diversity hiring for pilots, had just had a deadly crash on a runway in a big midwestern city in which a pilot, promoted from flight attendant and on her maiden commercial voyage flying a Boeing 787, overshot the runway and rolled the plane. Sixty people were dead and the airline's stock had crashed 40 percent before it was backstopped by a huge buy-in from RedGuard Capital.

"The real tragedy of this crash would be if it were to harm our commitment to diversity," the airline's CEO said. Less than six hours later a video of him posing naked with an alpaca made the rounds on Twitter; it had originally been posted at the OnlyFur fetish site.

The guys at the website were all over this stuff, and Billy Ray had dropped a half-dozen hilarious memes about the CEO. It struck me that we were a little close to the edge making jokes after a mass-casualty plane crash, and I planned on saying something about that with my team.

We had a quick business meeting after I told Karen that my relationship with Pierce was a commitment made and not soon broken, and if that meant she'd be scoring with the big leaguers on fees, then so be it.

At the meeting, I noticed that my folks were all smiles. They were energized. I cautioned the group that we really did want to take the high road, or at least try to, on our coverage of current events. But it was clear nobody was hearing that.

The FBI's visit had changed a lot of attitudes in that room. They were ready for war.

"Last week's podcast with Polk was the top traffic-getter in the history of Rumble," said Colby. "Site traffic is absolutely on fire. And you've got three of your old books in the Amazon top 20 in the American Politics category. You're a bigger deal now than you were when you did the ANN show."

"Ad revenues are way up, too," said Megan. "Especially since we just nailed down three new deals – the Dodge City Steak Company, Patrick Henry Rifle, and El Dorado Boots."

Those were pretty good accounts. Megan was beaming.

"Where's all this coming from?" I asked. "Did something happen that I missed?"

"It's Pierce Polk," said Tom. "He's rapidly turning into a folk hero. And the more they do to him the more the public is taking his side."

Lindzey Luger, who had the early prime slot on ANN and was a hard-core partisan Democrat, had uncovered some video of Pierce at a party somewhere yukking it up with Donny Trumbull, and she'd played it while declaring this was proof there was a "right-wing conspiracy to destroy our democracy" in advance of the 2024 election.

And somebody had put a microphone in front of Trumbull, who was heading into a courthouse in Chicago where he'd been sued for defamation of some woman that he'd been acquitted of sexually assaulting two decades earlier.

Asked about the old video, Trumbull didn't deny he knew Pierce.

"He's a hell of a guy," he said, "and it's a travesty what Deadhorse and Omobba are doing to him. You know this is all Omobba, right? Deadhorse doesn't go to the bathroom without Omobba's say-so."

Naturally, Trumbull saying that sparked the legacy corporate media into full outrage at the idea Deadhorse wasn't his own man, and there were plaudits and kudos heaped on Lindzey for having uncovered the "cabal" that Trumbull and Pierce were forming to destroy "our democracy."

Every time any of these people said "our democracy," it launched Colby into a furious diatribe. "That term describes nothing we Americans recognize!" he'd sputter. "And it definitely isn't democracy any honest person would accept!"

Boy, was Colby in high dudgeon over Lindzey Luger at our staff meeting. We all sat there smirking while the steam came out of his ears.

All of this seemed like a pretty normal Monday in 2024 to me.

Somehow, though, this media frenzy was turning me into a star. Tom told me *60 Minutes* had called asking to interview me as "Pierce Polk's last remaining link to the real world."

"Well," I said after the buzz around the conference table died down, "I guess the next podcast will be a big deal then."

"What are we doing?" asked Melissa.

"We're going to show Liberty Point to the world, and we're going to interview the folks building it."

"We're OK to do that?" asked Kaylee. "Pierce is good with it? I thought it was a secret."

"Not anymore it's not. And you and Melissa are coming, plus we're taking Craig Clifford and his good video camera."

I'd wrangled Craig for the trip over the phone while flying in. That didn't take much effort. Free-lance videographers tended to make themselves available whenever there was payment involved.

"This'll be big," said Tom.

"Huge," said Colby.

Then came a depressing night alone in my house, complete with a decision that I'd sell the place and just rent an apartment somewhere for a while. My next door neighbor had just sold her three-bedroom cottage for $1.2 million, which was double what I'd paid for mine 15 years before, and I figured that was a sign I should cash out.

Besides, Buckhead was turning into a shooting gallery. A couple of days before I left for Georgetown, a couple of ballers decided to trade lead in the parking lot of the strip mall down the street. The ambulances managed to take them both to Grady before they bled out, but it was nonetheless enough to put the neighborhood on a hair-trigger.

The next morning a car picked me up and Kaylee, Melissa, Craig, yours truly and an astonishing amount of luggage were flying out of Fulton County Airport on another private jet, this one a Bombardier Challenger 3500 owned by Leighton Industries – they were the manufacturer of Sentinel Telecommunications' satellites, and Tom Leighton had openly come out to defend Pierce and decry the feds' efforts to prosecute him.

A few hours later, we landed at Connor Polk International Airfield in the middle of a torrential downpour. That was a little surprising given that the rainy season wasn't supposed to start for another month. The plane taxied into a big hangar that hadn't been there the last time I'd been to Liberty Point.

"This place is a lot nicer than I thought it would be," said Melissa, as we descended the little jetway and made for a picnic table at the far corner where snacks were laid out and a bartender was waiting to mix us drinks.

"Oh, wait until you see the town," I said. "You're going to think you're in Barcelona or Genoa. They did a great job with it."

I noticed that the Challenger shared the hangar with a couple of planes that looked a good bit like Predator drones. I decided to file that bit of data away for later inquiry – and when Craig asked if I wanted him to film that, I shook my head.

"I'm imagining that has to do with Venezuela," I said. "I don't want it on my conscience if we give away any state secrets."

"Understood," he said.

The rain mercifully petered out while we sipped on capirinhas, and then a couple of Grand Cherokees rolled up into the hangar to fetch us.

And soon after, I noticed that the road from the airstrip into the town looked a lot different this time.

They'd landscaped it. The trees were cut quite a bit back, and somebody had planted shrubs off the shoulder of the road, I assume so as to serve as a barrier to the underbrush growing back. Plus, there were streetlights now.

"Looks like America," said Kaylee.

"Yep," said Craig, who had his video camera out and was shooting.

And then we passed through the big wooden gate and the girls gasped.

"I told you," I said. "It's got a European feel to it, dontcha think?"

"I'd say it's like New Orleans," said Kaylee, "but then I've never been to New Orleans."

"I know it's new," said Melissa as we turned onto the main drag, which the newly-installed street signs identified as Sentinel Boulevard, "but it looks and feels old, like it's been here for centuries."

"Maybe it has been," said Kaylee, "in a sense. And maybe Pierce just brought it out."

"Probably unlikely, K," I said. Melissa laughed.

"OK, OK," Kaylee whined. "Sorry."

A right and a left later, and our Cherokee brought us to the same building I'd stayed in on my previous trip. But it didn't look the same; this time I noticed they'd planted trees and bushes everywhere, and there were canvas awnings set up like the tops of tents – I immediately knew those were rain shelters – at intervals on the sidewalks.

And people. Liberty Point hadn't had nearly this many people the last time. I asked the driver, a new arrival from Chicago named Bill, if he knew what the population of the place was now.

"They announced it yesterday we just passed six thousand," he said. "Most everybody's here working for Sentinel Construction. There's great money in it. So that's why they're all in work clothes."

"How many are staying when the project is finished?" Kaylee asked.

"Probably everybody," said Bill. "No taxes? No stupid government? This place is just going to grow and grow."

We parked, and I led my little team through the same entrance to the concierge that I'd seen before.

"Welcome back to Liberty Lodge, *Senor* Holman," said the pretty concierge lady that I remembered from my last trip.

"Hey, Consuela!" I said. "This is Melissa Swindell, Kaylee Russo and Craig Clifford. They're here with me to make this place famous."

"I heard," she said. "Everyone here is talking about it."

A couple of bellmen, who I found out were members of the Patamona tribe who lived a few miles to the west in the village of Micobie, brought us up to what was Pierce's suite the last time I'd been in Liberty Point.

"Wait," I said, "where's Pierce?"

"*Aimu'nang Waica?*" said the taller guy, whose name was Sam. "He's at the new place."

"What's the new place? And Eye-moon-ang Wa-ee-ka?"

"It means White Warrior," said Sam. "We gave him an honorary title."

"Well, that was nice of you."

"It was the least we could do," said Lenny, the other guy. "He hooked up the whole village with cell service and satellite TV."

"It sounds like he's spoiled your pristine tribal lifestyle," Kaylee said, half joking.

"Is this lady kidding me right now?" said Lenny, looking at me.

"Yes, she is," I said quickly.

"OK, then," he said, smiling at us. And Sam and Lenny set our bags down and waved goodbye as they took off.

"Kaylee," I said, "come on."

"Hey, I went to Dartmouth," she said, "and I had a humanities class all about how European encroachment on native tribes is destroying their culture, and…"

"And you believed that bullshit?"

"You believe it if you want the 'A,'" said Melissa.

"OK, well, this isn't college. But yeah, we'll take a ride to Micobie and Mahdia and a couple of the other places around here and you guys can see what the indigenous folks think of their culture getting destroyed."

We got situated, then I recorded a couple of takes for an open of the podcast. I then got a message from Pierce inviting me to a meeting at his new place, which he said was a couple of blocks away along the Essequibo. I made my excuses to the rest of the team, as they were going to head out and explore Liberty Point and have Craig shoot a bunch of B-roll, and suggested that maybe we'd reconvene for dinner and go over our plans for podcast interviews we'd do the next day.

Consuela hooked me up with a golf cart ride to the new place, which she said was the Grand Waica. A little guy who said his name was Earl – he was an Arawak from Campbelltown, a few miles west – was my driver.

"Love your podcast," he said as we took off.

"You're kidding," I said. "How do you even know about it?"

"Because we're fans of everything Pierce Polk, and you're part of that. Anything you need, you just call."

And he gave me a business card. It said Earl Roberts, Toshao Region Eight, Construction; Mining; Communications.

"You're a man of many talents," I said. "Why are you driving a golf cart?"

"Because the work's easy and Pierce pays big. I also do drywall and some plumbing, too."

"What's a toshao?"

"Like a town captain, or maybe a mini-mayor, I guess."

"Got it."

Then we pulled up to a stately five-story building that looked like a hotel, which it was. "The Grand Waica" was chiseled above the large glass revolving door, and as I hustled inside I felt like I was transported to the Drake or the Plaza.

I could see along the far wall, which was mostly glass, that some of the building laid over the Essequibo. There was a mini-marina of sorts were people could park boats in the shade of the Grand Waica.

"Pretty cool, right?" said a friendly voice. I turned, and there was Roman Jefferson, the private security guy I'd met on my last trip.

"Definitely. Hey, Roman, how's it going?"

"Great, Mike. Just moved into my place, and my girl's comin' in on Monday to join me. We got a three-thousand square foot condo with a balcony up the street. But the bar here is where it's at."

"What exactly are you doing here?" I said. "Sorry if I'm being nosy."

"Call it a semi-retirement. But I'm helpin' with, ummm … contingencies."

"Like the Venezuelans?"

"Like that."

"Got it."

I didn't get the impression Roman was going to tell me more. Or that I wanted to know more.

So I found the elevator and rode it to the fifth floor, as Pierce's text had instructed. When the door opened there was a huge guy in a tan suit waiting for me.

"Come on through, Mr. Holman," said the guy.

He opened a door and there was Pierce, breaking off from a conversation with a group of people in a cavernous salon with windows overlooking the river. He was wearing jeans and a white t-shirt with "WAICA" in a bold font on it, and he flashed me a big smile.

"Here he is!" said Pierce. "Everybody, meet Mike Holman!"

There were probably two dozen people in the room at this cocktail party, or whatever it was, and they actually started applauding. I didn't know what to make of that.

Especially when I looked around and started recognizing some of the faces.

The two Guyanese politicos nominally in charge of the country, Ishgan and Jaganoo, were there. So was Burnham, the Exoil executive. I recognized Ravi Darke, who was Guyana's head general, from his photo. Pierce introduced me to a guy from Raytheon and another one from General Dynamics. The Brazilian and Argentinian ambassadors were there.

And then there was Brienna Givens, the tennis player.

I knew – or I had heard – that Pierce was seeing her, or at least to the extent that people like Pierce and Brienna would "see" anybody. But I could tell this was a real thing. She was sticking to him like glue.

What a knockout she was. Easily my height, and I'm right at six feet, and athletic as hell. Brienna would have been a dead ringer for a young Elizabeth Hurley but for her lighter hair and the fact that she's a little more masculine-looking, I guess. But wow. She'd done a lot of modeling, and she was good at it, but in the flesh Brienna was straight-up gorgeous.

At least, until she opened her mouth.

I didn't get the idea that Brienna was all that excited to be at Liberty Point. She said in that half-reformed London cockney accent of hers that she was here because she had to be in Mexico in a few days, and that Pierce had insisted.

Then she introduced me to Sarah, her sister. Who was a little older, not as tall, not quite as glamorous, but definitely more of a willing conversationalist.

Maybe it was the fact that I'm somewhat famous, but I got the impression that Sarah was interested in me. I got that impression when, just after Brienna told her who I was, she leaned in and put her hand over my heart and said she could feel a good man was in there, deep down.

"Thanks, I guess," I said.

She gave me a warm smile. I hadn't gotten one like that since Ashley dumped me. At that point I was suddenly very curious about Sarah Givens.

And that was just fine with Sarah, because she was quite keen to tell me all about her exploits. She said she was a photojournalist and the director of a nonprofit called EarthChampions.

"Brienna is on the board," Sarah said.

"Costs quite enough," said Brienna, and then I realized that Brienna *was* the board of EarthChampions.

"Wait – your nonprofit is with the UN?" I asked. I remembered that there was something similar to the name that had to do with some climate change something-or-other.

"Oh, no, love," she said. "You're thinking of Champions of the Earth. We're not the same."

"Oh, you do something different?"

"We do champion the Earth," she said.

"And how do you do that?"

"We inform the public about abuses of the ecology, air and water pollution, the climate, deforestation…"

"You've come to the right place, baby!" Pierce laughed. Sarah and Brienna gave him shitty looks for that.

"Don't agitate her," said Brienna.

"As I was saying," Sarah said with an irritated tone, "I'm here to investigate the effect your Liberty Point is having on the rivers, the flora and fauna, and the culture of the indigenous people."

"Interesting," I said, thinking to myself that Sarah's professional exploits weren't very interesting at all.

"You know, the capitalists see pristine places like this one and insist on paving it over. I've seen it all over the world – Nigeria, Eritrea, Tajikistan, Vietnam…"

"Vietnam is communist, though," said Pierce.

Sarah gave him a wicked side-eye.

"I should think this place is no different," she said.

"Well, I'm sure you two will have lots to talk about," Pierce said, leading Brienna off and giving me a devilish nod.

Thanks a lot, my look in response told him.

Sarah was saying that it was terrible that they'd disturbed the shore of the Potaro to build that hydroelectric power plant.

"Oh, you mean the converted land dredges along the riverfront?"

"Land dredges?"

I nodded. "Yep. They'd dug gravel pits all along the shoreline for mining purposes, and Pierce's guys re-engineered those to set up the hydro plant."

"Oh," she said.

"That's not all. There's a gold mine upriver on the Potaro, and there was a stone quarry right at the mouth of the Potaro where it flows into the Essequibo that they filled in around to make the little marina where the Landing is."

"It sounds as if you've been here before."

"Yeah," I said. "This hasn't been a pristine jungle for decades. Pierce just went ahead and built a town, but all around here there's industry. I'm not sure Liberty Point isn't a lot more environmentally sound than the mining operations they've had around here for a long time."

"It seems like you aren't very objective about this place."

"Are you going to interview the people?" I asked.

"That is my plan," Sarah nodded.

"Well then let's do that together. My team and I are recording a documentary starting tomorrow, and that was part of our plan as well."

"Is it dangerous, then?" Brienna, who had just returned, asked. "Tooling around in the bush with the natives?"

"Oh, the ones I've met are perfectly docile. And quite fond of Pierce, too."

"I'm not sure I believe that," Sarah said.

"Well, you'll get to see for yourself," I said. "Brienna, do you want to go and meet the locals with us tomorrow?"

I could instantly tell that she did not.

"Pierce said something about a waterfall," she said. "I think I'm for that instead."

Not long after, Burnham pulled me aside.

"You guys figure out how to dump your investment in Guyana yet?" I asked him.

"Nobody knows this," he said, "but yesterday the Venezuelans detained a supply ship as it was heading into the offshore complex. They're now demanding that all supply boats to the rigs have to come out of Venezuela."

"Sounds like a job for the U.S. Navy."

"Damn right it is. Know what the Navy is doing?"

"What's that?"

"Watching."

"What?"

"You heard me. They're 'observing.' And we've had lots of contact with the captain of the frigate which hangs around our complex. He isn't happy, but his orders are not to intervene."

"I thought the Navy was doing patrol flights over Guyana now. I thought they'd been doing that since December."

"They were. Not anymore. Stopped 10 days ago."

"The hell?"

"This shit is about to get out of control, Mike. The Vinnies are coming."

"The Vinnies?"

"Yeah. That's our nickname for the Venezuelans."

I considered that and nodded. It fit.

"This is all fun and games here now," Burnham was saying, "but I'm telling you, get back to Atlanta as fast as you can and stay there."

"That's your plan? Pull out back to Houston?"

"I don't know what my plan is. I know that you don't want to be here when the balloon goes up."

Then, as quickly as he'd pigeonholed me, Burnham gave me a smile and disappeared. I mingled for a while with the rest of the swells, and then Pierce collected me for a confab in a well-appointed private room off the salon.

There, I saw that Darke and Burnham were sitting at a table with Ishgan and Jaganoo. And an old guy built like a stone statue who had a handshake like a rock-crusher. I found that out when he introduced himself.

"Hal Gibson," he said curtly, as I felt the bones in my right hand come under excruciating strain.

"You're not the Hal Gibson who resigned from USMC over the COVID jab, are you?" I asked. "I think I remember you from Laura Ingraham's show."

"Yeah, that's me," he said. "That was my retirement after 20 years commanding men in battle. A vaccine shot is more important in the service now than competent leadership."

"Hal is now the security coordinator for Liberty Point," said Pierce. "He has lots of ideas on how to defend this place."

"I assume that includes the Predators I saw in the hangar," I said.

Gibson looked at me.

"I hope that won't make it into your podcast," he said.

"It will not."

He nodded.

The meeting in the little side room didn't last too long, but it was – what's the word? – declarative.

Gibson got into Darke's face and accused him of being a plant for the Vinnies. Darke hotly contested that and fingered Jaganoo. Things got ugly from there, and then Pierce stepped in and explained to the Guyanese that he was going to defend their country even if they wouldn't.

Ishgan said he was fully committed and that he welcomed whatever help Pierce and Gibson and Sentinel and Exoil were willing to offer.

Darke echoed that. All eyes went to Jaganoo.

"I don't understand why I am suspected," he said. "I've only ever attempted cordial relations with our neighbors. It doesn't make me a traitor."

"We can't afford traitors," said Burnham.

"And we won't have them," said Gibson.

Jaganoo shrugged. He was uncomfortable, clearly, but he was slick. He admitted nothing. And yet you got the firm impression there was a lot he could admit.

I felt like that was true of Darke as well, but Pierce and Burnham seemed interested in giving him the benefit of the doubt. And Gibson backed off his initial accusations. Darke was strangely unbothered by those.

Regardless, the Americans didn't talk very much about military hardware or strategy with the Guyanese bigwigs there. Which I understood, but it didn't give me much in the way of a good feeling about the planned defense of Essequibo.

Then Sarah found me after it was over.

"What are you doing later?" she asked.

"Back to the lodge to get together with my crew, then we'll get dinner," I said. "Why? Are you trying to get out of playing third wheel to Pierce and your sister?"

She nodded.

"It's boring," she said. "They're boring."

They were two of the most famous human beings on the planet and she was telling me I was more interesting than them. I had trouble believing that, but then again it was fun to get attention from a beautiful girl again.

"Well then, come and join us," I volunteered.

She nodded again.

Chapter 10

May 10, 2024: Miami, Florida

I'll bet you expected that Sarah and I were going to become an item. I'm sorry to disappoint you.

Which is not to say that my time with her was uneventful. Oh, it was eventful, all right.

She joined us for dinner at the Liberty Lodge; the restaurant there had Guyanese food that was amazingly good, and Melissa swore she was "moving down here so I can eat this every day."

"Oh my God, girl, you're gonna get *so* fat," said Kaylee.

"Shut *up*, Kaylee! Damn!"

"They've been griping at each other like this all afternoon," Craig groused.

But he said they got some amazing B-roll footage all around the town, and even managed to shoot the inside of one of the condos. It belonged to a retired Delta Force guy and his new wife; he'd just signed a contract as a security consultant for an oilfield services company working that offshore block of rigs and said he was going to be seven days on, seven days off starting in a week.

"There's more civilization here than anywhere else this part of South America," Kaylee had him on camera saying.

Sarah largely kept her mouth shut during dinner, at least until Melissa decided to interrogate her.

"So are you a tennis player, too?"

"Not since I was a girl. Brienna was the tennis prodigy in the family, not me."

"And when did you get into photography?"

"At university. And then I was on the job for the *Guardian* for a while, then a bit of fashion work…"

"You're a fashion photographer?" I said.

"It's not really my calling, but…yeah."

"That's *so* awesome," said Kaylee. "Must be really cool to get to meet all the celebrities and…"

"You don't really socialize with them," Sarah said curtly. "You're just there to do the work."

"Yeah, but afterward? I dunno, wrap parties or whatever?"

Sarah gave her a blank look and a slow shake of her head.

"Anyway," Sarah said, "I really do more non-profit work now."

Nobody in our crew cared about that, so the conversation petered out and then moved on to current events. The US Attorney in San Francisco had just announced a round of indictments against Trumbull, alleging that he'd defrauded a bunch of banks with "procedural deficiencies" in loan applications his real estate company had submitted. The banks underwrote the loans and the loans were paid off, but somehow somebody had been defrauded.

Melissa said the whole thing made her nervous. "It feels like there's no law anymore," she said. "Can we do a podcast on this when we get home?"

"We should," I said. "What we should do is get Trumbull."

"Oh, no," said Sarah. "You can't. He's horrid."

"He's about 80 million page views, easy," said Kaylee. "Horrid or not, that's a great idea."

I could tell that neither Melissa nor Kaylee were too impressed with Sarah. It seemed like that was the only thing they could agree on so far during this trip.

But after dinner, Sarah pigeonholed me.

"Care for a nightcap?" she asked.

"I maybe could," I said. "We're in Pierce's suite upstairs, so you're welcome to…"

She was shaking her head.

"I was thinking something more private."

"Oh, I see."

I knew it was a bad idea, but I went with Sarah back to the Grand Waica and spent the night in her room.

And everybody knew what I'd done when I made it back to the suite at the lodge early the next morning.

"I can NOT believe what you did," said Melissa, who was in her PJ's drinking coffee on the big couch when I attempted to sneak in. "How could you hook up with her? She's…"

"An adult," I said. "And so am I."

"Yeah, but come on, Mike. Nothing about her and you works."

"I'm not marrying the girl, Mel. Relax, will you?"

"But really," Kaylee, who had padded into the kitchen for coffee, said. "You're not down here to hook up. You're here to do a job. And she's a distraction."

"Exactly," said Melissa. "Exactly right. We're not distracted. But you are."

"Hey, I'm here. It's early. And we're working. We're leaving out of here for Micobie in an hour, and then we're going to Mahdia, and then this afternoon we've got interviews set with Bill Abbott and Ted Kournis, who built this place, and with

Mahandas Ishgan, the president. Does that sound like I'm distracted?"

Kaylee and Melissa both frowned at me.

"What's the problem here?"

"Ashley broke up with you and you're lonely," Kaylee said.

"You guys didn't like Ashley either. And why are you all playing Dating Nazi with my love life, anyway?"

"Because somebody has to," Melissa said. "You're a disaster."

"Dis-aster," Kaylee agreed.

I wanted to argue. I would have. I had nothing.

"Well, try not to be bitchy to Sarah. She's coming with us today."

"Great," groaned Melissa.

"Let's remember that we're also doing PR for Pierce, so having her along and being nice to her while she sees she's completely wrong about this place, and maybe changing her mind, is us earning some of the fat swag we're pulling down from Sentinel Holdings."

"Yeah, OK," said Kaylee, "but can you keep it professional?"

"Uhhh, yeah," I said, a little insulted. "Can *you?*"

A little later Sarah arrived, and just after that was when the whole project blew up.

We went down to Micobie and we interviewed no less than eight people, most of them women who were holding down the village while the men were working…at Liberty Point.

Universally, they loved Pierce Polk.

"He's absolutely the best thing that's ever happened here," said a charmingly pudgy middle-aged lady who gave her name as Betty. "The whole village is making money, we're getting a new road into Mahdia, and we're all fixing up our houses. He hired a guy who set up a learning pod for our kids and hooked us up to a bunch of online learning programs from the States. He's done so much for us."

"But why?" asked Sarah. "What is he gaining from it?"

"Probably friendship. He's a good neighbor and he takes care of people."

Sarah didn't like that at all. It didn't fit her narrative. And the more people we talked to, the bitchier she got.

Finally, she said she wanted to investigate the area around the village.

"I wouldn't do that if I were you," the village chief, an old guy named Patrick, told her.

"Oh, I know my way around a rain forest," Sarah said.

"Sarah, why don't you listen to him?" I said. "Besides, we need to get on the road to Mahdia. I don't want to make those people wait for us."

But she wasn't listening, and she fished a bunch of camera equipment out of the SUV and headed for the woods.

"Let her go," Kaylee said.

"I can't," I said. "Let me try to get her back."

So I chased after her, trying to cajole her back to the truck.

King Of The Jungle

"Look," I said, "you don't know the jungle here…"

"Rain forest," she said. "No one calls it a jungle anymore."

"Whatever. It's full of critters, many of them not at all friendly to humans. If you're going to go exploring in the wilderness you should do it with a local guide, don't you think?"

"I know what I'm doing," she said. "I've been in Africa, southeast Asia…"

"But you haven't been here. Do you know about which snakes are poisonous? Which plants cause a rash?"

"Do you?"

"No, which is why I'm saying let's get back in the truck and head to our next place."

She had her camera out and she was taking pictures. I was attempting to note, with less confidence than I was comfortable with, which way through the dense jungle led back to Micobie.

"Oh, here's something," Sarah said, snapping away with her camera.

I turned to look, and immediately yelled at her to back away.

She had turned over a log and found a nest full of snake eggs. And while she was clicking away, I could see a snake quickly slithering toward her.

"Sarah! Move!"

"What?" she asked, irritably, just before the snake – which I later found out was a brown labaria, or otherwise known as a fer-de-lance – struck at her leg and bit her two or three times.

"Ahhh!" she screamed as she went down.

I then did one of the stupidest things I've ever done, but I guess instinct kicked in. The snake had wrapped around her ankle and had pulled its head back to strike again, and I reached out and caught it just below the head.

Then I whipped out the retractable knife Megan had bought me with my credit card before my first trip down to Guyana, and I chopped the head off that snake.

Sarah was wincing. "Oh my God," she said.

"I need to keep the head of this thing," I said, "because it'll matter what kind of snake this is."

I made her get up, though I noticed she was bleeding a good bit from those bites on her leg, and helped her in the direction of Micobie.

We were a good 15 minutes before we were in sight of the village. The patient was clearly not holding up well.

Finally, I flagged down Patrick, who was walking his dog (a springer spaniel, if it matters), showed him the snake head and told him what happened. He wasn't pleased.

"Put her in that truck and take her to Liberty Point right now," he said, waving at the driver, who was sprinting to the Cherokee. "They don't have the hospital up yet, but the clinic is good. They can stabilize her and then you can get her out in time."

"In time for what?"

"To save her life. That's a brown labaria. It's one of the deadliest snakes there are. How'd you manage this, lady? Those snakes avoid people."

"We stumbled on a nest," I said.

"That was *stupid*," said Patrick. "You might have killed this poor girl."

Sarah was still somewhat lucid, and I expected her to defend me since this dumb escapade was her idea, but instead there was silence.

I gave her a shitty look, but I noticed she was in pain and I just felt guilty. Then I saw Patrick glaring at me and I got angry all over again.

We piled her in the back of the Cherokee and lit out as fast as the muddy dirt track would allow. Sarah was groaning. I was holding her hand and making her drink water. Patrick, while he was calling the clinic at Liberty Point and warning them we were coming in, had told me to keep her leg bent down so that the venom couldn't circulate as quickly to the rest of her system.

Melissa, Kaylee and Craig didn't say a word. They just looked at me. None of them gave off the vibe that I was a hero for helping to try to save Sarah.

We made it back to Liberty Point, and the Cherokee dropped us off at the medical clinic they'd set up next door to the Landing. There was a Guyanese doc there, whose name was Singh, and he grabbed a pair of scissors and cut the leg of her pants up to the knee as she had her lower leg hanging off the examination table. Sarah was wincing and muttering something about "man invading their habitat, and this is what happens."

Sarah's leg had swelled up like a tree trunk. She was bleeding profusely.

Singh looked at me and frowned. He grabbed a walkie-talkie and called the airfield.

"Give her water," he said, thrusting a bottle at me. I poured a little down Sarah's throat. She was shaking.

Then she threw up.

Singh was talking with the tower at the airfield, and there was a Cessna Citation owned by one of Pierce's friends that was headed back to Miami in a few minutes.

"Miami will work," he said, and demanded that they hold the plane.

"You must go with her," he said. "I would go, but I am the only doctor here. Someone must be on call. But I will tell you what to do for her."

"Well, the thing is…" I began.

Singh's look stopped me in my tracks.

A few minutes later, I was carrying Sarah from the Cherokee onto the Cessna, with the passengers – an aging hotel magnate and three very fetching young women who were quite certainly not his daughters – scrambling to get out of my way. I dumped her into a reclining seat in the front of the plane.

"Did she break her leg?" one of the girls asked.

"No," I said. "They put it in a splint when you get a snakebite."

"What's in that IV?"

"Antivenom. Hey, is there a bucket or something we can use?"

"What for?" asked the old man. The flight attendant closed the door and I could feel the jet begin to roll out of the hangar.

"Well, she might get sick. I don't want it to, you know."

I heard him sigh, and the next thing I knew there was a newly-empty ice bucket handed to me. I wedged it between Sarah's body and the edge of the seat.

"This bucket would have been more fun with what was in it before, I'll bet," I said.

"It's champagne," said one of the girls. "You want some?"

"Shit, yeah," I said. "Thanks!"

Sarah was mumbling nonsense and I could tell she was going into shock. Singh had given me an epi pen; I had no idea whether I should use it. He told me that if she was having trouble breathing or if she couldn't move, that I should give her a stick with it. But I had no clue.

And that was how it went for the next four hours until we landed at Miami Executive Airport. An ambulance was waiting for us on the tarmac, and off we went to Jackson South Medical Center.

And Sarah had a lucid moment as we hurtled east on 152nd Street.

"Mike," she said.

"Yeah, honey. Hang in there for me."

"You're very sweet. But it seems we're quite different people."

"Y'know," I said, "I think you're exactly right."

Sarah went straight into the ICU, and they deposited me in the waiting room. And my phone rang. It was Brienna.

"What happened?" she asked.

"Your sister started a fight with a snake and she lost," I said. "They just brought her into intensive care and it sounds like they think she's going to make it."

"Oh my God," came the response.

"I did the best that I could, but Brienna – that leg looks really bad. I don't know."

"She's always doing things like this, the stupid cow."

"I don't know what to say. She wanted to take a bunch of nature pics, and she wouldn't listen when the village chief told her she should take a guide…"

"No, it's not your fault, Michael."

"I should have tried to find you, but there wasn't time."

"I was at the waterfall with Pierce. But I'll come to you. Sarah isn't your problem."

"OK."

"I'm on the next plane out, which is in an hour. I'll be there tonight."

It struck me that it was after dark. I hadn't hardly noticed. Then I looked at the TV.

"Brienna, I've got to go," I said. And I hung up.

The chyron across the bottom of the screen said "TRUMBULL SHOT; WOULD-BE ASSASSIN TAKES OWN LIFE."

Chapter 11

May 12, 2024: Atlanta, Georgia

Kaylee, Melissa and Craig managed to salvage the podcast episode by doing the interviews with the folks in Mahdia and Liberty Point that we needed. They actually did a terrific job, I thought, and what we put together for that episode was great.

But as viewership went it was a dud, because of what happened with Trumbull.

The shooter who almost took him out was a 22-year-old male whose name was James Alfred Sterling, but he had demanded that people call him Shirley.

And yes, Billy Ray memed the shit out of that.

Sterling left a manifesto which held that killing Trumbull was a heroic attempt to save "Our Democracy," and a blow against "American fascism." It talked about how he had traveled back in time in a vision and killed Hitler before he took power in Germany, and that vision proved to him that he – well, they – was destined to take out "the modern Hitler which is so much worse."

Katrina Duvalier, Joe Deadhorse's press secretary, was caught on a hot mic saying Shirley Sterling was the greatest American patriot since the Rosenbergs. You'd think that would have been the absolute end of her career, but it only made a minor ripple when Dieter Poocey, the White House correspondent for Fox, asked her if she understood what a patriot was and then expressed doubt when she insisted she did.

When he got shot, Trumbull was at a rally in Terre Haute, having just won the Indiana primary and thereby sewing up the Republican nomination. At the time Sterling popped him he was talking about firing everybody at the EPA and letting the states take over environmental regulation. Such is the reduced state of American fascism, I guess.

The bullet broke his clavicle, missing his heart by six inches. Christy Hazel earned himself a two-day suspension from MSNBC by quipping that Trumbull had no heart to miss.

But the real problem was when the Secretary of the Treasury, under whom the Secret Service operates, called a press conference to decry a lack of cooperation and "shoddy practices" from Trumbull's private security contractors.

Guess who those were. Yep. Sentinel.

It was a huge PR problem, and we ended up pulling a couple of all-nighters to get on top of the situation. But when we dug down into the facts of the case, what we found was explosive as hell.

They'd changed out the head of Trumbull's Secret Service detail. DeAndre Taylor, who had been with Trumbull going back to his time in the White House, had been forced out because of some bogus sexual harassment claim filed against him. And his replacement, a lady named Pauline Chang, was the daughter of a San Francisco import-export guy who'd been a huge donor to both Omobba and Deadhorse.

It was a really bad look. And when we broke all this at the website, the shit hit the fan. Trumbull even called me from the hospital.

"Mike, Mike, Mike," he said, "you're gonna kill me. I can't use Sentinel for security, and now I can't get much from the Secret Service. I got crazies everywhere who want to take my head off and they're cheerin' 'em on at all the papers and networks. How'm I gonna run a campaign if I can't go anywhere?"

"Mr. President," I said, "we're just making sure the public knows the truth. But while I have you on the phone, I'd really like to do a podcast episode with you when you're back on your feet."

"Sure," he said. "Have your people call my people."

I asked him if he'd talked to Pierce.

"He's supposed to call later," he said, "but how's he gonna help? He's down in the jungle with that project of his. His business is falling apart and the FBI is taking all his houses."

Which was true. They'd raided Pierce's place in Jupiter, Florida that day. It was also cleared out, save for a house full of Walmart frog figurines set up in funny alignments. He'd texted me photos of those, and we put them up at the website and got a ton of traffic out of it.

That earned me a message from Karen, our new lawyer, asking me if I had a death wish. I responded saying maybe I did, but mostly I was just having too much fun to quit.

Pierce had stuff moving around everywhere, and the rumor had it he was stashing all of his gear at warehouses his friends owned to keep the feds from seizing it.

Pierce was now essentially a man without a country. The funny thing was, his businesses were very much still operational. For example, after what happened to New York State with the cyberattack, nobody dared put Sentinel Security out of business, and if Sentinel Port Management ceased operations half the country's supply chain would disintegrate.

And of course, his companies all had international operations. Pierce could have all of his stateside business go away and he'd still be one of the richest people in the world.

I wasn't sure Trumbull knew that. I also wasn't sure he cared that much, either. Donny Trumbull had a reputation for being hostile toward people richer than he was, though generally his experience had been that those people were hostile toward him. And while Pierce had been friendly, and publicly supportive, I got the impression Trumbull felt threatened by him.

Pierce had CC'ed me on an email he sent to Trumbull suggesting that his campaign hire Thurston Contingency Management as the new contractor, the upshot being that Thurston would retain the Sentinel team as a subcontractor, and that way everybody could save face a little. He also sent along a 14-page report from Sentinel Security's diagnostic team noting that there was a hole in his coverage at the Hulman Center at Indiana State University, where his rally was, and that where the shooter came in was a Secret Service responsibility.

And the details of that were really bad. Really, really bad. Which we'll get to a little later in the story.

Had the Secret Service deliberately botched the job and let a maniac in to assassinate a presidential candidate? And what would happen if that came out?

It had been a while since I'd been afraid to publish the truth. But on this, I definitely had to take a pause. Something Trumbull said stuck with me: because of what we'd reported about Pauline Chang, he was concerned the Secret Service was useless to him going forward. If I put this out? It would get a whole lot worse.

And social media, not to mention legacy corporate media, was full of people openly wishing that Shirley Sterling had done Trumbull in.

Things were getting exceptionally weird out there.

Then I got a death threat. It was just a stupid rant from an anonymous email, but I forwarded it to Agent Muhammad and asked if he wouldn't mind putting it through the proper channels.

"Not my department," came the response. I wasn't very surprised. So I sent it to Casey Crane, our contact at Sentinel

Network Security. He said he'd find out the source and "then we'll take care of it."

Then I called Pierce.

"I have a suggestion," I said. "I think you ought to get political. Like very political."

"More than I've been?"

"Yeah. If I were you, I'd go and set up a PAC and I'd buy up every ad impression and 30-second commercial spot you could get, and I would bombard the public with all the political dirt you have on Omobba and Deadhorse."

"It's a thought. What am I trying to accomplish?"

"For one thing, it gives you an opportunity to push back against these people calling you a crook. Especially when it's projection on their part. You've already uncovered enough on them that in a sane country the folks would be coming for their whole gang with pitchforks and torches."

"I would have thought we'd see more of an impact from what we've already put out there. Honestly, I would have thought they'd have backed off by now. Instead, it's getting worse."

"I don't think you can back these guys down. They don't back down. All they do is attack. Anybody who gets in their way, they wipe the poor bastard out. And that includes you, too, it seems."

"So you're saying play over the top of these assholes."

"I think that's all you can do. The thing you have, more than they have, is money. You've got an unlimited supply of that. You need to use it to bury them before they bury you."

"How's the podcast doing?"

"The one about Liberty Point?"

"Yeah."

"It got covered up a bit with the Trumbull shooting. But the numbers aren't terrible. And we've gotten some press inquiries. By the way, you talk to Brienna? How's her sister?"

"She's still in the hospital. She's all messed up, but they think they can save the leg. You saved her life, I think."

"Well, that's good."

"Mike did you sex up that girl?"

"It was a one-time thing. I was lonely, she was friendly. I don't think it'll be repeated."

"Brienna's pissed about that, but she won't tell me why."

"Do you care, Pierce?"

He laughed.

"Not really. I don't think my new existence as a hermit king is her style."

"It's not. You need somebody who's a wife, not a supermodel."

"Buddy, I've had two wives. I've had my last wife. They're expensive and they get mean. No thanks to all that. But you? You're the one who needs a wife. You're not like me. You actually would benefit from a normal life and a family. And let me tell you, Sarah Givens is not that girl."

"So I gather."

"Oh, yeah?"

"Pretty much."

I told him what happened that day in Micobie, including the part I didn't tell Brienna about how she didn't back me in front of the village chief and how she essentially broke up with me on the way to the ICU.

Pierce laughed.

"That's Sarah," he said. "Wait until she makes a fresh PR nightmare going public about the trip."

"What are you talking about, Pierce?"

"She told Brienna that snake-bite was all my fault. That between climate change and the loss of the snake's habitat, it's no surprise the wildlife are more aggressive."

"I'm thinking Sarah is the proximate cause of that snake-bite and not the climate."

"I don't think it matters a whole lot what the reality is. Not to her."

"Well, don't take that hit. Tell Brienna that she needs to let Sarah know that if she opens her mouth to trash you, after everything that was done to keep her from dying out there, that it's the end of that NGO of hers."

"That's not a bad idea. Brienna will probably end it with me if I do that, though."

"Again, do you care?"

"Not really. It's good advice. So is the political stuff. You know a guy I should use for that?"

"All the money you give to campaigns and you don't have a guy?"

"I don't care about that shit, Mike. Come on."

"Yeah, well, you're learning the most important rule, Pierce."

"What's that?"

"You might not care about politics, but politics definitely cares about you."

"Ain't that the truth. OK, so I'm going to go all mad bomber and essentially rig the election for Trumbull, and when I do I'll have a president in my pocket, and all of this bullshit will go away."

"I'm thinking that's your best call, yeah."

"OK. That'll work, I guess. But, dammit, I never wanted to be political. Why do I have to be political?"

"Because you do, Pierce. Modern America isn't interested in prominent people with no politics. It's bullshit, but that's how it is."

"That isn't a good look for modern America, Mike."

"I don't disagree. What about your situation down there?"

"We got a couple LM-100 Hercules planes makin' trips into the airfield regularly with pallets full of stuff, like military stuff, and we got shooters coming in from all over."

"Building a mercenary army, are you?"

"I'm tempted to go public about that. See if it scares off the Vinnies. But I'm apparently not as scary as I thought I was."

"The thing is, to impress them you'd have to let them know what kind of hardware your guys are packing. Small arms won't do it. And I'm no military strategist, but it's better, if you get in a fight, that the enemy doesn't know your order of battle."

"The point is to prevent the fight."

"The only way you fix that is to get Uncle Sam involved."

"Which won't happen if I keep up my war against Deadhorse and Omobba."

"That's about the size of it, yeah."

"Shit, Holman."

"Unless there's something else I don't know about, I don't know what to tell you. It's a rotten situation all around."

"Well, maybe there *is* something else. We'll see."

"That must be the something I don't know about. What is it?"

There was a short pause.

"Pierce?" I asked. "What's the story?"

"Not over the phone, man."

Chapter 12

May 15, 2024: Las Claritas, Bolivar

The mood in the camp was, in Cabrillo's estimation, less favorable than it had been since preparations had begun.

That had to do with the attempted coup d'etat, of course.

Things had deteriorated very quickly after the Madiera government announced that the second of the major opposition candidates in the elections set for December of 2024 had been disqualified. Jorge Rojas, who was the candidate of the new Primero Venezuela party and who in polling was holding a 15-point lead over the incumbent, was charged with collusion with America – a crime not specified in Venezuelan law – and stricken from the ballot.

Rojas was the second major candidate thus scratched; previously, Maria Lopez Morales of the Democracia Venezuela Party – who, like Rojas, had boasted a significant lead over Madiera at the time she was bounced off the ballot under dubious circumstances. And despite there being seven months until the election, it became painfully obvious to everyone involved in Venezuelan politics that Rojas would hardly be the last electoral threat Madiera and his government would block from running.

The people took to the streets. Violence ensued. The offices of the SENIAT, or *Servicio Nacional Integrado de Administración Aduanera y Tributaria*, Venezuela's national tax collection agency, were firebombed, and the mob refused to let the Caracas fire department put out the blaze. The building burned to the ground.

And then Pedro Ulloa de la Vega, the commander of the Army's First Infantry Division, stepped forward to offer himself as the interim president. De la Vega ordered that Madiera be arrested and tried for human rights abuses and vowed to restore Rojas and Morales to the ballot.

For three days no one knew who was running Venezuela. Then de la Vega turned up in Miami, conceding defeat and proclaiming Madiera the rightful president.

And hundreds of military and civilian supporters of the general were rounded up and shot as traitors.

That occasioned a fresh round of emigrations, including, interestingly enough, thousands of Venezuelans heading for Guyana. Not to mention a fresh round of condemnations from governments across the globe not to include China, Russia, South Africa, Bolivia, Cuba, Nicaragua, Ecuador, North Korea, Iran and Canada.

But more to the point, it occasioned problems in discipline for the 53rd Jungle Infantry Brigade which Cabrillo dealt with very harshly. Six of his men attempted to desert the brigade, but were found hiding in the woods a mile from their makeshift base. Cabrillo ordered that they be fired on by the helicopters sent to find them; the six tried to surrender and were cut down.

He knew that the men, who hadn't particularly liked or trusted him in the first place, were ready for an all-out mutiny; what saved him was that most of the brigade's leadership was Cuban and the only Venezuelan in the command structure was Carvajal, who was nobody's idea of a commander.

That, and Madiera paying the 53rd a visit and promising the men a loyalty bonus to be paid to their families.

That crisis resolved, things got much better.

The 53rd took delivery of four shipping containers full of food and water rations, dozens of crates full of new rifles, mortar systems, GPS locators, and even motorcycles.

And then there were the reinforcements.

The 53rd was to be supplemented by 500 additional troops, none of whom were Venezuelan.

Half of the additions were Cubans, a company of special-forces infantrymen from the *Avispas Negras,* or Black Wasps; these were the best jungle fighters the Cuban Revolutionary Army could offer, and Cabrillo had been asking for them for months. The rest were from elsewhere in Latin America: Bolivia, Ecuador and Nicaragua.

Cabrillo didn't think much of those.

He asked Xing whether China would be adding manpower to their effort, and the response he received was typical Xing.

"You have me," he said. "I'm your military advisor and procurement officer. And you don't need anything else to achieve your objectives, so stop whining."

That didn't sit well with Carvajal, who lit into their Chinese benefactor.

"We have enough trouble knowing that this action, which will cost many of our men their lives, ultimately results in more mines and oil rigs and timber for China," he said. "The least we should expect is that some Chinese might bleed alongside us before you earn your spoils."

"There are no Chinese to spare," Xing said.

"No Chinese to spare? There are more Chinese than anyone else! Why are you saying to me this *mierda?*"

"I mean that there are none to spare," said Xing. "Our people are working to the west of here."

"What is that supposed to mean?" asked Carvajal, angrily brushing off Cabrillo's attempts to shut him down. Cabrillo would discipline his adjutant later, but frankly, he wanted to hear what Xing had to say. Mostly he was curious to see if the rumors he had heard were true.

"It means that our people have a far larger project to work on than some shitwater jungle wilderness," said Xing, "and what we are doing will ensure you don't have to contend with that which you fear most."

"*Dios mio!*" Carvajal bellowed. "You speak in twisted riddles! What does that mean?"

"It means the Chinese are busy infiltrating up from Ecuador through to the *Yanqui* border," said Cabrillo, testing his theory.

Xing looked at him and smiled, and he knew he was correct.

"Meaning what?" asked Carvajal.

"Meaning that if the Americans attempt to block our adventure here, they will shortly find themselves dealing with much, much larger problems than Guyana," said Xing.

Carvajal cocked his head sideways. He clearly didn't understand.

"Hector," said Cabrillo, "our Chinese friends are playing the great game on a level much higher than ours. We need only focus on our mission, and all will be as it should."

"*Coronel*," said Carvajal, in perhaps the least subservient tone of his time under Cabrillo's command, "for an atheist you certainly seem to have a remarkable amount of faith."

"I have faith in *power*," said Cabrillo. "And that is something you must learn if you are to advance."

What Xing did provide, and Caracas then confirmed after Madiera re-established control of the government, was a much larger list of targets for the 53rd to occupy once the invasion began. Cabrillo could see that he would be in charge of one of three separate zones of occupation; each included every settlement, mine, quarry and other facility of any sort of value along the three tributaries to the Essequibo that were in the 53rd's area of operation.

One was the Rupununi River to the south. Then there were the two forks of the Mazaruni to the north. And, of course, the Potaro in the middle, which was Cabrillo's zone of operations.

They were going to have to drop in on and occupy well more than 150 different places in those three zones, though the vast majority of them wouldn't be resisting.

Most of the mission was simply a matter of getting his people to their objectives and then having them convince the locals that they were now Venezuelans and not a whole lot else would change.

They wouldn't like it much, but in Cabrillo's experience that wasn't particularly important. The Venezuelans didn't seem to be very fond of Madiera, but even after the failed coup attempt of a few days earlier it didn't appear they would do anything more dangerous than grumbling. All it took was for the regime to lay hands on de la Vega's wife and children and explain to him they'd either join him in comfortable exile or in a shallow grave. That was enough to get the general to choose exile. And when de la Vega wilted, the whole popular revolt did as well.

And now it was in doubt whether there would even be an election.

Cabrillo had learned to disdain the whims and wishes of the public. Especially when those people didn't have firearms. He knew Mao's old maxim that power comes from the barrel of a gun.

The Guyanese did have guns, though. Guyana had the highest rate of gun ownership in the Caribbean. And the people they were set to conquering were hunters and farmers used to shooting their dinners.

That wasn't the same as shooting people, though. Shooting people for the first time carried an injury to the soul profound enough to make many men hesitate, and that would give his troops an advantage.

He was training the 53rd very roughly, and most of them were becoming hardened. At least to an extent. Cabrillo hadn't adjusted upward his expectation that 60 percent of his men would perform in battle rather than melt away, but he did believe those 60 percent would acquit themselves quite well against what Guyanese resistance they would meet.

But at Liberty Point, it was different. Cabrillo watched the video of the American journalist Mike Holman who had done interviews of the capitalist exploiter Pierce Polk and his people there, and from those interviews it was clear that settlement would be well-defended by military veterans.

They'd have better troops than Cabrillo would. And maybe even more of them.

He didn't agree with Xing that he had everything he needed to take the territory he was assigned. It might take a division to capture Liberty Point, not a brigade.

And further, the order from the 5th Jungle Infantry Division headquarters in Tumeremo was to take the American town with as little structural damage as possible.

Chapter 13

May 20, 2024: Atlanta, Georgia

It was at about this point when things began happening faster than most of us could manage.

I had mentioned my reticence to go with the information I had about the near-assassination of Donny Trumbull in Indiana. That didn't last, because the story took on a life of its own.

First, Trumbull simply fired the Secret Service. He put out a statement saying that he'd hired his own in-house security team for the campaign, headed up by a guy named Ellis Marcado, who had been a staffer for the National Security Council when he'd been president. Marcado had done some heavy work as an Air Force special operator and he'd been a CIA contractor – he'd cycled out of Benghazi only a week or so before that whole thing had gone to shit. He was known.

And the campaign put out a statement saying that owing to his recovery and the effort to put a first-class security team together, Trumbull's campaign was going digital for the next few weeks. He was going to do a lot of remote-broadcast rallies, internet town halls and the like until the convention from his big estate in Boca Raton.

The truth was that Sentinel was taking over the entire thing, but it was going to be done on the sly with Marcado as the face of the operation.

King Of The Jungle

And on the same day Trumbull fired the Secret Service, Pauline Chang resigned.

Here was what I knew and was too chickenshit to go public with for fear I'd do more harm than good. It turned out that two key members of the Secret Service detail protecting Trumbull, that Chang was newly in charge of, had been taken off the job almost immediately before Trumbull's rally in Terre Haute.

And they weren't replaced. The detail was understrength when Trumbull was shot.

So in Terre Haute the Secret Service was missing somebody working one of the doors to the basketball arena that Shirley Sterling ended up coming through, and also missing was the Secret Service agent that was supposed to be next to the stage where Sterling ended up standing when he began blasting away at Trumbull.

That looked very, very bad for Pauline Chang. The fact that her father was a Chinese immigrant who'd made a few hundred million in the import-export game and had been a colossal donor to pretty much every Democrat politician in California, not to mention Omobba and Deadhorse, looked even worse.

But when Chang resigned, I got a note from Trumbull. "What you ought to do," he said, "is get her on your podcast."

"What the hell for?" I said.

"I think you'll like her," Trumbull replied.

I didn't know what to make of that. The one thing that came to mind was that she was, as my grandma used to say, "a swell looker." She was in her early 30's, about 5'8" and athletic as hell – apparently she'd been a pole vaulter at UCLA in college – and she had those amazing features you see so often in girls of mixed oriental and European ancestry. The high cheekbones, the clear complexion, the whole bit. But softer, if you know what I mean.

I wasn't even the first one to notice. Kaylee was. Which was not unusual.

"You know I'm not gay," she said when we were looking at the Breitbart story about her resignation which featured a wire photo of her standing near Trumbull. "But I would *totally* hit that."

"Well, there's a colossal case of TMI," I said, shaking my head at Kaylee.

"I'm joking, dummy. But seriously. That's the hottest Secret Service agent I've ever seen."

I couldn't disagree, but I still corrected her. "Ex-Secret Service agent, you mean."

"I'll bet there's more to this, Mike."

"Are you seriously going to take up for the chick who almost lost a president just because she's hot?" I said.

"No, of course not. I just think there's more."

And I remembered that conversation when Trumbull's text came in.

"Kaylee," I said as I poked my head into her office just after the former president's suggestion, "maybe we ought to look into booking Pauline Chang."

"You're kidding," she said. "I literally just got an e-mail from Jenny Wilson, who's doing her publicity."

"She has a publicist already?"

"I mean, people with a story to tell tend to get publicists, Mike. Oh, and now is the part where I tell you 'I told you so.'"

"Fair enough. When do we want to book her?"

"I think we ought to do it tomorrow night. Jenny said she's in Arlington right now and she can set it up. You're already scheduled to be in DC tomorrow."

I was. I had a speech scheduled at a PAC fundraiser lunch and I was supposed to interview Jim Jordan about the House Oversight Committee's attempts to prove the Mexican cartels had bought off the Secretary of Homeland Security. But following that, I could fit Chang in.

"Then let's do it," I said.

Kaylee gave me a big smile.

My speech to that PAC at the Waldorf was a big hit, although I thought I sucked, and while Jordan was good, he didn't say anything we didn't already know – it was probable that the cartels had corrupted the DHS bureaucracy, and maybe some folks even higher up than that, and there was circumstantial evidence that they had, but they were far too crafty to leave a smoking gun around.

But then I met Pauline Chang in Jenny Wilson's conference room in Arlington that night, and she was nothing like I expected.

For one thing, most of what had been written about her in the conservative media, and that was most of what had been written about her at all; the legacy corporate media barely covered anything about the Secret Service scandal, had it that she was a nepot who'd been pushed into the job of Trumbull's head-of-detail because of her family connections. There was even a story line out there which said Pauline Chang had been set up as the fall guy for the security failure because it was understood that she would then "fail up" and get rewarded with some plush job up the Secret Service chain or in the White House somewhere.

That was the Washington way, after all.

Except Pauline was not in that frame of mind.

When I met her, she told me straight-out that this would be different.

"Look," she said, "what I'm going to tell you is going to blow your mind. But I can substantiate every word. And I want it as public as possible because this stuff simply can't remain a secret."

"I think I know most of it," I said. "But hearing it from you means we can take it public. The real question is are you absolutely sure that you want to do this interview? There are people out there who really hate you right now."

"And if I didn't know the real story I'd hate me, too," she said. "It's more important I have a good name than a life. Going public is the only way I can get that back, so I'm all in."

"All right, then."

We started the interview with her life story – she grew up in the Bay Area, one of four siblings. Her three brothers all joined the Navy; one of them was a captain on a submarine in the Atlantic, while the other two got out and worked in the family business.

Pauline was supposed to be a lawyer like her mother, a tall blonde who'd been a Golden State Warriors dancer while she was putting herself through law school until she met Peter Chang. But after UCLA, Pauline decided what she'd rather do was law enforcement, and she chose the Secret Service over the FBI. She'd had a good career in the Secret Service, rising particularly quickly while Trumbull was president, and got onto the security detail for Perry Mince, then the VP. Then after 2020 she'd worked in a few other roles while they were grooming her for a big job.

And just a few days after she got one, they pulled the rug out from under her.

What I'd heard about Terre Haute was true. But what I didn't know was a lot worse.

They didn't just take two of the agents on her detail out of the field, they did it only half an hour before Trumbull's speech at that arena. And because of a "bureaucratic snafu," nobody informed her.

But it was worse even than that. Pauline alleged, and our contacts at Sentinel Security backed her up on this because they had terabytes of video from cameras all over the arena, that there were a pair of lookalikes who had stood in for Agents Eddard and Cole, and they'd magically disappeared just at the right time – Cole's doppleganger, just when Shirley Sterling made his way through Gate D into the arena, and Eddard's, just before Sterling started shooting.

So Pauline, watching the whole thing from mobile command, had absolutely no way to either recognize the problem or fix it in time to stop that almost-assassination.

She was hot about it, and I didn't blame her.

"I don't know how high up this goes," she said, "and I don't have enough information to accuse anybody specifically of anything. All I can say is what's obvious: this does not happen unless someone deliberately contrived it and executed it."

"My experience keeps telling me that accidents are a lot rarer than people think these days," I said. "It doesn't seem like this is one."

"Of course it isn't," she said. "And I guess I'm the perfect patsy, or maybe they thought I was."

"Because you'd have the family connections to survive it? There's a column out there by Robert Zane saying you'd have the opportunity to 'fail up' following this."

"Yeah, I saw it," she said, seething.

"I can tell you aren't very happy about that piece."

"No, I am not. But I'm not angry at Robert Zane. Based on what I've seen working inside the government I think he's probably right about most of what he wrote. What makes me angry is that the Swamp thinks I would just roll over and take it."

"So you think there is some entity out there, or some cabal, that would protect you if you'd played ball?"

"I'll put it like this: I had a couple of conversations with people inside the government who told me I could expect to be taken care of it I kept my head down. But it didn't get any further than that before…"

"Before you decided not to keep your head down."

"Exactly. The fact that this was even a possibility infuriates me."

"Why? At the end of the day, the plot – I'm assuming based on what our sources have told us and what you're saying that it had to be a plot to kill Donny Trumbull – failed. And the people responsible are almost certainly not getting away with it."

"You would think they wouldn't, Mike, but honestly? I'm not sure about anything."

"That's a little bit bleak, don't you think?"

"It definitely is. But what I'm most upset about is that the deck is now stacked against the honest professionals in government who just want to do a good job regardless of the politics. OK? What I wanted to do was to protect people from the bad guys who would do them harm. I busted my ass to get really good at my job. And what's what worth, at the end of the day? Here I am, 31 years old, I've put in maximum effort at everything I've done, and I'm a fall guy. That's it. I resigned because I'm always going to be considered a failure. I can't protect a president anymore; they'd be crazy to have me on the job."

"That isn't what President Trumbull told you, is it?"

"No, he was sympathetic once he understood what happened. But he fired the whole Secret Service off his campaign, and I can't blame him for that. We failed him.

"And if I'd just kept my mouth shut they would have shunted me off to some desk job until the coast was clear and then up I'd move through the bureaucracy, totally dependent on somebody's favor for advancement because I'd have this major black mark on my resume."

"So this was your one shot, is what you're saying," I said.

"Sure. But the thing I want to make clear is that this isn't just me we're talking about. Whoever's responsible for this has destroyed the Secret Service. The whole agency. It can't be trusted ever again because now it's clearly vulnerable to this kind of corruption."

"Well, that's definitely bleak."

"Absolutely it is."

"So what's next for you?"

"I want to get to the bottom of this horrible case, and I hope that you and your team can help because I know you're one of the best if not *the* best, and then after that? I don't have a clue. I'll have to start completely from scratch."

We finished the interview, I flew home, the next day we released it and bumped the release of the Jordan interview to the following day.

And Pauline got us 75 million views on X.

Pauline Chang went from a hated figure to a national heroine in no time flat. There was a big outpouring from people all over the place – lots of federal and state employees, especially, who echoed what she said about just trying to be a pro at a difficult job and finding it impossible because of all the bullshit politics and power agendas their agencies had been corrupted by.

Somebody caught up to Deadhorse outside a Planned Parenthood event where he was speaking and asked him about the Pauline Chang scandal. "She's lying," he said as he sloppily licked at an ice cream cone.

"What's she lying about?" the reporter asked.

He waved his hand dismissively. "All of it," he said. "All of…I was in the Secret Service. I know."

"Mr. President, you were never in the Secret Service."

"You're lying," he said.

And then he was whisked away to his vacation home on the beach an hour away.

Deadhorse's approval ticked down to 27 percent in a poll released the next morning, and Candy Abrams' gossip column in the *Times* suggested that it was only weeks away before he'd bow out of the race.

But back at Holman Media, we were ecstatic. Pauline had been gold for us. She was the perfect thing to push our traffic right back up into the stratosphere – and we needed it, because Megan had sold more impressions than we were even generating, and Tom had been freaking out about having to issue a make-good to the advertisers.

But the Pauline stuff was money in the bank. It didn't hurt that she looked absolutely fantastic on video, or that she disappeared – and I mean *vanished* – right after our interview hit the internet.

A couple of days later Kaylee got hold of Jenny Wilson to ask her about Pauline; we wanted to do a follow-up interview with her, because going back to that well was the best possible idea to stoke traffic.

"Oh, she's gone," said Jenny.

"What do you mean, she's gone?" Kaylee sputtered. "Jenny, you can't have a client as good as that and just let her disappear."

"Apparently, I can," came the response. "But tell Mike to ask his buddy Pierce Polk. I'll bet he can figure it out from there."

So I did, and the next day I was on a HondaJet 2600 to Guyana courtesy of the folks at Exoil. It occurred to me that I'd become a private-jet snob, because after you've flown on a Gulfstream 700 or a Bombardier 3500, pretty much anything else feels like coach.

Well, let me backtrack on that. I shouldn't blame HondaJet for my lousy flight down to Guyana. It had more to do with the company than the equipment.

For example, this was how the conversation went.

"Kaylee, that so gross," Melissa was saying. "I mean, you're a straight girl with a fiancé. Could you stop?"

"OK, I was joking. You know, *a joke?* Come on, Melissa."

"Yeah, but it doesn't seem like a joke the way you're making googly-eyes at pictures of Pauline."

"I'm not making googly-eyes. I'm trying to pick out a couple of still shots and maybe a little B-roll we can use if we do a follow-up podcast with her. It's just business!"

"Then what was all this you were saying about how interesting she is, and what a good interview she was, and how she's stunning and brave, and on and on?"

"Fine. I'll admit it. I'm a fangirl, OK? I mean, I think it'd be cool to be friends with her, that's all."

"All right, enough," I said. "That's all the bickering I can handle for now."

"Oh, yeah," said Kaylee, "because *somebody* got into the bourbon last night and has a massive hangover, and because of that we're not allowed to talk."

"I didn't 'get into the bourbon.' It was a business dinner. Megan had the XOX Communications people, and she and Phil and I took them out last night…"

"…and then you got into the bourbon. Got it."

I gave Kaylee a shitty look, and just then the flight attendant, an exotic-looking brunette named Francesca, dropped in on me.

"Can I get you anything, Mr. Holman?" she asked sweetly.

"Percocet, maybe?"

"Sorry. I think I might have some Aleve, though."

"That would be terrific. And some water. Thank you Francesca."

"Sure!" she said, and then she flashed me a million-dollar smile.

I noticed Melissa was looking at me a certain way.

"What?" I asked her.

"Nothing," she said.

Kaylee giggled. Francesca returned with a little bottle of Advil and a big glass of ice water.

"It's from my personal stash," she said. "I thought we had Aleve on board, but I was wrong."

"OK, great," I said. "You're a life-saver, Francesca!"

She smiled, dropped something in my lap, and sashayed back out of the cabin.

I picked it up. It was a business card. "Francesca Gianotto, Realtor," it said on the front. I guess the flight attendant gig was a side hustle for her.

And a little message on the back: "call me anytime. For any reason!" with a little heart as the top of the exclamation point.

That earned Francesca a grin when I caught her looking at me from the attendant station in the front.

And of course, Kaylee and Melissa both had their jaws on the floor when I turned to them.

"Sly...dog," said Kaylee.

"Don't do it," I told her. "It's none of your business."

"I'll bet she wants you to hook up with Pauline so she'll have to be friends with her," said Melissa.

"Oh my God! Shut *up*, Melissa!"

"Enough," I said. "Hush, or you're fired. Both of you."

That bought me a little time and I managed to get a tiny nap in, at least for a few minutes, until my phone rang. It was Karen.

"I just heard," she said, "you're being investigated by the FBI."

"Fabulous. What did I do?"

"Sharing classified information, apparently. The Pauline Chang interview."

"Are you serious right now?"

"Yep. You're going to want to protect yourself. I'll be sending you stuff on Signal. You do have the Signal app on your phone, right?"

"Yes. Go for it. I'll get with Sammy, our IT guy, and figure out what to do."

"Good. But between you, me and the NSA who's listening, I don't think you should take this lying down. You should get as loud as you can and see if you can scare these creeps off."

"Great minds think alike," I said. "On it."

So I pulled out my laptop and wrote an 800-word column for the website laying into Wreath and Ray Christofferson, the

King Of The Jungle

FBI director, calling them a pair of tyrants and criminals. Then I sent the link to Jim Jordan on Signal, with a quick message telling him his podcast interview was doing well traffic-wise.

"Not surprise about that investigation," he said. "It's par for the course. We've got Christofferson set to testify next week. You should come up and be on the panel with him."

"As much as I'm growing to hate DC, I guess I can't turn *that* down."

As we came in for a landing, I noticed that Liberty Point was noticeably bigger – but something else struck my eye.

Across the Potaro from town, right on the point where it met the Essequibo, there was a big circular concrete pavement that was scored to look like brickwork with a bunch of rectangles embedded into it. In the middle was a steel skeleton of…something.

Pierce was in the hangar when the jet pulled in.

"How about this?" I joked when I saw him. "I get the royal treatment!"

"It isn't really you," he said with a laugh. "I have the Venezuelans, the Guyanese, the Argentinians, the British and the Americans coming in, so I'm meeting them here. Big confab, trying to head off whatever is coming."

"That sounds like fun. Good news opp for us. I hope you'll have time to sit in for some interviews about the book while we're here, though."

"For sure, Mike. Absolutely. You guys want to go get comfortable first?"

"Yeah, but I've got a question: what's that you're building on the other side of the little river?"

"Oh, right. That's the Liberty Torch."

"The Liberty Torch?"

"It's going to be a big statue of a hand holding a torch. Two hundred and six feet high. Got a natural gas line going in so the flame will always be lit. Be able to see it for miles and miles around."

"That's pretty cool. Bet the environmentalist crowd is gonna love it."

He just smirked, and then Craig, Kaylee, Melissa and I caught a ride into town.

On the way, we passed what looked like a factory. The driver said they had some big 3-D printers they were using to make prefabricated concrete blocks to turbocharge the construction process.

"It's impressive," said Kaylee, "but why the rush to build all this if it's just going to get invaded?"

"Because they're building the stock exchange," said the driver, whose name was Vinod.

"The stock exchange?" I asked. "What stock exchange?"

"The Exchange of the Americas," he said. "It's not public yet, but they're going to trade stocks here in Liberty Point."

Melissa looked at me and shook her head. "Crazy," she mouthed.

"I keep telling you guys," I said. "Keeping up with Pierce Polk is impossible."

There was some time before we were supposed to meet at Pierce's place at the Grand Waica, so I decided to hang out for a while at the lodge's bar.

And that's when I saw her.

Pauline didn't look at all like she did when we met for that interview. She'd cut her hair into a short bob and she'd dyed it a dirty blonde, and she was wearing a denim miniskirt and a tank top with a plaid button-down shirt worn like a jacket, plus a pair of Tretorns. She was sitting alone at the half-crowded bar, drinking a Banks out of a frosty mug.

"Well, well, well," I said. "I'd search the whole world looking for you, just like everybody else is doing, and here you are in my building."

She didn't say anything. She just turned to me and beamed.

"You're the first guy to hit on me today that I was happy to see," she said.

"Is that a fact?"

"Yeah. Sit down, will you?"

"Sure, my dear. Are you enjoying your anonymity?"

"Anonymity? Not around here."

Just then a couple of guys came up to us wanting to take pictures. Grudgingly, I said yes, and grudgingly, Pauline did too. And the next thing I knew we were posing for pics for most of the people in the bar.

Finally, they left us alone.

"How are you holding up?" I asked.

"I'm good," she said. "Your friend Pierce set me up with a great condo that has a view of the park, and everybody here is friendly. I have no idea what I'm going to do next, but I can think of worse places to lay low while I figure it out."

"Maybe you could be the top cop around here. You could be the police commish or something."

"I don't think so, Mike."

"No?"

She shook her head.

"I don't know what I'm gonna do next, but I think I'm done trying to be a badass. Besides, I'm told I'm likely a felon now because I talked to you, so I don't think I have a great future in law enforcement."

"What a shame. You're my favorite badass chick!"

She laughed, and softly punched my shoulder. And those eyes looked straight into mine and I…was…hooked.

Chapter 14

May 23, 2024: Liberty Point, Guyana

To an extent, it was unfortunate that I ran into Pauline and hit it off with her. Because after a couple of hours of hanging out in the bar, I had to go. Pierce was having another one of his VIP receptions at the Waica and he wanted me there. Not to mention I needed to talk to those diplomats and see if we could set up interviews with some of them.

But on my way out, Pauline made me give her my phone and she texted herself with it.

"I think you're the only person in the world who has this number," she said with a smile. "It's new."

So I kissed her on the cheek. And she gave me a tight hug, which told me I wasn't the only one feeling something.

"I'm sending my producer down to keep you company," I said, taking back my phone and sending a quick text. "You remember Kaylee, right? She has a fangirl crush on you, or something."

"Cool. I need a girlfriend down here. With the job and all, I haven't had girlfriends in…hell, it's been since college, really. Please give me an actual life."

I smiled at her.

"Gotta go," I said.

"Go save the world, or whatever."

And she raised her glass as I left, wishing I didn't have to.

No sooner did I jump in a golf cart to catch a ride to the Waica, but it started raining like I'd never known possible. I'm talking sheets of it. Nick, the driver (he was a transplant from Texas who dropped everything and came down here a month earlier because, as he said, "it's all goin' to shit in the States and Pierce Polk might just be the guy to save it"), pulled under a rain shed – that's what those big canvas tent-looking things were, which struck me as a little stroke of genius - and had me help him roll down the plastic walls on the side and back of the cart.

"Won't keep us too dry," he said, "but it's better than you lookin' like you fell in the pool."

"This is what the rainy season is like here, I take it," I said.

"That's what they tell me. I'm as much a rookie about this place as you are, Mr. Holman."

A little better situated for the weather, Nick sped us to the Grand Waica and down the ramp into the underground garage.

I asked him if I needed to tip him. He shook his head.

"Instead, can we do a selfie?"

"Sure, Nick." I'd never thought of my image as currency, but he seemed happy.

But when I made it up to Pierce's party, it didn't really appear that happiness was the flavor of the day.

When I'd been to Pierce's VIP receptions before, it was usually a collection of business people and notable figures who did what I'd call "private-sector" things. A race car driver. An actor. Football players and other athletes. Writers and pundits like me. But this group was different.

These were the politicians.

Ishgan and Janaroo were there, like they always seemed to be, and both of them had a big retinue of staffers and minions. Then there was Sir Richard Montrose, the British ambassador to Guyana; the word on Montrose was that he was a military hero in Afghanistan who'd risen fast after joining the Foreign Ministry but his career had collapsed due to an over-affection for gin and they'd parked him in Guyana in hopes he'd dry out.

He definitely had not dried out.

Rigoberto Andujar was there; he was an envoy from Venezuela. Pierce told me he needed me in the room for the private meeting Andujar was asking for.

And then there was Valerie Wynn, the U.S. ambassador to Guyana. She'd been on the job for maybe a year. It was her first ambassadorship; she'd been in South Africa, Pakistan, Egypt, Belize, Iceland and a couple other places, essentially as a State Department office worker. Valerie was 38, never married, no kids, definitely not a fan of mine. She showed me a picture of her Siamese cat, whose name was Snookums. She made a big deal of the fact she spoke Urdu.

"Is the U.S. military going to come to Guyana's aid if the Venezuelans invade?" I asked.

"On the record?"

"If you want to. While I'm down here I'd like to do some interviews and I'd like to do one with you. But if you don't, we can just talk on background."

"OK, on the record, we're evaluating our commitments and have made no decision on an American role in what conflict might arise."

"In other words, no comment."

"It's all I've been authorized to say."

"Fine. Off the record, what's the deal?"

"Off the record, I have no idea."

"Wait, what?"

"Honestly, I don't think the administration believes this is a thing. They don't want to provoke a big international incident by coming in heavy. That just pisses off the Chinese and it's destabilizing."

"Destabilizing? Telling the Venezuelans they'll come out like Saddam Hussein did if they roll into Essequibo seems like the most stabilizing thing you could do. I don't get it."

She just shrugged.

"I don't think they see it that way."

"But it's different than what the administration was saying a couple of months ago."

"Well, this approach has worked so far."

I wanted to hit her with the "Bold strategy, Cotton" line, but thought better of it.

And she turned me down flat for a podcast interview. Which was par for the course. Nobody from the Deadhorse administration would do interviews with us, just like nobody from the Omobba administration would after the first couple of years.

Montrose was different, though. He said he was happy to sit down with me the next morning. And on background, in between gulps of his G&T – the pretty Patamona server knew to keep them coming when Montrose was around – he told me that the Brit government was considering preparations to deploy a naval flotilla and some troops for Guyana's defense.

"Why aren't they here?" I asked.

"Politics, dear boy. The London press would have a grand time skewering the PM over a return to colonialism if we were to go in. That must be managed."

"Yeah, but this is about Venezuela colonizing Guyana. It's the exact opposite of British colonialism."

"You know that, and I know that. Sadly, they don't know that."

"So what your government has to offer is empty threats to the Venezuelans."

"I should point out that it's more than your government is offering, my friend."

"Fair point."

When I finally ran into Pierce, he looked like he'd aged 10 years in the past couple of weeks.

"Hey, come with me," he said. "I need to talk to you before we sit down with the Venezuelan."

"Sure," I said, "but I don't know why you want me in there."

"Because I want him to know that whatever they do, the world will know about it."

We retired to that private study where Pierce and Hal Gibson had laid into Ravi Darke before, and it was just us.

"How's the book coming?" he asked.

"I'm crunching away at it in my off hours, but I have an outline and some parts written. By the end of July I'm hoping the first draft will be done and then we'll bring in an editor, and maybe a couple of months later it'll be finished. Shooting for Labor Day to have it out to the public."

He grimaced.

"What's wrong?"

"I was hoping maybe we could accelerate that."

"A book isn't really like one of your construction projects, Pierce. You can't 3-D print a biography."

"Well, you can use AI to…"

"Shut your mouth. There will be no AI in anything with my name on it."

"OK, fine. I was thinking maybe if we could publish the book it might generate public sentiment behind getting the U.S. involved down here."

"I talked to Wynn. I don't think there's much help there."

"No, there is not. And even if there was I don't think she's somebody who could handle it."

"You're not impressed with the cat-lady ambassador?"

Pierce just rolled his eyes.

"So what's the story with this stock exchange?"

Now Pierce lit up a bit.

"Right, that. So here's what we're doing – we're going to build an international exchange to trade companies that refuse to embrace DEI or ESG or any of that World Economic Forum bullshit. The Argentinians and Chileans have agreed to use it as a secondary exchange for their stuff and we've gotten some buy-ins from some Caribbean countries as well. We want to make it a place for companies from Prudhoe Bay to Tierra del Fuego to go public."

"Yeah, but you don't believe in public companies, Pierce."

"I don't believe in *my* companies going public. If somebody else wants to do that, I'm good with it."

He told me he had Ishgan and Janaroo behind the idea of turning Guyana into the world's biggest tax haven, more or less like a Switzerland of the New World; after all, the oil revenue would be more than enough to fund the government for a good, long time, and he said what was missing in places like the Cayman Islands was a stock market to capture more than just bank accounts here and there.

"We don't really have the banks in Guyana yet," he said, "so the money will actually get handled in the Caymans."

"Then why build the exchange in Liberty Point? Why not Georgetown?"

"Because Liberty Point is going to be the biggest, richest city in this part of the world in 20 years so long as we keep the Vinnies out. And actually, Ishgan wants it here. He wants the Vinnies to be scared to invade the place where all these stocks will be traded."

"I don't know, Pierce. It seems like a Hail Mary pass."

"It kind of is, but anyway…are you ready to have this sitdown with Andujar?"

"Sure."

Pierce pulled out his phone and sent a text, and a moment or two later, Hal Gibson and the Venezuelan came in and sat at the table.

"I take it everybody has met," said Pierce, "so let's talk."

"Are we in confidence?" Andujar asked. He was looking at me.

"I'll report what we agree I should report," I said.

"But if everyone agrees but me?"

"Then you're on the wrong side of a consensus, Rigoberto," said Pierce. "Mike stays."

The Venezuelan sighed.

"If that is the case, then I will just say this: my government is acting with the full will of the Venezuelan people when it moves to right a wrong done to us two hundred years ago. We will annex Essequibo and return it to its rightful place inside our borders. By force, if necessary."

"That's going to be very, very expensive for you," said Hal Gibson. "You should know that you're going to absorb catastrophic losses among the men you send here."

"We know about what you've got waiting at Las Claritas, Tumeremo and Santa Elena de Uairen," said Pierce. "You've forward-deployed your Jungle Infantry Division, but you can't move them through Brazil and that's the only road."

"Helicopters and planes are very, very vulnerable," said Gibson.

"It sure would be a shame if you tried an invasion and lost most of your guys on the way to the fight," said Pierce.

Andujar laughed.

"Your threats are not convincing," he said. "Let us not waste time with bluster."

"It isn't bluster," said Pierce. "I can recruit thousands and thousands of American patriots to come down here and fight you, and we'll hold the line for months. Maybe years. Can your government sustain a war effort for years?"

"Can your little town here? The Guyanese surely cannot."

"I'm prepared to put my entire fortune into this fight," said Pierce. "And given the debt-load of your government, which is what? Something like $450 billion? I think I might actually have more money than you do."

Andujar made a face, like he thought what Pierce had said was absurd.

"You've so destroyed your country that one American businessman has more money than your government which rules, what? Twenty million people? I don't know what your population is anymore because so many of them have left. And you think you can come in here and invade another country with guns and bombs?"

"Unless what you're actually doing is playing stooge for China," said Gibson. "But if you think doing their dirty work will save you, you've grossly miscalculated."

They were making Andujar uncomfortable, but I got the impression he wasn't in a position to stop anything. He held up his hands in a conciliatory gesture.

"What I hope to accomplish here is an accommodation. Your Liberty Point might maintain a sense of autonomy as part of Guayana Esequiba. We would even discuss having it become the capital of the new Venezuelan state."

"Not interested."

"Why not?"

"You make us Venezuelan, and now we're on the hook for your national debt. And since this place would be the only place that works in your whole country, you would sink your hooks in us so deep that we'd turn into your slaves."

"What if Liberty Point were to become a city-state in its own right, then?"

"In other words, you want us to stand aside and watch you conquer our neighbors who we've made great friendships with," said Gibson. "You want us to sell them out."

"And then we'd have to take them in as refugees," said Pierce. "So we'd have to pay to feed and house and clothe them after they've lost everything."

Andujar looked at me.

"As you see," he said, "it is *los Yanquis* taking an immovable position."

"The lamb refusing to be dined on by the wolf, one might say," I said.

"We don't care about these old territorial claims," said Pierce, "and we know Madiera doesn't care, either. He's trying to rally your people by ginning up bloodlust and blaming the Guyanese for the problems he's caused for his own country. Venezuela is in no position to annex anything. You're a failed state."

"We are not a failed state."

"You damn near had a revolution two weeks ago. I'd say that's pretty failed."

"And you think we are not aware of your involvement in that? That we are ignorant of your corruption of General de la Vega? That you didn't pay him to become your puppet?"

This was new, but it made sense. This would be the "something else" that Pierce had alluded to, rather cryptically.

"General de la Vega is a patriot who was attempting to save your country from its government," Pierce said. "What help I've provided to him and his family is a recognition of his efforts to bring democracy and freedom back to those people. You were going to execute his wife and children! You think I would willingly do business with monsters like that?"

Andujar shook his head and looked at the ceiling.

"We appreciate your efforts at peacemaking, senor Andujar," said Gibson, "but you need to tell your superiors in Caracas and their taskmasters in Havana and Beijing that the cost of this invasion will be utterly ruinous. It will bring down your government."

"I will see to that personally," said Pierce. "And you should know that when I take on a project, I complete that project."

"I will relay your statements to my government," said Andujar, "and I do admire your resolve if not your judgment. I hope that you do not all die here in this place when just across the river is safety."

Gibson smiled at him.

"We'll take care of that," he said, standing up and extending his hand to Andujar. The Venezuelan rose up and shook it. Then he nodded at Pierce and me and left.

"Well, that was a little less cordial than I was hoping for," said Pierce.

"Are you sure the city-state thing is a no-go?" I asked. "What if you could take this place and make it a Hong Kong?"

"No way," said Pierce. "We'd have a hostile army camped out next door and they'd be putting the arm on us daily. I'm not having that."

"And don't forget what happened to Hong Kong," said Gibson.

"OK, but this threat to make it expensive; what's that? A bluff?"

"We've got man-portable surface to air missiles distributed all over the villages around here," said Pierce. "I'm not saying we'll shoot down all their choppers or planes before they could put troops down, but we'll get a lot of them."

"And there's the four SAM batteries we've already set up around our perimeter," said Gibson. "They're gonna have a very, very hard time getting in here."

"You ever get a submarine like you were hoping to do?"

Pierce just smiled at me.

"You having fun so far, Mike? Bet you never thought you'd be getting this close to the great game."

Chapter 15

May 30, 2024: Pointe-a-Pitre, Guadeloupe

A week later, Pierce had turned me into a diplomat, or something like it.

And I had turned Pauline into a cameraman – er, camerawoman.

She said she'd been a shutterbug as a kid and she was reading up on how the latest cameras – and in particular, the Canon EOS R6 – incorporated video.

"All I know is still photography," she said. "I guess I have to learn."

"Is this your next career?" I asked her. "You trying to break into the lucrative world of press photography?"

"I'm just trying not to be bored," she said. "But I did think about maybe doing a blog or something, and photography could maybe be a part of that."

So I bought her a Canon EOS R6. Believe it or not, Amazon delivered it to the package station Pierce set up in Georgetown in two days and she had it in three.

And then Pauline was emailing us – we gave her a Holman Media e-mail address, because why not? - still photos, video, you name it. And for an amateur she actually wasn't bad. Colby even told her he wanted to use some of her stuff on the website, which was doing Guyana coverage every day now. A guy named Flip Hardison, who had been a correspondent for *Army Times* in Afghanistan and then went to work for Sentinel Security, ultimately answering the Liberty Point call earlier in the spring, had sought me out on my last trip down and talked his way onto our staff.

It turned out Hardison was pretty good. He was a ham radio enthusiast, and he brought all his gear down when he moved from San Diego. He also spoke Spanish, so he was talking with a bunch of the ham radio people in Venezuela – and you wouldn't think folks in a repressive country like that would be very chatty, but it turned out they were. So Hardison was getting all kinds of interesting intel about the Vinnies.

Most of it we were publishing at the website. Some we weren't.

But Pauline – or PJ, as she was now calling herself (the J was for Joan, which was her middle name), was snapping away with her camera and within a couple of days we had a Liberty Point bureau up and running.

You wouldn't think that would generate a lot of traffic for the site but, again, you'd be wrong. People were starting to become fascinated with Guyana, particularly on the Right, because of what Pierce was building down there and because the word was getting out about how that country was booming with oil wealth. Deadhorse kept going on TV and promising that America would be getting away from oil, and one blue state after another kept passing EV mandates even though sales of those things were dropping through the floor, and yet U.S. oil production kept setting record after record.

Glenn Beck did a show from Georgetown on what he called the "economic miracle" going on in Guyana, and Ishgan couldn't have put on a bigger smile for the BlazeTV cameras.

Everybody in the States seemed to think that (1) it was a bluff that the Vinnies were coming, and (2) if they did, we'd send the Fourth Fleet and some Marines down to wipe the floor with them. But when the Chinese sent a half-dozen attack ships through the Panama Canal and docked them at the Venezuelan naval base at Puerto Cabello, there was a palpable change.

Which led to a hastily-organized confab in Guadeloupe where all the players showed up.

The State Department sent the Deputy Assistant Secretary for Western Hemisphere Affairs, a woman named Fawn Bass-Weaver. She was Yale-educated and half-white, half-black, but wore flowing dashiki dresses everywhere she went.

There were representatives of all the CARICOM countries – that's the multilateral organization all the Caribbean nations are part of, including Guyana. The British sent somebody, so did the Brazilians, the Colombians, the Argentines and, of course, the Chinese.

All to kick around what to do about the dispute over Essequibo.

And Pierce got Ishgan to include me in the Guyanese delegation.

My job was to cover the confab, but more than that I had a couple of contacts they wanted me to make.

The most important one was with Sergio Roffler-Esquivel, the Argentine deputy foreign minister. Serge, as he insisted I call him, was a friend and ally of Miguel Sandoval, the new president of Argentina who was shaking that place up in a major way. Sandoval had fired half the Argentinian government and shuttered a third of the agencies upon taking office, and he was deregulating and tax-cutting his way into legendary status just a few months on the job.

Serge said Sandoval was "keenly interested" in the success of Liberty Point. He also said "it is the position of my government that any Venezuelan encroachment on Guyanese territory should be seen as an attack on the free world by the forces of communist tyranny."

This was at dinner the night before the confab got started. We didn't go anywhere fancy; we were at a seafood place on the water in Pointe-a-Pitre; I had on jeans and a Hawaiian shirt and PJ was wearing a beach dress she'd found at a funky little boutique in town. Plus her Tretorns; at that point I wasn't sure the woman was ever going to wear actual women's shoes again.

I had given Serge a letter from Pierce at the beginning of our meeting. I knew what was in it. It was a letter of intent to invest $10 billion into modernization of the ports of Buenos Aires, Quequen and Santa Fe, plus a commitment to provide satellite internet in Argentina over the next five years at cost plus five percent.

And Serge gave me a letter in return. In it – Pierce told me to read it to make sure what they'd talked about was in writing – was a commitment to deliver eight Lockheed Martin A-4AR Fightinghawk jets from the nation's inventory, with a minimum of two in working order, and a model TR-1700 submarine, the *Santa Cruz*, to the Republic of Guyana.

"We will deliver the items in that letter within 10 days," Serge said. "The work of fitting them for what action may be needed, that is for your friend and his friends."

"Understood," I said, "and I believe there is much reason for happy friendship between Argentina and Guyana."

"And the United States as well," Serge said, "once you have done as we are doing and chased the *zurdos de mierda* from your government."

That was a reference to Sandoval's term for communists. The best translation for it, I guess, is shitlibs.

The Argentines were serious. And PJ couldn't stop laughing later when I translated for her what Serge had said.

The other backchannel thing they had me do was to meet with Samantha Peale, the British foreign ministry rep at the confab, and deliver her the same kind of letter. Pierce was committing to make investments in ports and aerospace things, and in return the Brits were dumping, for a reasonable price, a nice little cache of weaponry on the Guyanese, including a whole bunch of small arms, a pair of Harrier

GR.9 fighter jets which had been sitting in a hangar in Somerset and a half-dozen Alvis Stormer mobile surface-to-air missile platforms equipped with Starstreak high velocity missiles.

On the sly, Pierce was doing a hell of a job cobbling together a well-provisioned little military. In the open, Sentinel was recruiting like crazy – putting ads on national TV for military and law enforcement veterans to become contractors for the company in Guyana and paying $50,000 signing bonuses, plus ten grand a month for a six-month hitch. They were flying people into Georgetown by the hundreds, and they were getting, from what Hal Gibson had told me, some really skilled operators across a number of needed disciplines.

Of course, the hope was that none of this was needed and all these guys would end up either going home or else they'd stick around Guyana and be butchers, bakers, candlestick makers and whatever else, because even with the threat the Vinnies would come the economy was blowing up in that country. I read a story about a kid still in college at the University of Guyana who was making a fortune launching a homefinder app, sort of a Guyanese Zillow-slash-AirBnB, and supplementing that by getting places turned around for move-in. And when the kid was interviewed about his business, he said his inspiration was…

I don't even need to tell you who. You already know.

Everybody hoped that something could be worked out at that confab. But it was a disaster.

All that needed to happen was for the State Department to commit to the defense of Guyana. But Bass-Weaver wouldn't do it. She mouthed a bunch of platitudes but otherwise said exactly nothing. And the Chinese and Venezuelans took over that summit and put the Americans, Brits, Guyanese and everyone else on the defensive by trashing the treaty of 1899 as a rigged farce and an injustice done to the Venezuelan people.

On the last day of the confab, of course, the Guyanese announced the results of the referendum they'd held in Essequibo the day before. It turned out that 88 percent of the people there voted to remain in Guyana, and there was something like 85 percent turnout. That Chinese bribe money of those villagers didn't mean a damn thing. They wanted no part of Venezuela.

Andujar challenged the results, saying that because Liberty Point was included and those people weren't Guyanese (despite the fact most of them had been granted citizenship by the government), the results were skewed. Ishgan responded by noting that 83 percent of everybody else had voted to remain in Guyana.

Guyana asked for a UN resolution condemning a Venezuelan invasion. That went nowhere.

It was crazy. It was like America barely existed, and nobody cared if we did. The center-right media was screaming that if we were going to spend a hundred billion on Ukraine all the way across the world the least we could do was show some interest in something in our backyard.

But asked about the situation, Deadhorse said that Guyana was already part of Venezuela. His press people went into turbodrive walking that one back. Then Pamela Farris, the vice president, went on TV and gave a speech about how Guyana was a country next door to Venezuela, which was also a country, and across the country the American people threw up their hands.

Another national poll came out with Deadhorse's approval notching down to 25 percent. And Trumbull was beating him by six points in a head-to-head race, including a nine-point lead in Pennsylvania and a 12-point lead in Georgia.

But illegal immigration, crime and corruption were the big-mover issues. Not our crisis in South America.

I expected the neocons to jump aboard the Save Guyana train. Not really. It was like the political class in America was simply out of gas. They went from not taking it seriously to being scared of getting into a war with China on our side of the world.

Or something like that.

While I was in Guadeloupe, ANN booked me to do a prime-time debate segment with Will Shue-Geldfarb, the publisher of the neoconservative webzine The Weekly Tureen and a chronic cable news talking head, especially on channels like MSNBC where he was trotted out as a pet conservative.

I hated doing it, because I hated being on the air with Shue-Geldfarb.

A couple of years back I'd interviewed him on the podcast about some of the insane things he was saying on Twitter, demanding that we send troops to invade Russia in retaliation for Putin's attacks on Ukraine, and when I challenged him on that topic he blew up like the Hindenburg. That segment got a ton of traffic, but it was an embarrassment. It felt like mudwrestling. But naturally, the cable news clowns had to get in on some of that action, and I got booked for another debate with him on Newsmax which was similarly a shitshow.

This was the third time, and it was no better.

Shue-Geldfarb – the story goes that he got his name because his mom was married to Geldfarb but was openly having an affair with Shue when he was conceived, and so the meme went that he'd been a cuck since birth – started the segment off by accusing me of being a shill for Pierce Polk, and the fact that we were doing all that coverage of the Essequibo crisis was checkbook journalism on my part.

I knew that was coming, and I was ready for it.

"Will, it's interesting that you're calling somebody else a shill. I expect we'll circle back to that question a little later, but I'd like to keep this discussion on topic. It's really strange, because based on your long history of demanding that America send troops to faraway places where there is zero evidence that our interests were well-served by fighting and dying there I would think you'd have a little Guyanese flag on those social media accounts you spend your whole day on. After all, Guyana isn't a failed state but instead a friendly, free country that we have some very big, and very rapidly growing, economic ties to. Not to mention there are tens of thousands of Americans living down there who aren't Pierce Polk. Why would you not be interested in preserving our sphere of influence?"

"Because there have to be limits. We aren't the world's policeman!"

"Why would Guyana be outside those limits and Iraq and Ukraine would be? Didn't you demand an invasion of Sri Lanka last year? I'm struggling to understand how that would be a place our interests involve but a place where Exoil and Enveron and Sentinel are employing thousands of our countrymen who could be in grave danger wouldn't be. You can call me a shill all you want, but that doesn't answer the question."

"There's no question to answer, because first of all Venezuela is not going to invade Guyana. And second, if they do invade they won't succeed. Third, they…"

"Wait, why won't they succeed?"

"Because Venezuela's armed forces aren't capable of invading another country."

"If that's the case, then all our administration needs to do is state that a Venezuelan invasion of Guyana isn't acceptable and will be dealt with rudely and decisively. What's wrong with that?"

"What's wrong with it is it's bullying, and if we've learned anything it's that the world is tired of the United States throwing our weight around. But of course, this whole thing is a perfect example of the latent racism of Mike Holman coming to the forefront. You're assuming that the brown Venezuelans are going to rape and pillage their neighbors, and…"

"OK, here you go again. You tried to call me a racist on my podcast a couple of years ago, and Colby Igboizwe, who runs our website and is a hell of a lot better American than you are, wrote a piece that absolutely demolished you on that subject. I don't think you have any black people working with you, and certainly not anybody as sharp or prominent as Colby is. So that's a pretty big fail right there. And…"

"You're dancing around the topic, Holman."

"No, I'm coming around to it. What I was about to say was that you're so ignorant about this subject that you don't realize Guyana's population is mostly Indian, as in South Asian Indian, and most of the rest of their people are black. And we're down here because the Guyanese face the prospect of being invaded by a country in Venezuela which is mostly white people. They're descendants of Spaniards, who are Europeans, don't you know. So the race angle here is beyond idiotic and I don't even know how you came up with that."

"Gentlemen," Kristina Walker, the host, chimed in, "we only have another couple of minutes left. Mr. Holman, what do you have to say to the accusation that this is simply about your relationship with Pierce Polk and not about America's interests?"

"I'm glad you asked that, Kristina, because what I can say is that the folks I've met in Guyana are some of the nicest

King Of The Jungle

people anywhere in the world, and they don't deserve to get run over by a communist dictatorship. It used to be that America was the country who would stand up for folks like them. I might not have gotten involved but for my relationship with Pierce, whom I've known since college, but now it's about the folks. Pierce could lose ten billion dollars down there in Guyana and still get on a private jet and go anywhere in the world without hurting at all, but they don't have such resources."

"He doesn't care about the Guyanians," said Shue-Geldfarb.

"Yeah? Well, Will, I managed to do a little research about what you care about, and it seems like you need to offer up a little disclosure of your own. Like for example, how much does that fat consulting contract you've got with Dragon Harvest, Limited, which is a Chinese Communist Party front company buying up farmland all over America, put in your wallet? Seems like that's a hell of a good explanation for why the neocon warmonger who wants our troops everywhere but on our southern border is all of a sudden willing to throw the Guyanese people under the bus. Your Chinese pals must be paying top dollar for that change of heart, I bet."

"There he is again," Shue-Geldfarb was screeching. "Racist!"

Walker was cutting in, trying to close the segment before the hard break. She didn't quite manage it.

The whole thing was depressing. What made it bearable was the nights back at the Maison Victoire, the decent little hotel where we were staying, with PJ.

And that was fun and torture at the same time, because we'd made a deal that we wouldn't fool around. "Nothing past second base until we know we mean it," she'd said, and I'd agreed. But by the second night there both of us had agreed we completely regretted that decision.

And yet we stuck to it.

PJ was laughing her ass off at Shue-Geldfarb after that debate, by the way. "Oh my God, what a tool," she said. "How did he get on TV?"

"Because he says whatever shit he's told to," I responded. "You don't think the people who actually know things are the ones they put on TV over and over again, do you?"

"Not really," she said. "But you were awesome, honey. I almost think that performance was worth a trip to third base."

"Yeah? That's encouraging."

"I said almost, Mike."

"Right. OK."

I was doing podcasts every day from Guadeloupe, interviewing some of the people at that confab, plus I did a Zoom call interview with Paul Vallely who caused a stir when he wondered if we were even a country anymore, and then suggested that Ron DeSantis ought to deploy the Florida State Guard down to Guyana.

I had a constitutional lawyer on the podcast the next day who said he was pretty sure that wasn't legal.

PJ was behind that camera the whole time, and when she wasn't, she was fussing over how my hair looked, straightening the tie she was making me wear, and so on. I told her it was hard to imagine her as a Secret Service agent now; she said she was having more fun doing this than she ever had with a gun on her hip.

I couldn't tell, and didn't want to ask, whether it was the de-stressing of not having somebody's life in her hands, or if it was just me. I was hoping it wasn't the former.

But when the confab ended, I had to fly back to Atlanta. I asked her to come back with me.

"I can't," she said. "I'm not ready to face all that."

So she went back to Liberty Point.

And when I got home, I read Hardison's story on the website that was blowing up about the Chinese People's Liberation Army general who'd flown in to hold talks with Madiera and the Venezuelan military brass in Caracas.

Chapter 16

June 10, 2024: Georgetown, Guyana

After all of the work that had been done in an attempt to stop it, the invasion happened anyway.

Which is not to say that it went smoothly for the Vinnies. It didn't.

I found out all of this either after the fact, or from the dispatches that my guy Flip Hardison was sending back from Liberty Point. Let me tell you something; if the Pulitzer Prize meant anything anymore, if it was for actual journalism, then Hardison was as hands-down a winner as you could get for what he was putting together every day once this thing got going.

The thing that was obvious from the very beginning was that the Vinnies weren't going to be able to stage the invasion the way, say, the Russians went into Ukraine, or the way the U.S. Army went into Iraq. In other words, going in with armored vehicles and troops in trucks was, simply, out.

There were no roads through that jungle, remember? The only road went south into Brazil and then back north into Guyana. And the Brazilians hadn't just said no to the Vinnies passing troops through their country, they'd deployed a sizable force of their own army to enforce that preference.

So the Vinnies had to drop guys from airplanes and helicopters into Essequibo, and they had to do amphibious landings from the Essequibo River after running a naval flotilla east along the Atlantic coast and then up the mouth of the river.

This was a logistical operation that would have been challenging for a first-rate military. And no, that's not what the Venezuelans had.

Of course, a third-rate military is better than no military. What the Guyanese had was essentially enough to defend their capital and not much more. And that meant that Hal Gibson was, for all practical purposes, the Supreme Commander of the military defense of Essequibo.

Hal had a little more than five thousand people, which was not what you'd think would be close to enough. The

Venezuelan Army's Fifth Jungle Infantry Division, augmented by Bolivian, Cuban, Ecuadoran, Nicaraguan and, we were later told, Iranian troops, plus some Chinese military advisors, had close to twenty thousand.

And Hal knew the Vinnies' plan was to supplement the Jungle Infantry with other regular army troops, plus thousands of *colectivos* – thugs on motorcycles from the barrios of the Venezuelan cities whose ordinary jobs were to ride around and terrorize regular folks.

But to get the Jungle Infantry in to take down all of these villages and other installations – the mines, quarries, road junctions and whatever else they needed to occupy – they'd have to do it with helicopters or maybe transport planes they'd parachute out of.

And that meant doing a good bit of softening up their targets with airstrikes. The Vinnies knew that Pierce had invested pretty heavily in surface-to-air missiles, and the way you'd typically go about suppressing SAMs is to roll in with fighter-bombers and take those out. Establish complete air superiority and then your choppers can ferry troops to all of your targets of opportunity, and now your invasion is going to proceed in an orderly fashion.

And a little defenseless country like Guyana is going to sue for the best peace deal they can get.

But Hal had ideas which differed from the Vinnies having air superiority.

And it didn't take him long to have a pretty good plan to insure his ideas, rather than those of Madiera's thugs, were the ones which became reality.

You wouldn't believe this, but the entire offensive capability of the Venezuelan Air Force came out of one place. El Libertador Air Base is located a little south of the city of Maracay, about 50 miles west of Caracas. At El Libertador, all of the Vinnies' attack jets – on paper, 18 F-16's and 21 Su-30MKV Flankers, but in reality a lot less than that – and their pilots and ground crew were housed.

And El Libertador was, frankly, not the most secure place. It certainly wasn't up to the standard it needed to be to hold up to the machinations of Hal Gibson and the Sentinel Security guys, who were some of the most devious, cruel bad-asses I've ever met.

They noticed that El Libertador had a grand total of one runway. They noticed that the base's fuel supply was set up in four very large, and very above-ground, fuel tanks. They also noticed that of the 17 attack jets that were in working order, 15 of them were parked on the tarmac under a row of canvas canopies, something like what the rednecks in the Atlanta suburbs would call a Carolina carport.

Gibson had told me in a private conversation during one of my sitdowns with him in May that the Vinnies weren't going to enjoy the early stages of their invasion. He didn't say how, but I was convinced he was right anyway. Hal didn't strike me as a bullshit artist, and his military record was a good indication that he knew what he was talking about when it came to killing people and breaking things.

What he didn't tell me, but I found out later, was that he'd already put a man on the inside at El Libertador.

Chris Rodrigue wasn't Venezuelan. He was actually a Cajun from St. Martinville, Louisiana. Rodrigue was one of those little guys who had boundless energy and would talk your ear off. He'd been a military policeman in Kuwait during the Iraq War; never saw action, and then he ended up transferring out of the MP's and landing in the maintenance crew fixing Black Hawk helicopters.

Then after he got out of the service, Rodrigue became an aviation mechanic. He'd worked on all kinds of airframes. Including some time he spent down in Chile as a civilian contractor for the Chilean air force.

So he knew Spanish. And he knew the F-16.

On top of all that Rodrigue even looked Hispanic. And what's more, he looked an awful lot like Jose Javier Jimenez, who had been a mechanic at El Libertador six years before he picked up and left for Miami and a job with a civilian aviation service company.

So thanks to a full briefing from Senor Jimenez, who was happy to tell stories of his time at El Libertador to the Sentinel Security guys who dropped him a nice check for the effort, Chris Rodrigue showed up at El Libertador with a cock-and-bull story about how he'd missed the old country and wanted to do his patriotic duty for the Bolivarian Republic and wouldn't he like his old job back.

None of the folks there really remembered him, but he was in the files and he was rated as an A-plus mechanic, and his story seemed to check out, so he got hired.

That was back in April. In May, Senor Jimenez' boss got himself laid up in the hospital after some unknown SOB t-boned him on a busy street. And that meant Jose Javier Jimenez found himself promoted as the guy who would be under those Carolina carports inspecting all the planes.

And the day before the balloon was supposed to go up, Senor Jimenez made a point of inspecting all of the landing gear of those 15 attack jets under the canopies, plus the two in the hangars with the rest of the planes which weren't service-ready thanks to various missing parts they'd had to cannibalize off them to keep the others running. Jimenez blew a gasket while he was in the hangars, because El Libertador was supposed to take delivery of several truckloads of parts that were to have been shipped in from China; it turned out that there was a Chinese part supplier that didn't just handle parts for the Su-30's – after all, the Chinese were now making Su-30's after the Russians had licensed the design to them – but also was knocking off parts for F-16's as well.

There's what free trade with China, the world's greatest practitioner of industrial espionage, can do for you.

Anyway, those parts had been on a ship which had docked at the port of Puerto Cabello, about an hour down Highway 1 from the base, and somehow they'd gone missing. It was a source of consternation for the brass at El Libertador that their parts should be *desaparecido,* and a frantic investigation had turned up the explanation that somehow there had been a mixup in the computer routing software. The trucks that were supposed to be carrying those aviation parts which would have made the other 22 jets airworthy arrived at the base with pallets full of diapers, ping pong balls and ceramic iguanas, and as best anybody could tell the containers carrying the base's intended cargo were put on trucks headed for Cumana.

Before anybody could figure any of this out, of course, those trucks had offloaded at the container port in Maiquetia, just a few miles north of the capital, and the containers were put on a ship bound for Spain which made a stop in Georgetown and just happened to offload them there.

But the Venezuelans at the base never found out about that. All they knew was that Jose Javier Jimenez was red hot about not getting his *malditas piezas de avión*, especially so close to the action.

So they all stayed far, far away from the *en fuego* head mechanic, and nobody said a thing when he attached thick rings bearing inspection badges around the front landing gear of all 17 of those attack jets. If anyone had said anything, he would have told them those rings, made out of what looked like bungee cords with a small plastic tag on them, were standard practice.

They didn't ask, and that answer would have satisfied them if they had. After all, Senor Jimenez had been a miracle-maker in getting airworthy the 17 planes which did have the parts, and that was thought to be more than enough to fulfill the mission over Guayana Esequiba.

What nobody knew was that those inspection badges were actually blasting caps and the bungee cords on those rings were made of Primacord, and when somebody sent a signal by cell phone all 15 of the attack jets still on the tarmac had their front landing gear blown off.

The two that were on air patrol over the Atlantic didn't. Not until they tried to land at the airport in Maiquetia, which is the main airport servicing Caracas, and somebody managed to get that cell signal to those two blasting caps and blew off the landing gear of both of those jets just as they were about to touch the ground. The twin little explosions led to a pair of larger ones as the Su-30's crashed on the runway, and that knocked out air service to the Venezuelan capital for a couple of hours.

Not only was there chaos on the tarmac in El Liberatador, just a few minutes later those four above-ground fuel tanks at the base went up in a giant ball of flame. It seems somebody managed to shoot an AGM-114 Hellfire missile from an

MQ-1 Predator drone into one of the tanks and crashed the Predator into another, and the explosions set half the base ablaze.

You'd think that an air base would be more than capable of detecting a relative slow-mover like a Predator. But there were some reversals. Specifically, the power to the air traffic control tower had gone out, which was a product of a truck bomb that had been delivered to the only power substation servicing the base, located right off the main road in. Nobody ever found remains of a driver picking through the wreckage of the Class 8 truck that had barreled into the substation and then lit off the fertilizer bomb in the back of the cab, and it was soon clear why; the truck was a drone in its own right, a prototype of a driverless vehicle manufactured by a company called Aurora in Texas.

And that was the end of the air cover for the first day of the Venezuelan invasion of Guyana.

Chris Rodrigue had slipped away from the base just before the carnage began and made his way to the airport in Maracay, where there was a little Cessna plane waiting to take him to Port of Spain. From there he caught a puddle-jumper to Georgetown and then hopped in a Land Rover for a ride to Linden, about 60 miles to the south, where Pierce had turned the little airstrip for whatever rickety old planes would land there into an air base.

They had a couple of old Harrier jump-jets at Linden, plus eight A-4AR Fightinghawk attack planes, which were the same airframe as an F-16; the A-4AR's were made by Lockheed Martin just like the F-16's were. The makeshift base at Linden also had a whole shitload of newly-arrived Chinese-marked containers full of parts to make airworthy the six semi-junked A-4AR's the Argentines had sent along.

Plus about three dozen Air Force and Navy veteran pilots and ground crew guys that Pierce's people had recruited, living in a little village of double-wide trailers that had been hastily put up a couple of weeks earlier.

Linden wasn't Miramar or Nellis. But it turned out that in this war it would be the center of air power. The Vinnies didn't realize how badly they'd been had until they started launching helicopters full of Fifth Jungle Infantry Division troopers out of the bases they'd set up at Tumeremo, Las Claritas and Santa Elena de Uairen, only to find those choppers torn to shreds shortly after liftoff thanks to the M61 Vulcan 20-millimeter cannons the marauding Guyanese A-4AR jets had been newly refitted with.

It got very ugly, very fast, on that first day. No sooner had Madiera gone on national TV in Venezuela to declare that "efforts to recover the long-lost Guayana Esequiba have now begun," but the power went down all over Caracas thanks to what appeared to be a cyberattack against the grid in the Capitol District.

As I said, this was all stuff I found out about either from what I was told later or from what Hardison was doing from Liberty Point. And what he was doing, as I said, was amazing.

Of course, Pierce helped him out a lot. Because there were cameras recording all of it, and Pierce made sure Hardison was getting the footage in real time. Dash-cam footage from the driverless truck, which caught the drone strike on those fuel tanks and then the explosion at the power substation, cockpit camera footage of those choppers getting torn to pieces by the A-4AR's, footage from the El Libertador security cameras (that they'd hacked, of course) showing the explosions under those jets on the tarmac.

And footage of the runway wrecks at Maiquetia.

He had all of it.

What he didn't publish, at least not then, was the fact that the Sentinel Security guys had set up cameras everywhere in the jungle along a double perimeter outside of Liberty Point and around Mahdia as well. Actually, the guy who did most of the camera setups was Earl Roberts, the tochao from Campbelltown, the village next door to Mahdia, who had been my driver that time. Earl told them "give me that bag of cameras. You guys have more important work to do."

And he just tromped around in the jungle setting the cameras up perfectly on those trees, so that before long they had a full ground-level view of the entire jungle.

Then Hal's guys went in and set up anti-personnel mines in strategic places that could be detonated with a smartphone app.

While all this was going on I was back in the States, suddenly dealing with all kinds of crap. Karen had demanded that I sit for an interview with the two FBI agents Smythe and Muhammad, who proceeded to pepper me with questions not about PJ and her story but Pierce.

They wanted me to turn informant on Pierce. Karen had to stop me from telling them to do something anatomically impossible. I got up and left the meeting, which was not what Karen was hoping for but she didn't yell at me for it.

"They don't have anything on you," she told me. "I expect this will go away, but they're squeezing the tube from the bottom for sure. They want him."

"I'm not severing my ties with Pierce, Karen. I know that's what's coming next out of your mouth."

"Nah. This is out of control. My politics and yours might be totally different, but the feds are crooked and somebody has to call them out for what they're doing. Keep fighting."

Then there was the domestic news, which just got weirder and weirder.

There had been a standoff on the border in Texas, the third one in the past four months, between the Border Patrol and the Texas National Guard over the former's attempts to take down blockades the latter had set up to keep migrants from coming across.

This was the biggest issue in the country, and it had been all year. The Deadhorse administration had every big-city mayor in America screaming about the flood of migrants into their cities, and there had been the whiff of chaos in the air. In Chicago, the police had barely managed to squelch a race riot on the city's south side after an illegal from Honduras had run over a black kid while driving drunk, and Illinois' governor had brought in the Illinois National Guard to help to keep the peace.

And when the Albuquerque Police raided the warehouse of a local taco-stand chain and uncovered a large cache of weapons – we're talking several thousand AK-47's, hand grenades and RPG platforms – the issue of the border turned into a galvanizing one.

Texas, with the help of some 25 other states sending National Guard and State Guard personnel, had largely halted the flood of migrants at the Rio Grande. But all that did was turn New Mexico and Arizona into war zones. I flew to Tucson to interview the sheriff of Pima County, who was a Democrat but who together with his counterparts in Yuma, Cochise and Santa Cruz Counties was openly defying both the governor and the Deadhorse administration by turning away people at the border with a huge army of volunteers funded by a nonprofit some grocery store magnate had set up.

Arizona's governor was threatening to call out the National Guard against the sheriffs, but she wasn't doing it because there was a whole lot of discussion about whether the state legislature had the votes to impeach and remove her.

None of that was happening in New Mexico, but the polls were increasingly ugly for Deadhorse there. Our Sentinel investigations partners had come up with a bunch of dirt on the governor, who had made an uncanny investment return with an off-Wall Street international hedge fund called Pan American Partners.

We had a couple of reporters digging on Pan American Partners and it turned out it had extensive real estate investments both stateside and throughout Latin America, including a significant amount of the huge skyscrapers going up in Monterrey.

But Pan American Partners wasn't just collecting rent. It was a front for a pair of the cartels – specifically the Sinaloa cartel and Cartel del Noreste. And it had a stake in a whole host of other companies.

Among them was Plum Solar Industries, which operated a couple of large-scale solar plants in the New Mexico desert that delivered a disappointing amount of energy, and a network of dealerships in solar panels for residential housing.

Plum Solar was also delivering an uncanny investment return for lots of political figures who were disclosing their income on state and federal disclosure forms.

And that included Alexis Mallorca, the Secretary of Homeland Security. Mallorca had survived an impeachment attempt earlier in the year, and the House cranked up another on June 1 after our report on the Pan American Partners and Plum Solar Industries connections hit the internet.

You would have thought all of this would have had people in the streets. Not really. The mainstream legacy corporate press barely noticed, other than to run a few "Republicans Pounce" stories on how members of Congress and conservative media were making a big deal out of those reports.

They didn't even flinch when Fox News broke the story quoting an unnamed cartel boss who said that the migrant invasion was a front for a Chinese infiltration of the southern border.

Just…nothing. There was a daily debate over whether Travis Kelce would pop the question to Taylor Swift before the Chiefs' preseason camp began.

And there was a real conversation about Deadhorse, who was rapidly getting worse. In a speech to the SEIU convention in Las Vegas, he addressed the crowd by welcoming them to Miami, and then – because of a teleprompter malfunction – he proceeded to ad-lib a speech for eight minutes and forty-two seconds before the music went up and he was escorted, protesting "you can't do this to me, I'm a United States Senator!", off the stage.

That eight minutes and forty-two seconds was probably the worst stretch of video in American politics since the Kennedy assassination. He set off no less than three international incidents and earned the condemnation of eleven different left-leaning advocacy groups in addition to every conservative organization in America by the end of the day. There was something to offend and alarm everyone in that eight minutes and forty-two seconds. His handlers didn't know what to do.

Either that, or they were instructed, many thought by the Omobba machine, to let it happen.

A poll on June 4 actually had Deadhorse behind Paddy Moynihan, Jr., the longtime liberal gadfly who was running as an independent. And the media stories were full of nonstop speculation about how this was the end for him and he'd have to come off the ticket.

But at a Rose Garden press conference on June 7, Deadhorse issued an angry denial that he was leaving the ticket. "Why would I go anywhere?" he barked. "The other guy is going to jail. They're all going to jail."

Moynihan publicly blew a gasket and demanded to know by what charge he would be convicted and imprisoned, going so far as to set up a press avail outside the White House to demand answers.

And since he didn't have a security clearance he actually did get arrested and was given a ticket, which was a piece of PR brilliance on his part.

The House voted on a non-binding resolution demanding the invocation of the 25th Amendment against Deadhorse. It fell three votes short, even with four Democrats voting "yes." The Speaker announced he was throwing six Republicans off all their committee assignments in retaliation for not voting the way the leadership wanted.

King Of The Jungle

Politics had turned into a circus. The American people were whipsawed back and forth over the advancing decline of the public sector. It was impossible to fully cover the mounting idiocy and instability.

I had a lot going on, but in the meantime I'd already made a commitment to head down to Georgetown to interview Ishgan, and to meet PJ, whom I'd convinced to make a trip up from Liberty Point to join me at the Grand Coastal Hotel.

Chapter 17

June 12 2024: Tumeremo, Bolivar, Venezuela

"I should point out, *General*, that there were certainly elements missing which were not under my control."

"We are aware, *Coronel*. Nevertheless…"

"Sir, if I may. We had no air defense capability at Las Claritas. This had been discussed for weeks prior to the invasion date but Division Command judged the enemy would have no air power and as such it was not provided."

"The intelligence failure was not yours, that much is true…"

"And I should also point out that I voiced misgivings about launching our adventure without our attack jets from El Libertador."

"But *Coronel* Cabrillo, when ordered to continue the launch, you disobeyed. That is why you are here at this tribunal. Orders must be followed."

"I still have a brigade because I shut down the invasion and sent our helicopters away. *General* Velez and the 52nd Jungle Infantry Brigade have lost half their strength attempting to launch amid the *Yanquis* firing on their helicopters."

"But they have nonetheless taken more than a dozen of their objectives in the south. And *Coronel* Fernandez and the 51st Brigade have achieved seven of their objectives in the northern sector. It is your failure to execute your orders which has cost us the tactical initiative."

"Tactical initiative? The enemy knew not only that we were coming but when we were coming and how. I have lost only four of 24 helicopters and 44 of more than 5,000 men. Mine is the only combat-effective brigade in the division. Sirs, I should point out that the *Yanqui* Pierce Polk and his hired men are the only effective opposition we have and they are billeted in my sector. This was discussed in the briefings prior to the action."

Cabrillo was torn between the strain of keeping his cool amid the struggle session Division Command was putting him through and not really caring if he was relieved of duty.

Everything about this Guayana Esequiba operation was a mess. Cabrillo expected it to end badly. And he knew he had enough walk-away money that if they wanted to sack him he could be gone, comfortable and free to live in a place where he wouldn't have to take orders from slack-faced functionaries like these.

What else he knew was that he had done the right thing in shutting down the attack as soon as the enemy's jets zoomed in and riddled four of his helicopters with 20-millimeter shells upon takeoff. It was clear that the enemy had them under surveillance, almost certainly with a drone, and the A-4AR jets were patrolling along the border with the ability to turn and blaze a path to their position as soon as the choppers were spotted taking off.

He'd had to act quickly. The four helicopters crashed to the earth in giant fireballs, which sent the men into a panic. Many who had boarded other helicopters for the short rides into Guyana jumped out and ran, creating a scene of utter chaos in the 53rd's staging area, and Cabrillo knew that what would come next was the enemy jets strafing – or worse, bombing – their position with those 20-millimeter cannons to take out all of their helicopters.

He made a split-second decision, ordering the chopper pilots to disgorge their troops and fly away to the west, and the enemy had not engaged them. Which saved his brigade to fight another day.

Cabrillo knew that it was a mistake for the Americans to show such mercy, but here, in Tumeremo, he was enduring the fat Venezuelan generals in charge of the Jungle Infantry Division attempting to make a bigger one.

Namely, firing him.

He'd reported the enemy action and notified Tumeremo that he was unable to fulfill his mission with neither air support nor air defense while his men were busy attempting to douse the fire from a crashed helicopter as the wind blew it dangerously close to the command trailer from which he was communicating via cell phone. And when he was ordered to fight anyway, he had simply said no.

"I will not meaninglessly sacrifice my men," he said. "I will spend every one of them on a mission with a chance of success. This is no such mission. We will go when circumstances indicate it is possible to achieve our objectives."

Carvajal was looking at him with a mixture of admiration and amazement, which he later explained by saying he had never seen an officer disobey an order openly and on principle before.

"Don't get any ideas," he told Carvajal. "You aren't capable of what I've just done. You do as you're told."

Xing had disappeared, which Cabrillo figured was a blessing, but then he worried that their Chinese military liaison might have perished in one of the chopper crashes. But no, he turned up just before Cabrillo was summoned to Tumeremo to answer for his disobedience.

"It's been nice knowing you," he said. "For the record, you were correct. No air defense, no air support, no invasion."

"Thanks for all your help," Cabrillo snarked in response.

"You're welcome. I'll have you know I've gotten you a lot more supplies and equipment than the other brigades have. You should be grateful. And let them know about it in Tumeremo."

But when Cabrillo made it to the 5th Jungle Infantry Division's forward headquarters in that dingy little town an hour and a half away by jeep, he didn't feel very grateful. He felt what he imagined his grandfather had felt when the Castros stashed him in those prisons.

Trouble.

In the northern and southern sectors, it was true, the Venezuelans had managed to land troops at their objectives. But losses – both from air attacks from the A-4AR's and also from enemy surface-to-air missiles fired by villagers and others on the ground – had been catastrophic.

And discipline had broken down, as the men of the 51st and 52nd brigades who had landed at their objectives had engaged in horrific, barbaric abuse of those villagers. Which caused an even larger set of problems.

Especially in the ill-fated village of Port Kaituma in the north, ironically enough near to the site of the People's Temple at Jonestown, where the locals had attempted to resist the 55 men who landed there. Someone on the roof of a restaurant had set up a South African Vektor SS-77 machine gun and unloaded some fairly accurate fire on a pair of the choppers which set down at the site, killing eight men before they'd even had a chance to set foot on land. But a rocket-propelled grenade fired from one of the other choppers had scattered the defenders on that roof, and when the Venezuelans hit the ground they killed every last man, woman and child in Port Kaituma, and even chased many of its 1,200-odd inhabitants into the jungle to murder them.

Making the Venezuelans more guilty of murder in that place than even the psychotic Jim Jones, who had murdered or induced to suicide some 909 of his followers at Jonestown seven miles away in 1978.

Similar massacres took place in Towakaima, Monkey Mountain, Isherton and several other places. Worse, the enemy had installed cameras in most of the villages, so that when the Venezuelans had taken their revenge they shortly found the images of the slaughter broadcast to the entire world.

And that had created an international incident which led to countries all over the world cutting off trade and diplomatic ties to Venezuela. The only major countries sticking with normal relations with Venezuela were Russia and China, and Cabrillo, who as a Cuban didn't particularly care but as an observer of geopolitics couldn't help but notice, recognized this only cemented his employer's country as a Chinese economic colony.

He wondered if those massacres were a breakdown in discipline at all, or whether they were purposeful and strategic.

But things got even worse for the 51st and 52nd, because the Guyanese wasted no time in exacting their revenge by air against those responsible. The A-4AR's returned with a vengeance to strafe the places the Venezuelans occupied, though conspicuously they did not have bombs.

Which was a saving grace. None of the places the 51st and 52nd captured were retaken, though both brigades were down to a collection of skeleton crews. The plans were to replenish their strength by bringing in *colectivos* and reinforcements from other infantry divisions, but both brigades themselves were now collections of understrength platoons strewn across parts of their assigned territories.

Cabrillo knew that his objectives were largely far better defended than in the north or south sectors. And without air support or air defense, it would be impossible to take any but the most tertiary of their objectives.

The division command was attempting to make him the scapegoat for the disaster that was the invasion to date. He was lucky, however; General Luis Montoya de Loyola, a fellow Cuban who had been his mentor and who served at Army General Command, had flown in to his rescue.

Montoya de Loyola took over the meeting and proceeded to browbeat the division's generals for their own incompetence. The shouting match that ensued resulted in Cabrillo getting a reprieve in Las Claritas, if just barely.

"You are down to your last life, Manuel," said his benefactor. "Reacquire your helicopters and go tonight with your men."

"General, with no air support it is suicide."

"Things are better than they seem, Manuel. Be of good cheer! And do not make a fool of me again."

Chapter 18

June 14, 2024: Liberty Point, Guyana

I guess I made it to Liberty Point at the best, and worst, possible time.

I did my interview with Ishgan, which was basically a forum for him to directly plead with the Deadhorse administration to send in the Marines before things started getting ugly, and then the next morning I hopped on a chopper that was headed down to Liberty Point from Sentinel Port Management's facility. With me was a guy whom I'll call Kurt. He had the look and sound of somebody who'd done some wet work for some agency or other.

"Are you heading down to get involved?" I asked him.

"I'll do what I can," he said. "Price is right, and so's the cause."

He didn't have much more to say than that. I felt it would be rude to pry, and Kurt didn't seem like a guy I should be rude to.

We touched down at the airfield close to one of the hangars and the chopper immediately took off again, heading quickly to the east. My old buddy Earl was waiting for me in a Cherokee. He was beckoning me from the driver's seat.

"Hop in, quick!" he said.

"Hey," I said, as I hustled my bags into the back and myself into the passenger seat. "What's with all the rushing around?"

"Worried about an air strike," he said as he gunned the engine. "And we expect they're going to hit CPX any minute. I can't believe they let you fly down here on a chopper."

"I think the guy I came down with is a somebody."

"Yeah, he is," Earl said as we shot past the open airfield gate and up the road heading for the town. The 3-D printer factory, I saw, was surrounded by sandbags and there was a…

"Is that a SAM site?" I asked, gawking.

"Starstreak," said Earl. "They got one last night, I understand."

"Got one what?"

"Attack jet. I think it was one of those Su-30's. I can't really tell 'em apart, and definitely not at night."

"Wait, I thought you guys knocked their air force out day before yesterday."

"It sounds like they lifted parts off the destroyed planes and got the other ones running," said Earl. "I think I heard 'em say last night after we made it in that the Vinnies had nine jets in the air."

"After you made it in?"

"Got the whole population of Campbelltown evacuated here. It was a hell of a good operation, let me tell you. Just in the nick of time, too."

"I'm way behind here, Earl. Can you tell it to me like I'm stupid?"

He gave me a quick smile, which turned into a grimace.

"OK. Yesterday the Vinnies invaded to our north and our south. You know about that, right? And you heard about the massacres at Port Kaituma and those other places."

"Right. Yes."

"Well, here in, what's I guess, the middle, our jets busted 'em just as the helos were taking off and they broke up the attack. The enemy actually got their choppers away, and Hal was worried they'd lead our guys into a missile trap so they didn't pursue."

"Right. I heard about that, too."

"Then what you don't know is that last night, they got their act together and came back. Got air cover from those nine, or maybe it was ten, zoomers – I heard a couple were these J-16 jets which are actually Chinese-made – and while we did get three of their planes either with a missile or with one of our pilots shooting one of them down, we also lost three jets. And in the air-fight, they managed to land choppers at a bunch of places. So we've definitely been invaded."

"Ahh, damn. I'm sorry, Earl."

"Yeah, well, they managed to put 500 or so troops down at Mahdia last night. When the word hit that they were coming, I called an immediate evacuation of Campbelltown. Had to. They'd be not three miles away and we didn't have the resources to hold out."

"That's right. I forgot that you were the mayor over there."

"Yeah, well, anyway, I got every last one of us out and Pierce has us sorted with a place to stay. So I'm now the head of the IM. I guess that's my reward for bein' a hero."

"What's the IM?"

"Indigenous militia. Which is a shitty name. Pierce wanted to call me the Grand Waica. I told him not until I've earned it."

"Damn, Earl. You ever serve in a military?"

"Hell, no. But I hunt, and I know this jungle. For what we're gonna do that's enough."

"Which is what?"

Earl pulled under the arch. We were at the Liberty Lodge. He stopped and looked at me.

"We're gonna be the bogeymen these bastards dream about. Come to my country like this, and I'll make you pay."

I'd met Earl a couple of times before. He'd always seemed so nice. He definitely didn't seem that way now.

"I hear you," I said.

"Stay safe, Mike. I think your girl is in your suite with that Flip guy."

And she was.

When I went in the door, Flip and PJ essentially mobbed me, fighting to blurt out all the latest scoop they were going to post to the website. Flip was damned proud of the fact that Pierce was letting him get all the footage from the cameras they had virtually everywhere, though he had to run each clip by a guy named Rivers Sutton, who was Hal's security officer, before posting it.

"They don't want to give away any tactical advantage," he said, "but we've got imagery – good imagery – from all over."

"What we should do," said PJ, "is make a documentary about the invasion."

I could tell that this was what she wanted to do when she grew up. And it struck me that here I was hooking up with my second photojournalist in a row.

Though clearly this was a trade up from Sarah Givens.

I said I was good with the idea for PJ's documentary film, though it was contingent on surviving what was coming.

"Are we sitting ducks here?" I asked.

"Be hard to get at us," said Flip. "This place is absolutely covered with MANPADs and the four Starstreak pods. I don't think they have enough jets to spare trying to hit Liberty Point."

"But Hal thinks they're going to try to take out the airfield next," said PJ. "They're going to try to starve us out."

"Don't like the sound of that."

"We should get to the bunker," Flip said. "The meeting's gonna start in twenty minutes."

He and PJ hurriedly gathered up their gear, which made me pick up my computer bag, and then Flip led the way to the elevator. He punched a button and soon we were down in the garage in front of a golf cart.

"You wanna ride shotgun?" PJ asked, and handed me…not a shotgun, but something a bit more interesting.

"What is this, an M4A1?" I asked, noting the grenade launcher under the barrel.

"Yup," said Flip. And I looked at PJ, who was settling into a back seat which faced behind the cart. She had an M4A1 rifle as well.

"Try not to shoot yourself," she said.

"It's really nice to see you, sweetie," I said to PJ as Flip drove us out of the garage and into the street heading northwest toward the Potaro. She blew me a kiss and told me to watch the sky.

Just then I heard a whoosh, and I could see a contrail forming behind what looked like a fast-moving missile heading to the west.

"Oh, shit," Flip said. "Here they come."

And in the distance I could see three jets on the way in. Another whoosh, and then another. Then two more.

"Those are our missiles?"

"Yeah," said Flip. He parked the golf cart. "We're here."

PJ had her camera out and she was filming the sky to the west. Two of the planes had, it appeared, begun to bug out. The other was banking, attempting to evade that first missile. It was flying low over the jungle.

A second missile exploded as it hit a wing on that plane. The Su-30 – I could see that it was an Su-30 – rolled and then dived into the trees, where it erupted into a large fireball.

"Splash you, motherfucker," said Flip.

"OK, let's get inside," said PJ.

The building was sort of an all-purpose facility that was going to house the police and fire departments and administrative center of Liberty Point. In the basement was a bunker. We were passed through a phalanx of a dozen guys, all of whom looked like they'd just come from the battle of Fallujah, and into a war room filled with TV and computer screens. The full breadth of the security camera coverage that Pierce and his guys had laid on was glaringly apparent now.

"Jesus," I said, gawking at the wall-to-wall imagery.

"Hey, Mike," I could hear Pierce as he motioned for us to join him in a glass conference room to my right. "In here."

He had Hal with him, plus a half-dozen other guys I didn't know, plus my old travel buddy Roman Jefferson.

And Earl.

They were sitting around the table looking at a satellite image on the far wall.

"...and so they're going to make the police station their headquarters and I bet that's where the Cuban is," one of the strangers was saying. "Should we take the chance at hitting that building?"

"I'm worried about this rumor," said Earl.

"What's the rumor, Earl?" Pierce asked.

"That they stashed the kids on the second floor."

"It's not worth the risk just to take out the Cuban," said Hal.

Pierce motioned for me to grab a seat next to him. I did.

"Who's the Cuban?" I asked him quietly.

"Cabrillo," said Pierce. "He's the colonel in charge of the 53rd Jungle Infantry Brigade. He's their Norman Schwarzkopf."

"So you take him out, and, what?"

"That's just it. They'll send somebody else. Hal thinks this guy is better than the others they have, though."

"…not a problem," one of the guys I didn't know was saying. "We get in close and we just do it."

"They've got to have 500 troopers, though," said Roman. "And now that they've established an airhead at the Mahdia airfield they're going to just pour people in."

"This is what we need to break out the Predator for," Hal said to Pierce. "That airfield has to go."

"Use it or lose it," Pierce was saying.

"Yeah. Durandal."

"I'll make the call."

A few seconds later, Pierce was hanging up his cell after barking a few cryptic words to someone.

"What's going on?" I asked him.

"You remember the Durandal bombs from the first Gulf War?" he asked me.

"Not really."

"They're bombs for busting up runways so they can't get fixed any time soon. We need to take out Mahdia so they can't land planes on that runway. The Vinnies can carry in way, way more troops with planes than in those little Chinese helicopters of theirs, and we can't have them landing a whole damn army just up the road."

"Exactly how bad is this?" I asked.

Hal jumped in. "Mr. Holman, the enemy is in possession of Mahdia, with the bulk of its population currently hostage. Adults are penned into a collection camp surrounded with razor wire, children we believe are human shields in the police station. They're now organizing in at least company strength and they're going to build and build until they can make a ground assault on Liberty Point."

"Shit," I said. "Guess that's better than them dropping in out of the sky here."

"We've got too much air defense to try to take us from the air," Pierce said. "They could come from upriver, though that won't be easy, but the main problem is Mahdia. These guys are jungle infantry, meaning they train to fight in those woods."

I suddenly felt like I really didn't want to be here. I'd covered a couple of armed conflicts before; I'd been to Afghanistan, and I'd seen a little bit of the Colombians' fight against the FARC rebels. But this seemed a whole lot more personal.

"Look," Roman was saying, "the most important thing is to pin the enemy down where he is and deny him freedom of movement. This isn't complicated. They're still getting organized. I imagine they haven't even started patrols yet. So let's do this the smart way."

Hal smiled at him.

"Whom shall I send?" he asked. "And who will go for us?"

Roman smiled back. "Here am I. Send me!"

The book of Isaiah had made it to the Guyanese war.

"Take two guys with you," Hal said. "You're there to disrupt and lay chaos, and after you've kicked over the anthill, you know which way to lead them."

"Through Candyland," said Roman.

"Candyland," echoed one of the guys. Roman pointed to him.

"Where's Kurt?" Roman asked.

"I think he's still at the airfield," I said. "The guy who flew in with me?"

"Yeah. Fine. Come on, Charlie, let's gear up."

Charlie, the guy Roman had pointed to, shot up from his seat and followed Roman out. Flip plopped down in Charlie's vacant chair.

"So what's next?" asked Pierce.

Hal scowled.

"Hit the runway this evening, pray the Predator comes back intact, pray your shipment of munitions gets in here, pray the river is protected, pray we get some international help."

"That's a lot of praying," I said. "Are you concerned you can't hold out here?"

"We'll hold out," said Hal. "My concern is that we're Stalingrad. They're landing their people in all of their other objectives, and they're going to be in a position to hold the locals hostage."

"What about Micobie?" I asked. That little village between Liberty Point and Mahdia had been the only other indigenous settlement I'd seen.

"Got them out, too," said Earl. "Really, around here it's Mahdia."

"How many prisoners are we talking about?" I asked.

"About twenty-one hundred," said Hal.

Most of the rest of the day was spent in that basement watching the security footage – which included camera shots of three men riding west on motorcycles through a barely-discernible trail through the jungle. There had been a road running parallel to the Potaro west to Micobie and then to Mahdia, but when the enemy came, Pierce told me, they'd blown a few trees so they'd fall and block it.

He'd also told me that they'd ringed all of the areas around those fallen trees with Claymore mines, so if the Vinnies tried to clear them they'd take some heavy losses.

So Roman, Charlie and Kurt were on their way to Mahdia, or parts near it, where they were setting up as snipers. And at the airfield they were preparing the one Predator drone Liberty Point had available with a spread of old French Durandal runway-buster bombs that the Argentinians had donated to the cause. Meanwhile, the inhabitants of Liberty Point had been fully mobilized for its defense and were standing guard all along those high wooden walls and on rooftops watching the skies.

Hal told me they had more than 50 shoulder-fired surface-to-air missiles, not counting the four Starstreak missile emplacements. I'd already seen what those could do.

It seemed like Liberty Point was about as safe a place as you could be, considering it was on the front line of a war.

There was a monitor high on the wall to my left, and Pierce pointed it out to me.

"That's our runway cam in Mahdia," he said.

"You have a runway cam there."

"Yeah."

"Well done."

"Thank old Earl over there. He's the one who set it up."

Earl just nodded and smiled.

"OK," I said, "is this where we're going to see a show?"

"Should be less than a minute now," said Hal. "Can we get that image on the main screen?"

A freckly-faced kid sitting at one of the war room's computer terminals nodded, moved his mouse, and the runway cam occupied the large screen in the middle of the display.

"Oh, would you look at that," said one of the guys I didn't know.

"Some kind of timing, isn't it?" said Hal.

I could make out in the fading light from the runway camera that there was a plane on its way in from the west. It looked like a big C-130 Hercules plane. I didn't think a big monster like that could land on a little runway like Mahdia had, but it looked like its pilot disagreed with me.

Except just as the Hercules dipped down over the trees on its final approach, the camera caught a flash of light and a fast-rising smoke cloud over the runway. It was too late for the Hercules pilot to pull up, and the plane touched down just in time to run into the sizable crater the bomb had made on the asphalt.

The Hercules bounced, and then skidded to its right. It crashed into a stand of trees and broke apart in a fiery mess. I felt a wave of nausea pass over me when I could see bodies being thrown from the ruined airframe; these guys might have been the enemy, but a worse death than this was hard to imagine.

"It's good," said Hal. "Mission accomplished."

I looked at PJ, who was sitting next to me. She stared back.

"I need to get you out of here," I said.

"No way," came the response. "This is home. I'm defending it."

Chapter 19

June 14, 2024: Mahdia, Guyana

"Pop! Pop!" rang out the shots, and Cabrillo could see his men scrambling near the barbed-wire enclosure where the adult villagers were held from of the window of the police station.

He figured this was the work of a sniper, and Cabrillo could see that the tall trees and medium-sized rise to the west of the little town center of Mahdia held a fertile habitat for enemy shooters to pick off his occupying force.

He needed to make his forward headquarters here, because in the Potaro valley this was the biggest objective of them all.

Except for Liberty Point, which they were to take as intact as possible.

Cabrillo saw that to do that would be a nearly impossible mission, so his best option was to clear the rest of his objectives, try to isolate the Americans at Liberty Point and then pressure them into a surrender. And if that didn't work, then build up enough of a concentrated force here, with reinforcements and *colectivos* relieving his troopers at the other small villages, mines and other objectives so that he could have virtually his entire brigade available to overwhelm the enemy in what would surely be a bloody massacre of a fight.

He didn't want to chew up his brigade. But at the end of the day, most of its men were Venezuelans, and Cabrillo was not. If Division Command was willing to sacrifice their lives for Liberty Point, which they were already calling Ciudad Chavismo, after the former Venezuelan president, then who was he to protest?

Of course, his adjutant Carvajal was apoplectic.

Cabrillo could tell Carvajal was near to the point of desertion after the first day. He was a sensitive little man, overprone to emotion. Cabrillo was near to the point of wanting to relieve him, but he was too deep into the fight to attempt to break in a new adjutant. So he tolerated Carvajal's womanly protests.

Xing was a different matter.

He'd showed up after the initial assault on Mahdia, flying in on a little Cessna turboprop plane with crates full of Puerto Rican rum for the men in order that they might celebrate their great victory. And then he left again, after picking one of the women out of the barbed-wire camp in the soccer feld across the street from the police station and having his way with her in the bed of an old Toyota pickup truck. The men saw it, and they were inspired.

Cabrillo didn't want to see him again. He'd told Xing that abuse of civilians was off-limits. Xing asked him just who he thought he was to give orders.

He thought about shooting the bastard, but he knew doing so would be his end. Perhaps that was Xing's grand finale as the 53rd's procurement specialist and liaison with the Chinese.

And shooting Xing would certainly dampen the victory for his brigade.

Some victory. What they'd done was land about a hundred men in 10 helicopters in the middle of the night while their jets were keeping the enemy's fighter pilots and SAM operators busy, and then those men went house to house kidnapping the civilians and bringing them to the soccer field across the street from the police station where they had set up a small, crowded concentration camp. Cabrillo didn't like it, and he especially didn't like it when, inspired by Xing, some of the men had taken certain liberties with their female captives – liberties which had led to some suicidal attempts by the men to fight back. Several dozen dead residents of Mahdia were the result.

And the helicopters kept ferrying in more and more of his men a little at a time.

There were few amenities for the prisoners in the fenced-in camp at the soccer field. On the second day they'd managed to string together a few canvas tents so the angry civilians were at least somewhat out of the rain.

But Cabrillo's men needed billeting, so the Venezuelans would be occupying the houses of Mahdia. And there would be a whole lot more of them as he staged for the attack on Liberty Point.

At least, that had been the plan. It was now coming apart to a substantial extent. The C-130 Hercules plane that was supposed to ferry the rest of the 53rd Jungle Infantry Brigade from the airfield at Tumeremo, where they had relocated for the follow-on deployments, to Mahida had crashed and blown up on the now-unusable runway at the airfield.

Cabrillo figured it was a drone strike which had destroyed the runway just before the C-130 landed; 71 men and four pilots had been killed, with six troopers seriously injured and flown back to Tumeremo by helicopter and three, amazingly, walking away from the crash shaken but otherwise unhurt.

They'd have to bring the rest in by helicopter, and resupply was going to be a problem without the use of that runway. And reinforcing the garrison at Mahdia in advance of going on offense was going to take a long time.

At least, Cabrillo expected, they'd have air superiority. The enemy's fighter pilots were vastly superior. Their intelligence had it the American Polk had recruited three aces, two from the U.S. Navy and one from their Air Force, who were retired and had been flying private jets. He'd also recruited three or four others with experience as fighter pilots. Interestingly enough, they were British and Argentinian, which marked a strange mix since those two nations had been at war some 42 years earlier.

But in one of the few strokes of luck he'd had, the Americans hadn't been able to get missiles for those planes. They were limited to using their guns. And while the pilots were good, they had to get in close against the Venezuelan jets to fight. So far Polk's force had lost three of the 10 planes from their airfield on the other side of the Essequibo where his troops were not allowed to go, while the Venezuelans had lost four of what looked like it would be at least 14 jets able to fly. They would likely win the battle of attrition in the air.

The Chinese who were taking over jet maintenance and repair at El Libertador were hard at work replacing the landing gear on the planes not too badly damaged in the sabotage attack which ruined the invasion's first day, and in the coming days the word was that they'd be adding planes.

And the Chinese were supplying their J-16 fighters as well, which were essentially the same thing as the Su-30's they were using now. They had two; there were three more coming, was the word.

With time, he felt like he had the advantage. If he could cut the enemy's ability to resupply Liberty Point, he could starve them out. It would just take a while.

But those gunshots in the street were a reminder that Cabrillo's plans had every possibility of going awry. He peered out of the corner of the window of the little office of the Chief of Police on the second floor, the only room upstairs not occupied by the captive children of the village, and he saw three of his men dead in the street and the rest running for cover as the shots rang out.

And then he saw something which both amazed him and frightened him at the same time.

It was, he would call it, a robot. It looked almost like a toy car, but with treads instead of wheels, and it had a stem on which was mounted a small fisheye camera and, as he stared at it through binoculars, a pair of pistols.

Someone was remotely piloting this thing, and it was rolling along the street pot-shotting his men.

"Ernesto!" he yelled at the private he was using as a messenger.

"*Si, coronel?*" said the young man as he came running.

"Go out there and tell the men to shoot that thing! It's just a toy!"

Ernesto nodded and thundered down the stairs. He could see him running from the front door in an effort to flag down the sergeant who was in charge of the camp. But almost as soon as he came into view Ernesto's head exploded.

That was not from the toy. Cabrillo knew the enemy now had at least one sniper as well.

The toy car was quite agile, he saw. It would move quickly in the open, and then it would hide under a car or truck. A bullet would glance off it; it seemed to have a steel outer casing tough enough to protect its motor.

Cabrillo knew someone would have to hit its camera to render it unusable. But that was a shot which would need to be taken up close.

He figured he could perhaps do it himself, so he slid the window open just a bit to poke his rifle out, and…

A loud crash ensued as the window exploded. Cabrillo could hear, or more accurately he could feel, a bullet whizzing past his head barely three inches away.

Whoever was out there, the man was good. Damned good.

The drone was continuing to pop off shots, this time from underneath a truck, and the men were firing back to no avail. Someone managed to throw a grenade in an attempt to blow it up; but the damned thing hit the truck's fender and bounced away before exploding in front of the police station and blowing out the front window.

"This is bullshit," Cabrillo seethed.

He found the stairs and bounded down them, crooking his finger at Carvajal who had been hiding behind the station's reception desk.

"I want you to kill that thing," he said, pointing outside.

"*Senor*, it is…"

"No excuses, damn you. Lead. Take eight men and kill it. Tackle it if you have to. It doesn't have an unlimited supply of ammunition."

Carvajal knew he couldn't disobey a direct order, Cabrillo could tell, but he wanted to.

"Go, dammit!" he screamed at the stubby little major.

Carvajal nodded, the fear on his face rendering him utterly pathetic in Cabrillo's eyes, and he picked a squad of men to run out to the street and attempt to defeat the drone.

Through the window, Cabrillo saw the muzzle flash from a distance, and he saw the impact of the bullet as it hit Carvajal center mass. He was dead before he hit the ground.

There was a sniper in a tree on the hillside to the west of the soccer field. He had to be a thousand yards away, but his accuracy was nightmarish.

Carvajal's men were now pinned down behind a police car parked on the street. One by one they attempted to re-enter the safety of the police station; only half survived.

And now the drone was moving again. It rolled to the sidewalk in front of the police station and began shooting through the blown-out window. Cabrillo retreated to the back of the station where seven of his men had taken refuge.

"We have to get that thing!" he yelled. "Who is with me?"

Silence and stone faces were his unexpected response.

Just then he could hear a loud bang, and then a cheer from his men across the street in the soccer field. One of them had scored a hit on the drone with a grenade, though a big chunk of the building's façade had been taken out in the process. The station might no longer be functional as a headquarters. Cabrillo figured that Mahdia General Hospital a block away could be a suitable replacement.

The shots continued ringing out, and his men kept dying in the street.

Cabrillo could see that at least one of the shooters was to the west or southwest. He got on his walkie-talkie and gave orders to the 531st battalion to charge that position.

A few moments later, they were. Two ragged columns of men were hustling around the soccer field, a few of them dropping as they were hit, and making their way toward the hillside.

But as they went, Cabrillo could hear a familiar sound.

Motorcycles. Two, or was it three?

He caught a glimpse of them zooming through the trees to the south of his vantage.

The enemy had three snipers, and they were escaping.

"Get them!" he barked into the walkie-talkie. "They're getting away!"

There was a lot of radio chatter after that, and the men were boarding requisitioned trucks to follow the motorcycles as they made their way east through the trees that sectioned the main part of town off from the ruined Mahdia airfield. Others were in a dead run attempting to cut off the enemy's escape.

A few minutes later, Cabrillo could hear what sounded like a stuttering detonation to the east. Boomboomboomboomboomboom.

He knew what it was, and he cursed himself.

He'd sent his men right into a jackpot the snipers had laid in for them. They must have run into a massive mine field in that jungle.

Cabrillo could see smoke rising from the trees. A lot of smoke. It sickened him.

And, as if on cue, the rain came with a vengeance.

Chapter 20

June 21 2024: Linden, Guyana

I managed to get PJ out of Liberty Point. It practically took an act of Congress to get her out. And it's a good thing, too.

Not that she's ever going to give me credit for that. As far as she's concerned, letting me talk her out of that place was the worst example of me manipulating her there is.

And honestly, I'm OK with that.

When Roman, Charlie and Kurt, not to mention the mini-army of deadly drones Kurt carried in his rucksack as they headed off to Mahdia, stitched up the Vinnies as they did, the effect was not what Hal and Pierce were going for.

They figured they'd waste a nice percentage of the Vinnies' main invasion force at Mahdia as it was gearing up to come after them at Liberty Point. That's exactly what they did. And by all reasonable recognition it should have brought cooler heads to the table for a parlay about how this thing was going to be resolved.

Clearly, Pierce and Hal had lots of Romans, Charlies and Kurts. They also had lots of high-tech weaponry that would make for colossal casualty counts the more the Vinnies wanted to press their occupation of Essequibo.

But the analysis failed from there, because this wasn't about Venezuela. It wasn't about Madiera and his government. And the forces controlling them.

After the first couple of days, when the Vinnies had absorbed such massive losses in occupying all those little villages and other assets in Essequibo, it was time to start negotiating. After all, it was clear that to hold them would be to commit the kinds of abuses the world is unlikely to tolerate for long, Even then, they would be getting an ever-increasing amount of trouble from the indigenous opposition rapidly building thanks to guys like my friend Earl. I'll get to that in a minute.

What I'm saying is that if you're Madiera, you'd do this not because you wanted to occupy Essequibo. The expense associated with that alone made it a bad idea. Throw in the cost of governing a whole shitload of little bitty villages where everybody hates your guts, plus the international sanctions from being where you're not supposed to be, and it just looks bad and worse.

I think this is where that Latin mindset kicks in. The Venezuelans didn't want to admit they'd bitten off more than they could chew. If they were able to recognize that, they'd have bluffed their way into a deal that would have gotten them what they were looking for, or at least some of it, with their Essequibo adventure.

Especially when somebody – I think it was Pierce and Hal, but they wouldn't admit it, and there were other sources saying it was the CIA, though it's been a while since I saw those guys do anything effective outside of our borders – started a pretty well-organized amount of domestic trouble for Madiera.

Remember General de la Vega? You thought he'd gone away when Madiera kidnapped his wife and kids and traded them for his exile to Miami. Well, de la Vega showed up on Univision trashing the invasion as a disaster, claiming that the

Chinese were in charge of everything and calling for Madiera's resignation.

Asked what changed given that he'd tabbed Madiera as the rightful ruler, he said that he'd been under duress when he'd relented, and that the war changed everything.

While de la Vega's first emergence as a dissident leader had fizzled before it ever got going, this one was different. The Venezuelan expat community in South Florida got behind him and raised a bunch of money practically overnight, there were rumors of a couple of camps in El Salvador that sprang up to train guerillas to fight the government – and it was easy to get recruits given the flood of refugees who'd left Venezuela for Central America on their way north – and the streets of Venezuela's cities turned bloody.

Madiera couldn't reinforce his gains in Essequibo. Not the way he wanted to. He all of a sudden needed every boot he could get on the ground back home. His recognition of that fact was…well, let me tell that part a little bit later.

De la Vega reiterated that he would take power only as an interim president through the election in December. He said he would negotiate an honorable end to the war in Guyana and he would restore both market economics and human rights.

"Venezuela must be a prosperous democracy again," he said. "That starts with peace, the rule of law and then elections. I can accomplish those between now and the end of the year."

All of those things sounded good.

Anyway, I talked PJ into coming with me to interview the pilots at the air base in Linden and then back to Georgetown. I'd had an email from her dad saying she wouldn't talk to him; he'd said something immediately after Terre Haute that had really, really hacked her off. He said that if I could get her to come home, he'd fix everything.

"I don't know what you've convinced her of," he said, "but she has a future back in California. I'm begging you to let me make that happen."

"Mr. Chang," I said, "your daughter is a very smart, very strong woman. I'm making no decisions for her. She's quite capable of handling herself. I think you should be proud of her."

I didn't get a response back, but the exchange was unnerving enough – Peter Chang had the kind of influence with the Deadhorse administration which could result in a whole lot of trouble for yours truly. And with the FBI already nosing around back in Atlanta – Karen messaged me that the U.S. Attorney for the Northern District of Georgia had a grand jury going about my dissemination of "classified information" about the Secret Service and Terre Haute, and that I was likely to catch a subpoena.

It occurred to me that I would need to come home soon or else I might not be able to.

Anyway, the effect of the war on PJ was fascinating. It turned her on. She was glowing. The night Roman, Charlie and Kurt made it back to Liberty Point, and there was a big celebration at the Grand Waica about their huge win, she cornered me behind a big fern not far from the concierge desk and just about choked me with her tongue.

"I think we've passed that point we talked about," she said.

"Oh, you mean…"

"We don't need to stop at second base anymore."

"Are you sure?"

"I feel so alive right now I can't stand it. Don't you?"

"Well, I'm older. I've been in a war zone a couple of times. It's not as new. But yeah, this thing between you and me has some legs on it."

She gave me a big smile. We caught a ride back to the suite at Liberty Lodge and that was that.

PJ was a very early riser, and she insisted I become one too.

"OK, Mike," she said, nudging me awake just before the crack of dawn, "if we're going to become a, you know, I'm going to have to train you. Get up."

I did, bitching about it, but PJ made it worthwhile. She was a clean freak, it turned out, and the best shower-helper I've ever seen.

After breakfast, we made it down to Pierce's bunker and control room. The joy of the previous evening had settled into what seemed like a satisfied calm.

"Good day yesterday," said Hal, as he sipped his coffee and surveyed the wall of surveillance screens.

"Yeah, sounds like it," I said. "What comes next?"

"We're going to keep harassing the enemy, force him onto the defensive."

"How does this end, do you think?"

"Either badly, or maybe we do a deal, or, best hope, either Deadhorse wakes up and sends in the Marines or there's a coup in Venezuela and this melts away."

"So you don't think there's a winning scenario here."

"Not from a military standpoint, no. Not if the Vinnies are willing to escalate this."

"So you're about making Liberty Point as hard a target as you can, and hope for the best."

"I think later today we might have a development. We'll see."

That was cryptic enough, so I took out my laptop and checked emails and messages.

Which was when I had my interaction with Peter Chang. That I didn't tell PJ about.

Back home nobody was paying any attention to the war in Guyana, and it was starting to become awfully clear overt American help wasn't coming our way.

There was an incident in Washington that morning which made it obvious any hope of robust U.S. involvement down in the jungle was a fantasy.

Dr. Diego Cardoza, a geopolitics expert who'd spent time on Trumbull's National Security Council, was giving a speech on the threat China posed to America's interests worldwide and, more specifically, to the homeland.

Cardoza had written an op-ed at the *Wall Street Journal* warning that there were more than 35,000 military-age Chinese males who had come across the U.S. border in the previous 10 months, and he said he was in possession of proof that some or most of those illegals were not migrants but invaders – they were saboteurs, guerillas, hackers, terrorists and spies. And Cardoza had mentioned, in a follow-up interview on Fox News, that the war in Guyana was all about the Chinese getting their hands on the mines and oilfields of Essequibo.

All of which generated some calls for Congressional investigations, and it was awfully splashy on the radio talk show circuit. A few days later, Cardoza was at the National Press Club to show the proof he claimed he had about Chinese infiltration.

But he didn't get to show it. As soon as Cardozo took the stage, he was rushed by three dozen Chinese men from the crowd who were calling him a racist. "Stop Asian Hate!" they screamed, as they rushed the podium and proceeded to beat him bloody.

No one in the audience did much of anything. Not even the DC Metro Police officer who was there to provide security; he called the incident in, but of course it was streaming live on CSPAN and everybody knew in real time what was happening. The Chinese left Cardozo with half his teeth knocked out, a detached retina, seven broken ribs, a fractured skull and a severe concussion.

And the legacy media were covering the case as outraged citizens taking their frustrations out on a deranged racist. Even though it was by no means in evidence that any of these guys were citizens.

The Chinese ambassador said that while he "abhorred violence," the claims Cardozo had made were inflammatory and could not be allowed to poison Sino-American relations.

And then around noon, a satellite image on the control-room wall showed a flotilla of vessels – dozens of fishing trawlers, houseboats, small freighters, and pleasure craft – leaving the harbor at Puerto Cabello escorted by that Chinese naval task force, heading east along the coast.

If you weren't allowed to talk about the Chinese infiltrators in America in Washington, DC, then you certainly weren't going to get any American help in stopping a Chinese-protected invasion fleet in Guyana. That was obvious.

Hal was watching the Cardozo event on one of the monitors on the wall. Pierce had joined in, having been off doing something else in the morning.

I could see from the expressions on both of their faces that the implications of that event were disturbing – and devastating.

Pierce found me and whispered quietly, "I think you've done what you can in Liberty Point for now. Take your girl and get the hell out of here, quick."

"I was thinking the same," I said.

So we caught a chopper to Linden. I told PJ that I needed a photojournalist to document the goings-on at the air base.

But when we landed at Linden, the relative calm of Liberty Point had become something else.

There were pilots and ground crews scrambling around, and a huge hustle to get the four working A-4AR's and two old Harriers in the air. They managed it, and everybody seemed to be jumping in cars and trucks to get the hell out of there. A few minutes later we found out why.

The guy in command of the air base in Linden was a retired Air Force bomber wing commander named Bob Arness. When we landed, he and his assistant, a heavyset black lady whose name was Lucille, drove up in an old Jeep and he demanded we get in.

"Now!" he said. "Hustle up unless you have a death wish!"

We got in the Jeep and Lucille hit the gas.

"What's going on?" I asked, as we shot west along the runway toward the Linden-Kwakwani Road and the Demerara River.

"Missile…" said Arness, just as we could hear a very loud ripping sound and a series of huge booms behind us. Almost immediately thereafter, the Jeep was shaken – hard – by a series of shock waves.

When I looked behind, there was a fiery smoke cloud which reminded me of the pyroclastic cloud from Mount St. Helen's eruption in that old Pierce Brosnan movie. Perhaps not quite that dramatic, but more than enough for me to let loose a string of expletives.

And that earned me a nudge from PJ, who had her camera out and was filming the entire thing.

"We got all the good planes out," said Lucille. "And the guys should…"

"Yeah, I hope so," Arness muttered.

"How'd you know the missiles were coming?" I asked.

"Early warning radar," he said. "And real-time satellite imagery. They fired from the central part of Venezuela, which was their mistake; they should have had those missiles in Tumeremo. Gave us an eight-minute head start."

"I'm shocked you got your jets in the air that quickly," said PJ.

"Well, we got lucky there. We were launching anyway. The enemy is usually patrolling in the late afternoon, and with the boats they have coming it's almost certain they're going to be out to provide air cover."

"You're attacking those boats?"

"We're attacking their planes."

"Seems like it's a suicide mission."

"It is what it is. Our tactics are better. But we've got to be perfect, because they have air-to-air missiles and we just have guns. And now we're not going to have anything since it's a pretty sure thing they just took out our weapons stores along with our fuel."

"And your runway, I imagine," said PJ.

"I'd say that's correct," said Arness. "We have a last-ditch mission today and then it's bug-out time."

"How come you don't have missiles?"

"Because the A-4AR uses Sidewinders, and those are damned hard to find. Deadhorse raided all the stocks he could, all over the world, to send to Ukraine. They've been using them as surface-to-air missiles against the Russians. So we've really been up shit creek getting the weapons we need. We were lucky enough that I had a contact who could get us the M-61 Vulcan cannons to replace what those planes came with."

It struck me how desperate this situation really was.

Lucille was taking us over the Wismar/Mackenzie bridge into the town of Linden, which wasn't all that happening a burg. Arness was on his cell, though I couldn't hear what he was saying.

Finally, he hung up, turned back to look at us and said "You're in luck. Your chopper turned back around and he's going to pick you up at the ballfield."

I could see that he was telling the truth, because as we traveled that road toward a sports park only a couple miles away there was a helicopter vectoring in and landing.

"What's next for you guys?" I asked Arness.

"Suriname," he said. "Our secondary base is at the Kabalebo Nature Resort in Suriname, about 130 miles southeast of here. They've got a decent little airstrip there and the government is willing to get out of our way for a nice fee Pierce negotiated."

"Man," I said. "This is some wildcat operation, isn't it?"

"Never seen anything like it."

I shook his hand, Lucille wished us well and we hopped on the chopper.

"Back to Liberty Point?" I asked when I put the headset on.

"Nah, you don't want to do that," said the pilot. "They got hit with a missile strike at the airfield and a few other places. I'm taking you to Georgetown."

"Oh, no," said PJ.

"How bad are the casualties?" I asked.

"They don't know yet. It's pretty chaotic down there."

"We should go and help," PJ said.

I shook my head. "No. We need to get to Georgetown. We've got to get the word out about what's happening down here."

Things weren't better in the capital. We were supposed to land at the helipad at Sentinel Port Management's facility on the Demerara. That wasn't possible, because the whole place was a blown-out wreck.

So were a whole host of other targets in the capital, including the Parliament building.

And the Guyana Police Force headquarters. And Camp Ayanganna, which was the military base in the capital.

And the airport.

And Exoil's office complex next to the airport.

There were pillars of smoke rising from close to a dozen large fires around Georgetown.

So instead, he set us down in the parking lot in front of the Marriott.

The place was heavily guarded, but it seems like I was known. The two big black guys in berets and what looked like Guyanese military uniforms guarding the front door waved us to the concierge, where we were directed to one of the little ballrooms. There, we were given ID badges on lanyards and directed to the grand ballroom.

Because the Marriott had become the seat of government now that most of the government buildings had been hit by missiles.

I remembered Ravi Darke, the head of the Guyanese military. He was there, surrounded by a host of minions and it looked like they were keeping awfully busy. People were sitting at banquet tables with their faces inches away from laptop screens, and it looked a little like a war room.

But of course, these guys were helpless. Missiles were raining down on every security asset in Guyana at this point, and they had no defense for it.

There was a flotilla headed from Venezuela that was almost surely going up the Essequibo, and they had no defense for that, either. Hell, they wouldn't have much defense if that flotilla was coming for Georgetown.

The only defense they had was Pierce and his operation, and for all we knew that was out of commission, too.

We hung off to the side, but then Jaganoo, the Prime Minister, saw me and collected us. Jaganoo led PJ and I to a second floor suite, and then sat us down.

"Beer?" he asked. It seemed like a bizarre offer, but I couldn't turn it down. Neither could PJ.

"Been a long day," I said, tipping my bottle to Jaganoo. "I'm sure yours has been the same."

"I am glad that you are safe," said Jaganoo, "and I thought you should hear it from me first. We are in contact with the Madiera government about a cease-fire."

"You're surrendering?"

"There is no choice. Earlier today the Venezuelans took Bartica. Because of that, they now control the mouth of the Essequibo. They've killed half our parliament and they have cut off the capital from the rest of the country by destroying the airport."

"They can't hold what they've taken," said PJ. "They're going to fall apart. The whole Venezuelan government is going to topple."

"We must save as many lives as we can."

"You mean like at Port Kaituma?"

"OK, PJ, take it easy," I said.

"How can he just give his country away?" she said, her face screwed up in a rage.

"It's been decided," said Jaganoo. "No one wants this, but we are without options."

Just then my cell rang. It was Pierce.

"I have to take this call," I said. Jaganoo pointed me to a bedroom.

"Are you all right?" I asked him.

"We're good," he said. "Airfield is shot up pretty bad and they whacked the hydro plant, but we still have some juice. And what pisses me off more than anything, they hit the Torch."

"How chickenshit. You guys were almost finished with that."

"Tell me about it. Mostly we're just shaken up. About a dozen wounded, nobody too seriously, nobody dead which is a miracle thanks to our early-warning radar and real-time sat imagery. But it's not all bad news here. We have the Cuban."

"You what?"

"Cabrillo. We nabbed him."

"How in the hell did you do that?"

"Ol' boy made the mistake of going out to check on the progress of his airfield getting rebuilt. Somebody hit his ride with an RPG, and then he got dragged off into the woods."

"Well, that sucks to be him. Roman and his guys are good, right?"

"This wasn't Roman."

"No? Who was it?"

"Believe it or not, Earl and the IM's pulled it off. They also shot up the guards at that soccer field in Mahdia and got the civilians out. Or at least the adults – the kids we'll go get next."

"You're kidding."

"Nope. So right now Cabrillo is making a little hostage confession speech we'll send back to Caracas, and maybe that'll put a stop to these damned Iranian missiles they're shooting at us."

"Pierce, we're with Jaganoo. They're surrendering."

"They're what? The hell they are."

"The Vinnies hit Parliament. They took out the airport, the army base, the police headquarters, a bunch of other stuff. They hit your port facility, too. Plus they took Linden out, but you already know that."

"Yeah. I know about the port. They didn't hit it in time."

"What's that mean?"

"Probably find that out later today."

"Jaganoo says they took Bartica, too."

"Yeah, that was the Black Wasps."

"The what?"

"*Avispas Negras.* Cuban special forces. They shot up the Guyanese army guys who were guarding the town with an airstrike, and they gave up almost immediately when the Black Wasps showed up in choppers. They had plenty of MANPADs; nobody bothered firing one."

"Not great."

"These guys might be soldiers. They aren't warriors. And there's the question of leadership, too."

"So what's the play?"

"Well, we're not done. We're gonna hold out. And any Guyanese who want to keep fighting, we'll get 'em weapons and comms and whatever supplies they need. I still have procurement guys around the world and we've got lots more stuff coming."

"Pierce, you don't think it's over? What if Ishgan calls on you to give up?"

"Ohhh, it is *not* over. Not by a long shot. In a few hours things are gonna look completely different on the ground."

"Yeah, but if Georgetown sues for peace…"

"This is what I need from you," he said. "*Don't let him.* That's the key. You've got to stall Ishgan – if it's even Ishgan who's still calling the shots, because we found a whole bunch of interesting things."

"Anything on that you can tell me?"

"Check your email when you get off this call."

"All right."

"But do *not* let these guys throw in the towel. Not just yet. All right? Whatever it takes, I need another three or four hours."

"OK. I'll do what I can."

Chapter 21

June 22, 2024: Georgetown, Guyana

PJ and I didn't have a place to stay in Georgetown. The Grand Coastal was out of rooms, and so were all the other hotels in town. We ended up crashing in the poolhouse at Tom Burnham's place in Lusignan, which frankly was a sizable stroke of luck.

After I finished my call with Pierce, I went back to the main room of Jaganoo's suite at the Marriott and saw that he was becoming more and more agitated with PJ. She was giving him what-for about the idea of giving up.

I was quickly scanning the email that Pierce had sent on my phone, so I didn't say anything. I just listened.

I could tell that Moses Jaganoo was not in the custom of listening to lectures from women. And to be fair, from what I knew of PJ it wasn't all that customary for her to talk to anybody like she was talking to Jaganoo. PJ was always very polite and friendly. But I think she had seen, heard and endured enough over the past few days and weeks, and she wasn't very friendly anymore.

So finally, I turned on the "record" app on my phone. And I stepped in.

"OK," I said. "Let's turn the temperature down."

"But Mike, he's…"

"No, PJ, let's calm it down. Please."

"Thank you," said Jaganoo, who was recovering his carefully-practiced composure.

I took PJ's hand and I smiled at her.

"The thing is, Mr. Prime Minister, she's absolutely correct. It would be treason for you to surrender right now."

That took him aback.

"And sir, you're not really in a position to defend against accusations of treason."

"Why, I am deeply offended at the statement, Mr. Holman…"

"Stabroek-Penitence Holdings. That ring a bell?"

"Yes, of course," he said, stammering a little. "What of it?"

"You've been a fairly broke lawyer and politician all your life, Mr. Jaganoo. Three years ago you ended up in a partnership now worth more than $150 million with real estate property all over the Caribbean. How did you pull that off? Where'd you get the equity for that?"

"What are you accusing me of, sir?"

"I'm not accusing you of anything. I'm just asking what about you made Mr. George Ling of Sino-Americas Harvest Limited, who in reality is the Chinese Communist Party's number one espionage operative in Latin America, interested in cutting you in for a one-third share of his real estate company. You guys must be close, right?"

"He's a business partner. I know nothing of espionage."

"Yeah, I don't think that's right. I think you know plenty about espionage, and I think you've been waiting for this invasion from the very beginning. Where is the president?"

"He's in the presidential suite."

"I think it's time we go and see him."

"He's indisposed."

"Indisposed?"

"President Ishgan has had an emotional breakdown. He is resting comfortably under sedation."

"I see. And are we free to leave?"

There was a very, very long pause.

"Of course," he said, quite shakily. "But I should caution you that the capital is a dangerous city given the missile attacks. Be very careful out there."

"Is that a threat?" PJ exploded. "Did you just *fucking* threaten us?"

"Easy, girl," I said, squeezing her hand. "Easy. We're going to take our chances. Mr. Jaganoo, what I'm here to ask you is that you do nothing until tomorrow morning."

"As I said, it has already been decided. I'm sorry."

"Decide what you want, sir, but the deal I will make with you is that if you do nothing publicly, if you announce no cease-fire or surrender, then your commercial history similarly will not go public. My team back in Atlanta has it all, and they await my instructions."

"Now it is *you* making threats."

"No, sir, I'm not making threats. I'm proposing a mutually beneficial arrangement which could work out very well for all involved. Give me and Pierce Polk twelve hours, and you might find yourself with very superior options to those you currently have, but if you act now it'll be…"

"Messy," said PJ, following my lead.

Jaganoo looked at me for what seemed like a long time. I could see sweat forming on his brow.

PJ started to say something. I squeezed her hand and she shut up.

"I require certain considerations," he said.

"I think we can work something out. What are you looking for?"

"I want to be on the board of Polk's stock exchange."

"I'll let him know."

"And I want his endorsement of my candidacy for president in the snap elections we will call for next month."

"Well, it would seem like if an arrangement were made it would be to Pierce's benefit to do something like that."

"And I want $100 million in cash."

"A very reasonable number. I'll relay that to Pierce."

"I require a response in one hour's time."

"OK, then. Let me get to work."

We grabbed our bags and left. I could tell PJ was ready to explode, but I managed to keep her quiet until we got outside of the hotel.

"Holy *shit*!" she said. "You just bribed the Prime Minister to keep him from treason! You're a lot more interesting guy than I thought, Mike."

"I haven't done *anything* yet," I said. "What I did do is make sure Mr. Jaganoo is done in politics, though."

I pulled out my phone, selected the app and tapped the "play" button. When PJ heard the recording, her eyes lit up.

"Oh, that is *sooo* hot," she said after a few seconds.

I stopped the playback and sent the recording out to Pierce, Flip Hardison, Colby, Tom Burnham and a bunch of other people, with a message asking them not to share it until further instructions.

Burnham immediately messaged me back.

"You in Georgetown?"

"Yes."

"Where?"

"In front of the Marriott."

"Wait five minutes."

There was a Land Rover with an Exoil logo on the side door pulling up to us in three.

"Mr. Holman?" the driver, a black guy I could have sworn was Idi Amin's cousin, said out of the window.

"Mr. Burnham sent you?"

"Yes, sir," he said. "Please do hop in."

So PJ and I did, and he took off to the east down the Seawall Public Road.

The guy's name was Desmond. He was Jamaican. He was an engineer, or at least he was until around lunchtime.

"They struck our offices," he said. "Seventy-four people dead. I will have my vengeance. You and your man must succeed."

I could feel PJ shaking in the back seat next to me. She was trying to hold back her rage.

We turned onto Railway Embankment Road, still heading east. Desmond was talking about how the public was inflamed by the failure of the government to do anything to fight the Venezuelans and how citizens' militias were springing up.

"Your man Polk had the right idea," he was saying. "But the people don't have the resources he has."

"It's a problem," I said.

"Ultimately the people are what will solve this. The people are who pay the price for their poor leaders."

"No doubt."

"I have a Heckler & Koch 416 rifle," he said. "I'll be going home and getting it after I drop you off. I'll stand with the militia in Lusignan, where I live."

"What's Lusignan?" asked PJ.

"It's the ritzy neighborhood on the golf course where all the Exoil people hang out," I said. "East of the city."

"You know your Georgetown well," said Desmond.

Burnham's house had turned into a headquarters facility of its own, since they'd blown up Exoil's offices with that missile.

"I leave you here," said Desmond, "and then I join the militia. This isn't even my country, but it seems we have to fight shit politicians everywhere. The enemy, the traitors among us…"

"Best of luck to you, Desmond," I said.

He nodded and waved, and we made our way through the crowd in the front yard.

"A lot of angry folks here," said PJ as we picked up shreds of conversations along the way to the front door.

"Yep," I said.

There was a twenty-something kid who answered the door when I knocked on it. Unlike Desmond, I could immediately tell he was an engineer. The glasses gave it away.

"You're Mr. Holman," he said in a brogue-y East Coast accent. "I've seen your podcast! I'm Sal O'Reilly."

"Nice to meet you, Sal. Irish-Italian mix, huh?"

King Of The Jungle

"I'm a mutt, yep."

"Classic white-privileged kid from…"

"South Philly."

"Got it. This here is PJ."

"I know you, too. You're Pauline Chang. They did you wrong, ma'am."

"Thanks," said PJ. "But call me PJ."

"Mr. Burnham wouldn't be around, would he?" I asked.

"Yes! Sorry. He's upstairs in the office with some people, but I know he needs to see you. Go right up."

So we did.

"Do you think these are, like…" PJ was saying.

"This is who the Vinnies didn't take out when they hit the Exoil Guyana headquarters," I said, "and now there are two super-wealthy American companies at war with Venezuela."

"I don't understand. Why would they hit Exoil?"

"Because if there's nobody left to run Exoil's operations in Guyana, Exoil sells the thing to…"

"China," she said. "Damn."

"Sino-Petro is already a partner in those offshore oilfields. It's nothing to just get a check over to them and bow out, and then nobody cares when the fields are licensed through the new conquering lackey government."

"I hate everybody," she said.

"Well, all these people standing around looking for a fight to get in might be an indication they've grossly, grossly miscalculated," I said.

Finally, after dodging a host of people hanging around in the upstairs den we managed to get into Burnham's office. He had a Zoom call going with his corporate people in Houston and, surprisingly enough, Ravi Darke, the head of the Guyanese military.

"Mike, glad you're here," Burnham said. "I heard you almost bought it at Linden."

"I felt the shock wave," I said. "It was pretty lucky stuff."

"Well, there's no time to fill you in, so I'll try to do that later. But as we talk this through, feel free to jump in. You've talked to Pierce? I can't get through."

"Like 20 minutes ago, yeah."

"OK, good," he said and then pointed to the Zoom call screen on his wall. "First, Mike Holman, this is Brett Gilchrist, Exoil CEO. Rob Owens, head of field security, Tina Williams, VP of corporate external relations, Walt Zeiling, governmental affairs. And Brigadier Darke you already know. Also, everybody, this is PJ Chang; she's with Mike. I understand she's a hell of a photojournalist."

They all nodded their greetings when PJ and I sat next to Burnham and entered the video frame.

"Sorry, guys. Brigadier, please continue."

"The issue," Darke said, "is that the surviving members of Parliament are with Jaganoo. And so the votes for surrender are there."

"What's the state of the GDF?" Gilchrist asked. He was talking about the Guyanese Defense Force.

"We lost a third of our men when Bartica surrendered," Darke said. "The rest will have to hold the capital and the eastern coast in case the enemy attempts to swallow all of Guyana."

"Will your men hold the capital?" asked Owens.

"We will certainly do our best," Darke said.

"That's not what I'm asking. Will your men hold the capital against this cabal trying to give away two thirds of your country?"

"You're asking about a coup d'etat."

"Brigadier," said Gilchrist, "it sounds a hell of a lot like you've already had one. The question is, are you going to sanction it?"

I leaned to Burnham.

"Are we saying that Jaganoo had his allies in Parliament hang back and let the patriots get killed by that missile strike?" I asked him.

"We don't know that," said Burnham, "but it sure does come off that way."

"What about Ishgan? Has anybody talked to him? They told me he had a breakdown and they had him sedated."

"Out of pocket and out of the picture. I don't think he's the president anymore."

"Then it's definitely a coup d'etat."

Burnham shrugged and nodded.

"I don't know that I have the authority," Darke was saying. "A majority of the remaining parliament voted earlier today to make Jaganoo acting president, and…"

"Hang on," I said. "If I can jump in, I might be able to contribute a few things."

Gilchrist and Darke both nodded, and I relayed what Pierce had said about the situation at Liberty Point, and I noted that they were going to relocate the little air force to the jungle resort airstrip in Suriname.

And then I noted that Jaganoo had told me his price for holding off on the surrender until morning. Burnham uploaded the recording to the Zoom call and everyone heard it.

"Jeez," said Owens.

I could see in Darke's face that we'd had him wrong. He wasn't a traitor. He was just in over his head.

"I will do as you ask," he said, "but if I am to assume power it will be for a very short time and then, when a new election is held, I will retire."

"I have to talk to Mr. Polk," I said, "but would anyone here object if we told Jaganoo his terms are acceptable? I want to stall him so there's time to put whatever plan in place that we can."

"I think it's the only play," said Burnham. "Rob?"

"Tell him whatever. We need to buy some time."

"Mr. Zeiling, maybe you guys talked about this, but is there nothing the U.S. government is going to do?"

Before he could answer, Gilchrist stepped in.

"The Navy offered to evacuate our offshore platforms. And they recalled the ambassador in Caracas."

"That's it?"

"So far," Zeiling said.

"But Trumbull is interested in doing a fly-in," said Gilchrist. "We're trying to figure out how to get him into Georgetown with the airport knocked out."

"Boy, that would send a signal," I said. "Pretty good politics, too."

"Almost certain to get him indicted under the Logan Act," Zeiling said, laughing.

I looked at Burnham. "I need to call Pierce," I said.

He nodded, and he pointed to the balcony.

"Go out there. Cell reception in here is atrocious."

Mine was a satellite phone, so it didn't matter, but I went on the balcony and called Pierce. He answered immediately and I told him where I was.

"You're on speaker," he said, "and I've got Hal and a couple of his guys with me. By the way, the Vinnies just surrendered Mahdia 10 minutes ago."

"They what?"

"Yeah. We've been using a swarm of these quad-copter drones that drop grenades on 'em, and we've been picking them off all day. Finally they all came out and waved the white flag, and they brought the kids out of the police station. So that's over and Earl and the IM's are retaking the place. We have the Vinnies fenced in at the soccer field now, but there aren't a lot of them left."

"Hang on," I said, and I leaned into Burnham's office. "Tom, Pierce says the Venezuelans just gave up in Mahdia."

"Oh," said Pierce, "tell Burnham I just emailed him a link he's going to want to see, in about four minutes."

So I did, and Burnham put up the link in the "share screen" function on the Zoom call. I was looking at it through the window from the balcony.

It was footage from a drone, and you could see the flotilla of Venezuelan boats escorted by those three Chinese warships as they made their way eastward near the coast.

I then quickly filled Pierce in on the conversations with Jaganoo and Darke.

"OK, OK," he said, "but wait up a minute."

Pierce was telling me that the IM's had set up a training camp at a little place in the far south called Yupukari, which was along the Rupunari River, and people were coming out of the woodwork to join up. He said the Venezuelans had sent two choppers down there to occupy the place on the first day of the invasion and both of them had been hit with MANPADs. Only six Vinnies managed to survive the crash landings and the locals had managed to dispose of them after about three days. There was a former British SAS lieutenant who was running a research station for the black caiman down there, and the guy turned out to be a pretty kick-ass military commander.

"Too bad he can't train the caiman," I said.

"Well, apparently one of the Vinnies ran and jumped in the river as the locals were chasing him down," Pierce said with a laugh, "and the caiman got him. So maybe he did train 'em."

Just then his voice changed. "OK, here we go," he said.

I looked at the drone footage, and it showed a couple of big explosions on two of those Chinese ships happening almost simultaneously.

"Biiiig badaboom!" said Pierce.

"What the hell?" I said.

"That would be the ARA *Santa Cruz*," said Pierce, "newly equipped with an upgraded power plant and the Mark 48 Mod 7 Common Broadband Advanced Sonar System torpedo," he said. "I'm not even going to tell you how much this cost. Worth every penny."

Three more explosions hit the third Chinese ship and a couple of the bigger boats in the flotilla. The Chinese sailors were lowering their lifeboats as the warships began listing.

"You just declared war on China, Pierce," I said. "Holy cow."

"Nah," he said. "They've been at war with me for a good while now. I just started fighting. Oh, by the way, tell Tom I have another link for him."

I did, and another window popped up on Burnham's wall.

This looked more like satellite imagery. Pierce said it was from a town called Tumeremo, which was where the Vinnies had been staging the bulk of their invasion from.

The satellite camera was zooming in on what looked like a fairly deserted road, and there were six trucks, or what looked like trucks, parked along it.

"Those would be our Iranian friends," he said, and I realized he was talking about missile launchers.

"That's what hit…"

"Linden. And Liberty Point. And Georgetown," Pierce said.

Just then, there were two shadows moving quickly across the image, and shortly behind them were four large explosions.

And then several secondary explosions behind them.

"Fatteh you, you bastards," said Pierce. I think he was talking about the Fatteh 11 missile, the Iranian-made weapon the Vinnies had used on us. "We're settling all family business tonight. *Keyser Soze!*"

I laughed. "Good grief, Pierce. Could you butcher your movie references any worse? And why didn't you tell me you had all this going on?"

"Operational security, I guess. In case they got you."

"Well, I need to tell Jaganoo something. He's the key to this, I guess. Tell me what you want to do."

"Sure. Call him and tell him he gets everything he wants if he holds off. And then Ravi can go and arrest him and run his coup."

"OK, will do."

King Of The Jungle

"Hey, Earl is here. Earl, how'd you like to be president of Guyana?"

Chapter 22

June 24, 2024: Georgetown, Guyana

Jaganoo was as good as his word in not surrendering to the Vinnies that day, but his people put out a statement that he was going to address the nation at 9 a.m. the next morning.

And then he was arrested by the Guyana Defense Force at 8 a.m. It was Darke who addressed the nation. When he did, he said that Jaganoo had been arrested for treason and that Ishgan, the president, was out of commission for a "medical condition."

Which turned out to be a fentanyl overdose.

Somebody had dosed him with three times the fatal amount, and the only thing that saved him was a miracle; Ishgan's personal doctor had been a block away from the Marriott and had a Narcan pen in his bag.

But he was still practically comatose a day later. For all practical purposes, Ishgan was knocked out of the game. That made Darke effectively the interim president. And as his first act, he announced that Guyana would not surrender to Venezuela under any circumstances, and he openly called for help from "the community of nations to help us restore the internationally recognized borders of the Republic of Guyana."

There was good news and bad news on that score.

The good news came in the southern part of the country. The Vinnies who had been dropped into those little villages in the Rupununi river valley had generally been scattered into very small units, and they'd suffered a lot of losses to helicopters getting shot down. Not to mention the locals tended to be pretty well armed and fairly decently led, and the Guyanese were for the most part kicking their asses.

Of course, the plan had been that the Venezuelans would reinforce their initial gains. They couldn't really do that in the south because of the trouble back home.

And that got worse and worse for them because just after the naval attack somebody hacked the central bank in Caracas and wiped out, well, everything.

Yes, you read that correctly. The hack all but destroyed all of the Venezuelan central bank's current records and locked the Madiera government out of most of its financial resources.

Not to mention those hackers also hit the power grid in Caracas, Maracaibo, Ciudad Guayana, Puerto Cabello, and Barquisimeto, which plunged a big chunk of the population into darkness.

Then de la Vega flew to Curacao and took a helicopter into Coro, a coastal city west of Caracas. He said the revolution was afoot, and that Madiera no longer had the consent of the people of Venezuela to continue as the president.

Burnham, Darke, and Pierce were on a Zoom call that PJ and I sat in on that morning after Darke had taken over, and we had a surprising guest join in.

"Mr. President," said Burnham. "It's a pleasant surprise to have you."

"I'm happy to be here," said Trumbull. "And Tommy — I can call you Tommy? — Gilchrist says you're a hell of a guy, so you're all right with me."

"Yes, sir," Burnham laughed.

"Hey Pierce, how ya holdin' up down in the sticks?" said Trumbull.

"I'm the King of the Jungle," said Pierce. "I might never leave. No army is about to dig me out of here, I can tell you."

Trumbull chuckled.

"Wait a minute," he said. "Mike, is that Pauline you've got with you?"

"Yes, sir," she said.

"Wow!" he said. "I like what you've done with your hair. You look like that girl, oh, what's her name…"

"Thanks, Mr. President," PJ said, and I could tell she was in no mood to be compared to any dye-blond Chinese starlets.

"Right. Anyway," Trumbull said, "I heard what's going on down there and it seems like it could be at least a little helpful if I did a quick fly-in and endorsed Ravi here — it's Ravi, right?"

"Yes, Mr. President," said Darke.

"Ravi. Hell of a guy, and bold stuff you're doing. Anyway, if you guys think it'll help, I'll fly down from Palm Beach, say hi, give a speech about how Venezuela has got to go back, and I'll say that when I'm back in office all of this will get put right, and in the meantime Ravi will keep up the fight. Y'know, buck up the folks a little."

"I think that could only help," said Pierce.

"If nothing else, it'll shame Deadhorse into doing something," said Burnham.

"I believe things will ultimately turn in Essequibo," said Darke. "The southern part of the region seems to be returning to our control thanks to the efforts of the indigenous population."

"That's good," said Trumbull. "That's really good. You've gotta hang on. And Pierce, your guys have to hang on, too."

"We're doing more than that," said Pierce.

King Of The Jungle

"Right, great. I want you guys to hang onto that oil! You can't let China" — he pronounced it CHY-na — "get those offshore rigs. Yuge to hold on to those. I mean it."

"No, sir," said Burnham.

"We have some plans in that regard," said Pierce.

"So look," said Trumbull. "They tell me you can't really fly into Georgetown now, right? Airport is messed up?"

"The runways were hit with missiles," said Darke. "It will be a few days before they're operational again."

"Well, then we could wait, or maybe I could do something else," said Trumbull. "What if I flew in someplace close and then you came and got me in a chopper and flew me in that way?"

"That's the best idea," said Pierce. "We'll fly you in to Paramaribo, in Suriname, and then chopper you to Georgetown. It's like 200 miles away."

"Oof," said Trumbull.

"Oh, come on. You'll get to ride in on the Sikorsky V-92. You'll be here in an hour from the tarmac in Paramaribo."

"You brought your Sikorsky down, Pierce?" Trumbull was impressed.

Pierce shook his head. "This is the second one."

Trumbull chuckled. "They say I'm rich, but nobody's loaded like this guy."

PJ leaned in.

"We're out of place with all these super-rich guys," she said. "They're talking about private helicopters."

"Excuse me," I whispered back, "but isn't your dad rich like this?"

"I'm not my dad."

"That's why I love you."

Blurting that out surprised the shit out of both of us.

"Oh, I…" she whispered.

I didn't know what to say.

"Hey," Trumbull was saying, "Mike, are you paying attention?"

"Yes, sir," I said. "Sorry, Mr. President."

"What I'm thinking is that maybe you could do the interview on the chopper tomorrow. Meet me in Paramaribo, we'll get on the helicopter and then that gives us an hour."

"It's a great idea," I said. "But PJ here — er, Pauline — will come with, because she's pitching in as my cameraman now."

"Yeah? Nice. She's definitely welcome. Plus, she's muscle. You always need as much muscle as you can get, right?"

"That's my experience, sir," I said, humoring him.

Trumbull signed off, and so we now had a former, and possibly future, American president coming to Guyana to raise awareness about the war. But when the president checked out, the conversation turned.

"The issue," Darke was saying, "is the north."

Pierce's hit on that naval flotilla was a success, but the Santa Cruz didn't pick off all of those boats heading into the Essequibo River. It would have been impossible. They didn't have enough torpedoes. And more important was to protect the oil platforms to the north, because the Vinnies sent a bunch of their naval ships in the direction of the platforms. The sub gave chase and hit one of them with a torpedo, which turned away the little armada.

But in the meantime, the flotilla along the coast simply went ashore. And when it did, it disgorged several thousand Venezuelan troops, which were shortly commandeering vehicles from the locals and holding all of the lightly populated western coastline from the Essequibo to the Venezuelan border.

And they already held basically everything north of the Potaro in the interior.

Darke was saying that what was needed was impossible, namely, a counterattack to dislodge them before they could consolidate those gains and — we all knew this was coming — bring in the Chinese to begin exploiting them.

"Wish we had an army to do that," said Burnham.

"You guys are thinking about this the wrong way," said Pierce. And I could see him moving aside to make room for Hal Gibson in the Zoom call.

"Hi everybody," said Gibson. "Look, the day after tomorrow there is a ceremony at the waterfall. Madiera is coming and he's going to declare victory at Kaietur Falls."

"Is he really?" I said.

"We think they're going to call a ceasefire and try to claim what they took," said Pierce. "It's really the only move they've got."

"And the north has more economic assets," said Darke.

"That they can sell to China," said PJ.

"Well, how do we break up that party?" I asked.

"You let us handle that," said Pierce.

"Do we want to know more than that?" asked Burnham.

"No," said Hal. "You do not."

"OK, then," I said. "Brigadier Darke, can you make security arrangements for a Trumbull pop-in?"

"I believe so," he said, "given that we have a true professional with us to show us the way."

"OK, security pro," said Pierce, "what do you need from us?"

I think PJ was the last to realize they were talking to her.

"Oh, wait," she said.

Once she realized she had a job to do, PJ moved fast. She had Pierce send her six guys from Liberty Point, and she got Darke to set up the ballroom at the Pegasus Hotel, which was the other nice place in town, as the venue for Trumbull to speak.

Still, I sat there watching her work the phones, and then I rode with her as Desmond came to get us and brought us to the Pegasus, and she had the folks at that hotel jumping as she rearranged their whole setup in preparation for Trumbull's arrival. Everything from closing the pool bar and rearranging the beach chairs, eliminating any possible vantage from which a shooter could get at Trumbull from the time he got off the chopper in the parking lot just on the ocean side of the hotel to his speech in the ballroom, to his exit out of the hotel's side entrance to the convoy of SUVs she organized and to the reboarding of the chopper at the police college a block away. She spent the whole night, practically, coordinating with Trumbull's team and the Guyana Police Force and Darke's people. She was still doing it when I decided to head to bed.

"Can I do anything?" I asked.

"Nope. This is my stuff."

I didn't see her the next morning. Not until about 11, when Desmond came to pick me up and take me to what was left of the airport, where Pierce's Sikorsky was waiting.

PJ was there, wearing a black business suit that reminded me very much of the Secret Service agent she'd been so recently.

"You look rumpled," Holman," she said. "You don't have a tie?"

"Trumbull isn't going to wear one," I said. "So I'm not."

She rolled her eyes, and we boarded the Sikorsky. And an hour later we were landing at the airport in Paramaribo, or better put the airport south of Paramaribo, because it was really nowhere near that city, and not long after, Trumbull's plane zoomed in from the north and he got off on the tarmac.

The president of Suriname and a few of his people insisted on welcoming Trumbull as he debarked, and Trumbull spent a few minutes making pleasantries before he shook my hand.

"Hey, Mike," he said. "Big times, huh? And look at Pauline! Back to the old tricks, right?"

"Mr. President," she smiled. "I'm wearing two hats on this trip, but you know which one is most important."

"Right," he said. "So let's go!"

He shook all the Surinamese hands, and Pauline and his two security guys hustled him into the chopper. I followed.

And for the next hour we did an interview which, honestly, I would have liked to take back. Trumbull, I could tell, was nervous.

Halfway through, he stopped.

"Hey, off the record?" he asked.

"Sure," I responded.

"I'm kinda thinking this was rash, comin' down here. I mean, it's still a war going on, right?"

"Well, yes and no. It's something of a stalemate and we're hoping Venezuela's government falls apart."

"Yeah, I know your guy is doin' everything he can to dick 'em over. Think that'll work?"

"I learned a long time ago not to doubt him, but this is a pretty big project."

"I'm just saying, Mike. I don't wanna be a pussy. But I got shot in Indiana of all places and here I'm goin' to Guyana."

He more or less mumbled his way through the rest of the interview, saying his usual things, trashing Deadhorse and promising that if he got put back in charge it would be "no trouble at all" to put the world back right, and to kick out all the Omobba spies and saboteurs embedded in the Executive Branch.

"These guys," he said, "my first term they had an advantage over me. It's gonna be different the second go-round. You know, the presidency's a big job. You need a lot of help. Gotta have the right people or it's all fucked. Wait, edit that out, will ya?"

"We'll bleep it."

"Right. OK, whatever. But Deadhorse, I mean, come on. I told everybody he was senile four years ago and they weren't listening. But now? Nobody's arguin' anymore. Did you hear what he said yesterday? He said he was the lead singer for the Eagles before Don Henley. Where does he even get shit like that?"

PJ was happily rolling away with her camera. I thought it was interesting; she'd been a giant ball of stress from the time she'd gotten drafted back into her old job, and while she attacked it with a passion I found amazing she'd gone from friendly and polite to irritable and grumpy. But now? I was convinced that camera was therapeutic for her.

We ended the interview early, mostly because Trumbull was more interested in asking me questions.

"Mike, you've been down here most of the last month. What do you think of Guyana? What's the deal here?"

"I think if the Vinnies…"

"Who's the Vinnies?"

"Sorry. The Venezuelans. If they can get chased off, I think Guyana has some real potential. And I think what you're going to want to do is knock out some sort of free trade deal with them."

"Yeah?"

"Yeah. And because they're going to need a big infusion of labor, especially for construction with all the industry that the offshore oil will bring in, I'd make plans to deport a bunch of those illegals you're talking about getting rid of to here."

"Oooh. That's an idea. So the Guyanese would take 'em in and make 'em guest workers?"

"I bet they'd be open to it."

"Who? This guy Darke?"

"They're going to do elections in a few weeks. He's not going to run."

"Who is?"

"Not sure, but the guy I imagine might win is Earl Roberts."

"Guy named Earl? Sounds like he fixes cars."

"He's actually a war hero. Pierce's guy. I think you'll meet him in Georgetown."

Trumbull nodded. "Well, good. After this, have him call me and I'll help if I can."

We landed in a cleared-out parking lot, and I could see PJ tense up again. She and Trumbull's bodyguards made a phalanx around him and walked him into the hotel. Security was tight as we made our way to the ballroom, where several hundred people had taken seats. The applause was thunderous as Trumbull and his party made their way through the side door.

Darke was on stage, applauding, and he and Trumbull shared a quick exchange and a handshake as the former president came to the podium. Then it was Trumbull's turn.

And he held forth for about a half hour about how "lousy communists" were ruining the world and how the good folks of Guyana were the front lines against them.

"I know you guys have the fight in you," he said, "and soon you'll have your country back. All of it."

That took the roof off, and the crowd rose to their feet yelling, screaming and clapping. It was like a rock concert.

And Trumbull shook hands with Darke and a few other Guyanese politicians, not to mention Burnham and a couple of other American businesspeople who were there. Then he shook Earl's hand and took a picture with him and told him,

"Call me, and I'll make sure you get elected. You're a hell of a guy."

Then it was time to take Trumbull out of the hotel to the SUVs parked at the side exit.

That happened without a hitch. Then we were headed east along Seawall Public Road for about a block, then came a right turn into the Guyana Police Depot, which was half-destroyed by the missile strike, and then a left into the grass parking lot where the chopper had relocated and was whirling away, prepared for a fast takeoff, and then we all got out…

"Wait, no," PJ said. "That's not how we set this up."

"What's wrong?" I said.

"That pile of timber was supposed to be cleared!" she said, pointing at an unwanted obstruction to the right.

Two of Pierce's guys took off running for the woodpile, and then PJ looked back to the left.

"Get down!" I could hear her say as she brushed past me…

…and then I heard the shot.

King Of The Jungle

It would probably have taken Trumbull's head off. He'd crouched down in front of the chopper, and the shooter had positioned himself behind one of those decorative cinderblock walls that was constructed in a checkerboard-type fashion, next to the road.

Instead, it hit PJ. She dove in front of Trumbull just in time.

Everything was a bit of a blur at that point. Immediately, the guns began blazing in the direction of that wall, and Pierce's six-man team closed on the shooter in no time flat and before he could get into the getaway car he was down. So was the getaway driver.

Meanwhile, Trumbull's bodyguards whisked him into the chopper, and it launched about as quickly as I've ever seen. Up and away it went, and for a moment it was just PJ and me on the grass field.

"PJ!" I said, rolling her over gently. "How you doing, honey? Are you hit?"

"You know I'm hit, dummy," she said. "You saw me get hit."

"Where?"

"Think hard. No, wait — please don't roll me on my back."

"Oh, no. You didn't…"

"My ass," she said. "I got shot in my beautiful, half-Asian ass."

She was laying on her side, crying and laughing at the same time.

"Well, you saved Donny Trumbull's life, hon," I said.

"That's it," she said. "I quit."

The shooter didn't die despite taking eight bullets from Pierce's guys and the Guyanese cops who fell asleep rather than stopping that car when it drove around their barricade on Seawall Public Road. It turned out that his name was Mohammed Hosseini, and he was Iranian.

Because of course he was.

And the getaway driver's name was Enrique Contreras of Cienfuegos, Cuba, who turned out to be in the employ of the *Servicio Bolivariano de Inteligencia Nacional,* or the Bolivarian National Intelligence Service, headquartered in Caracas,

Venezuela. Contreras even had his SEBIN ID on him. That's how arrogant these assholes were.

All of that we found out later.

I helped as Pierce's guys gently laid her across the back seat of the SUV, with her head on my lap and my belt tightened across her hip, her jacket pressed tight against her derriere in order to manage the bleeding, and tried to joke with her as we raced the few blocks to St. Joseph's Mercy Hospital down the street. They took her immediately into an operating room, and the next time I saw her she was in a hospital gown lying on her side with a big wad of gauze wrapped around her stitched-up right butt-cheek.

PJ was all tranked up on whatever they'd given her, but she still had plenty of gas left in the tank. And as soon as they let me in to see her, she was awfully chatty.

"I got an email from Trumbull," I said. "He wanted me to pass along his thanks for saving his life. He said you can have any job in his administration that you want. Just name it."

"Forget that," she said.

"Really?"

PJ shook her head.

"You're gonna give me a damn good job as your videographer," she said. "Like, I'm not hearing no from you. That's the last bullet I'm taking for a politician. So it's on you now. Make me a job offer."

"What is this, emotional blackmail?" I said.

"Hey, I get to do that to you."

"Since when?"

"Since you said you love me."

She had me there.

EPILOGUE

July 31, 2024: Lake Lanier, Georgia

I finished Pierce's biography a lot faster than I expected. It's coming out on August 15, and we went with the obvious title:

King of the Jungle: How One of America's Greatest Industrialists Held Off a Communist Invasion

I think it's going to do well. We've got over 400,000 copies already sold via pre-order.

And I'm publishing it through Holman Media. Tom did a fantastic deal with a printer and a distributor, plus we already had the online store on the site, so we're going to make a killing off this thing.

It's a good book, though I feel a little guilty taking credit for it when Flip, Colby, and a couple of the other writers at the site pitched in with the writing and editing. It was really more of a community project than something I did. Of course, all of the background and history leading up to Guyana was my stuff. That was the part I could write in my sleep, and I practically did. The rest came from a bunch of group interviews we did with Pierce via Zoom. He was starting to turn into a hermit down there, though I guess I couldn't blame him.

And we didn't put that in the book.

The title is accurate, by the way. Guyana did win that war. In fact, they managed to get their whole country back.

How? Well, the government changed over in Caracas, and General de la Vega was only too happy to pull his troops out of there.

Especially after what happened to Madiera.

Anybody could have told that arrogant bastard that going to Kaietur Falls and bragging about winning the war, when they'd really done anything but, was a bad idea.

It was the last idea he ever had.

King Of The Jungle

Madiera was at the little airport a little ways from the waterfall, and they'd put a little podium festooned with Venezuelan flags out for him to speak in front of the cameras and the little crowd of sycophants he'd brought with him. His party had walked up to the waterfall to look at it, and then they actually toasted each other with champagne. Then he came back to that podium to give his dumb little speech about how they'd decided to split the difference with the Guyanese *en aras de la paz.*

In the interests of peace. What bullshit.

You probably know what came next. The bullet came next. Right in the forehead.

Nobody saw the shooter. It was estimated he'd had to have been in one of the trees set back from the little airport building. The shot had to be a good 1,500 yards away. To this day it's completely unknown who's responsible.

And I don't know, either. I don't even have a theory.

I do have an idea, and it makes me smile. My idea is it was a very well-preserved, handsome middle-aged black guy. My thought is that he lined up his shot, and under his breath he said, "Here am I. Send me."

Then he took a breath, then slowly exhaled and pulled the trigger.

And when Madiera went down, on national TV in Venezuela — interestingly enough, the power came back on all over the country just a couple of hours before the proceedings at the waterfall — there were people in the streets.

Not rioting. Celebrating.

After that it was de la Vega, and the end of the war. The Venezuelans came home from Guyana, and even, in a surprising number of cases, from the U.S. and elsewhere in North America. And the Cubans all got packed off and sent home, where they could be a problem for the Castro gang instead of the Venezuelan people.

Pierce even cut Cabrillo loose and let him go home, though we found out that his wife had filed for divorce and split with all of his money as soon as he was captured. One rumor had it that she was in Panama. Another was that she'd taken up with a cartel boss in Monterrey.

Meanwhile, Darke proved to be a lot cleverer than anybody thought, though I suspect he had help. Sino-Petro found their portion of those offshore oil fields nationalized and then leased to a brand new public company, Guyana Petroleum Export Company, or Guyanapec.

Which is expected to have its initial public offering when the Exchange of the Americas opens on January 6.

And yeah, I did get around to selling my house in Buckhead. I was thinking maybe I'd hold onto it after all. But when I brought PJ home a few days after that incident in Georgetown, she waddled around the place and just looked at me with her nose scrunched up.

"No?" I said.

"I can see you living here by yourself," she said. "But we can do better. You're big-time now, and you've got me."

Instead, she found us this VRBO on Lake Lanier. I almost passed out at the price, but she told me not to worry about it.

I suspected her dad was going to foot the bill, and I later found out I was right. He might have hated the idea of her throwing in with me, but at the end of the day PJ was his little girl.

"It's so you can take care of me while I recover," she said about that ritzy rental. "Then we'll find something more our style."

I will say this — there are few things more conducive to getting a whole lot of writing done in not that much time than a big, luxurious lakehouse with a deck out on the water. And a hot chick in a bikini watching you from the lounge chair a couple of feet away as you bang away at your laptop.

Even if she does have a telltale scar on her ass.

Trumbull had us come to Milwaukee for the convention. He brought PJ up on the stage and said she'd saved his life.

"She's a hero," he said, as the crowd went wild. "And believe it or not she's with that guy Holman. Can you imagine that? There's no accounting for love, right?"

King Of The Jungle

I didn't mind taking shit from Trumbull in front of the whole country. I was too happy for PJ. She was beaming. She told me that her career exit was even better than John Elway's, if maybe a little more painful.

By the way, there are rumors that Deadhorse is going to drop out of the race right before his convention next month. Are they true? Maybe. But after that incident at that black church in North Carolina where he went off script and told the parishioners, "You dumb n***ers had better turn out the vote for me," it's a good bet he's done.

But if he goes, who knows who they'll replace him with?

Maybe we do. You might have to watch our next podcast if you want to find out.

AUTHOR'S NOTE

As some of the readers of *King of the Jungle* may know, this is actually my fifth novel. The first four of them were a series of epic fantasy/action-adventure stories I called *Tales of Ardenia*.

They were also about war, though in a much different setting.

I learned a lot about writing fiction with those books. Hopefully those lessons were useful.

One of the most important lessons was how effective it can be to use the world of fiction to make observations on reality, which is one of the driving impulses which led to *King of the Jungle*. It's a novel, but not much in it would be very surprising if it happened in real life.

How likely is it that Venezuela would invade Guyana? Not overly so, but it could definitely happen under the right circumstances. How likely is it that such an invasion could happen without the U.S. government taking action to stop it? Much more likely than it ought to be, at least with the current administration in office.

How likely would some red-pilled billionaire put his fortune, or a sizable chunk of it, on the line to fight essentially a private war against an aggressor backed by China, Russia, Iran and others? Here we enter the world of pure fiction.

And that's too bad.

If you've read my writing at *The American Spectator* or my two websites, TheHayride.com and RVIVR.com, you know that I'm not bullish on our ruling class or the administration they've produced. America is declining because those people entrusted with great power and privilege are alarmingly corrupt and stupid, and to the extent *King of the Jungle* doesn't represent how bad it's gotten, what you've read in the pages before this one is, I think, a good summation of where it's going. Maybe this story simply got the dates wrong.

At least we can laugh at them. A little.

I need to give thanks to a few people before I let you go. First, Melissa Mackenzie, the publisher of *The American Spectator*, has been supportive, almost outrageously so, since I first bugged her with the idea of a novel based on the Venezuela-Guyana mess back in the fall of 2023. So much so that

Melissa committed to running *King of the Jungle* initially as a serialized novel in 10 parts at *The American Spectator's* website.

Also, I'd like to thank the editors at *The American Spectator* – Lucy Van Berkum, Ellie Gardey, Seth Forman and Wlady Pleszczynski – for their work cleaning up the initial manuscript and rounding it into its final form.

And I'd like to thank my partners at RVIVR.com, J.D. Perry and Hollis Day, for their feedback and efforts in building a distribution channel – and their forbearance in allowing this project to serve as a test run for our efforts to join the publishing and bookselling world.

And finally, I'd like to thank the beta readers, and there are too many of them to list here, for helping the project through its initial stages.

Will Mike Holman, Pierce Polk, PJ Chang and the rest be heard from again? That might depend on you. If you liked this book, feel free to make that fact known in an Amazon review and on social media. I'm happy to turn this into a series of adventures through a world gone not just mad but hilariously dumb, but I'd like to know there's an audience for it. If you want to see more, help us spread the word!

Made in the USA
Monee, IL
29 July 2024